THE CAT CAFE

Caroline Bell Foster

www.carolinebellfoster.com
Editor: Alec Hawkes
Cover design: Heidi Hargreaves at Dukki Design www.dukkidesign.co.uk

To all those cat lovers who have no problem being called 'The mad cat person down the street.'

CONTENTS

CHAPTER ONE

Whoever said cats weren't trainable? Trinity Peters mused as she watched all twenty-two rescue cats downstairs stare intently at the door that separated her living quarters from the café below.

Today was the day, Trinity thought, her heart skipping a beat as she walked through her small living room into her equally small bedroom with a smile on her face, placed her tea on the dresser and pulled out her work uniform of jeans and T-shirt.

Her appointment with the bank wasn't until ten so she had just under four hours to sort the cats out, go for the meeting, and be back in time to open half an hour before lunchtime.

Pumping a little hair lotion into her hand, she rubbed her palms together, smoothed the light olive oil concoction over her hair, making sure to get the ends and then using a wide paddle brush put her hair into a low ponytail before going into the bathroom to freshen up.

Mercy, her white Persian, was sat on the wicker clothes basket going through her grooming routine yet, watching with half an eye trained on Trinity who was brushing her teeth.

"And what will you be doing today?" Trinity asked the cat around the frothy paste in her mouth.

"Meow," the cat stopped licking the tip of her tail and turned to look at her full on with startling blue eyes.

"You know you're my number one kitty don't you?" Trinity gushed at the cat, "and today that lovely man at the bank is going to give us loads of money so we can extend into the shop next door and we can have even more space. Wouldn't that be nice Mercy?" She asked the cat as she gargled, rinsed her mouth and then washed and dried her face. She then picked up the white ball of fur—who really needed to go on a diet—and placed the cat on the windowsill to look out.

"I'll see you later." She told her as she shut the door and carefully walked down the steep staircase that led to the café below.

She knew the cats would now be gathered at the door and she prepared herself for the barrage of complaints and meows of adoration she was going to get as she unlocked the door and stepped carefully inside.

After giving each one a cuddle, she put on her apron shared out bowls of dried food, changed their water and, while they were eating, went to tackle the litter trays in the storage room at the back of the building.

She'd come a long way she thought, as she picked up a tray and emptied it out into the bin before placing the empty tray on its side ready for a hosing down and disinfecting.

Trinity had always loved animals, cats especially, and had wanted to become a vet, but an aversion to anything remotely bloody put paid to that dream, and she'd done an English Degree instead, finishing off her last year in Japan where she taught English at an exclusive school for girls.

She'd fallen in love with the city and the numerous themed cafés that were dotted around.

Saving every penny, she returned home and leased a large shop space. She sectioned it off into a 'living room' where the cats interacted with the humans, a smaller, partitioned, cats only space for when one of her little felines wanted to be left alone, and then there was the backspace where two vending machines dispensed luxury hot and cold drinks.

She wanted to expand into the shop next door so that she could sell cat merchandise, have a proper reading area and sell cakes. After cats, Trinity loved books and cake.

Scrubbing the last of the litter trays, she stacked it against the wall to drain off and started dispensing heavy-duty litter in some trays as well as fine sandy litter in others.

Cats could be very picky when it came to how they liked their litter, she now knew, as she'd once spent a fortune on bulk litter and only two of the cats used it. Now she had a variety of textures.

Placing the trays in various spots Trinity washed and dried her hands before closing the door, knowing the cats would make their own way to their toilet when they were good and ready.

Giving the café a quick vacuum and dust she watched as Lance the vending machine man parked on the double yellow lines with his large white van. She went to the door, being careful to close the inner door behind her.

"Morning Lance," Trinity said as she opened the door, wedging it open with a rubber wedge. Wednesday was vending machine change over day.

"Morning lovey," he said handing her his clipboard before going to open the back of his van. "Same as usual?" He asked.

"Please."

She watched as he took out his trolley and placed boxes of hot chocolate, powdered milk, varieties of coffee onto it before turning to her with a gentle smile.

"How's my favourite cat lady?" He asked, walking past her with the laden trolley, putting it aside as he toed off his shoes to put on a pair of plastic disposable socks over his own brightly coloured stripy socks.

The café had rules. No outdoor footwear was to be worn around the cats.

Trinity supplied disposable socks and lockers.

"Heading to the bank today Lance," she told him, watching as he rubbed sanitiser in his large hands, being careful to get the gel between his fingers. "Seeing if I can get the shop next door."

"That'd be grand," he told her, as, at her nod, he lifted a box and walked into the living room. "Who'd have thought a place like this would do so well?" He said conversationally as he placed the box on the floor and unlocked the machine. Two of the cats Odin and Rodney immediately went to have a snoop. He bent and scratched their ears before opening the machines.

Trinity watched as he swiftly cleaned and refilled it, going back and forth to the boxes.

"Pity you don't allow kids though Trinity, my granddaughter would love it here."

Trinity smiled. "I know, but you know how cats are? Not that fond of kids and all that."

"Hmm too true. Did I ever tell you about the time..."

And so their conversation went on, he sorted out the machines, and she used disinfectant wipes to wipe down all the surfaces.

***

Trinity watched Lance slowly reverse up the narrow lane and, carefully closing the door behind her, went upstairs to have a quick shower and change into one of her suits from her teaching days.

Today she would sign on the bottom line. An injection of cash to deposit on the shop space next door and enough money to furnish it. It wasn't a lot of money and Reece the loans officer assured her it was hers. Trinity was so excited, excited enough to sweep a touch of lip gloss and several brushes of mascara on her lashes.

"Mercy?" Trinity turned to her cat that hadn't moved from the windowsill where she'd left her earlier. "Mummy is going to go get us some money. I'll be back soon baby." She told the cat as she closed the door and instead of going into the shop, used the narrow front door that opened right onto the street.

She crossed the street and paused to look over at her shop, smiling at the purple painted brickwork left over from the jewellery shop that used to be there. The words The Cat Café were painted gold, and she had a large silhouette of a black cat sitting in a pink teacup above the door. All cats are black in the dark, it said in smaller gold lettering on the silhouette. It was just as she'd pictured it all those months ago when she returned to England to settle in the East Midlands.

She loved the region, the three cities, Nottingham, Derby and Leicester, weren't too big, but large enough to get everything she needed including good coffee. She would need a really good reason to live in London again. It was too large, and although born down there she had enough country blood to make her want to settle in Nottingham.

"Morning Trinity,"

"Morning, Michelle," she told the florist as she walked past the shop.

"You look nice,"

"Thanks, business beckons."

"Oh?"

Michelle seemed to know everyone's business on this section of May Hill Lane in Hockley. They were a select range of shops that skimmed the main hustle and bustle of the city centre. They got a lot of foot traffic on the cobbled lane, university students and business people, needing a tea break or browsing the charity shops or simply passing through as they headed towards Market Square.

The buildings were old factory warehouses that had been converted to shops in the 50s and built using local sandstone that was orangey pink in colour. The council were thinking of making the whole area into some sort of creative quarter.

"I'll tell you when I get back Michelle," Trinity promised walking on.

"Here," her friend held out a red rose with a smile. "Tuck it into your hair."

Trinity smoothed her hair self-consciously. She didn't normally wear her hair down, but as today was a suit day she thought a down hairdo would soften the shoulder pads in her black jacket.

With a grin, she tucked the flower into the lapel of her jacket instead. "As I said, this is business. You can give me another one when I'm going on a hot date."

"Hot date," her friend huffed. "You haven't been on a date since you moved onto the street a year ago."

"Too busy,"

"You'll turn into a crazy old cat woman, you will," Michelle warned.

Trinity laughed and turned away. "See you later Michelle."

"See you."

With a smile still on her face, Trinity followed the tram lines, as they ran parallel to Market Square until they turned off and she continued on, up a lane and onto Maid Marian Way to her bank.

Tomorrow, she would be making plans for her expansion. More space meant more cats. More cats meant a higher chance they could be re-homed. It was a win-win.

***

From his vantage point on the mezzanine, Blake watched with boredom as his staff tried to look busy. He should have been laughing, really, but when was the last time he'd even ventured this far north without the invitation of a party and promise of slender thighs wrapped around his waist. London gave him everything he needed. Why was he even here?

Ah yes, he thought leaning on the shiny mahogany bannister, his grandpop had sent him here to buy some Godforsaken building, just because he'd heard whispers the whole area was going to get an injection of cash to make it into some sort of pretty artist delight.

Since grandpop had married his first love, Annalise, he'd taken to buying art. Blake really didn't see the necessity for art, well maybe a beautiful face he thought about to turn away, but stopped with his hand still on the bannister when a beautiful girl in a too large suit opened the door and smoothed her hair.

Blake watched as she looked around, skimming a slender hand up and down the leather strap of her handbag before smiling over at someone. He wasn't able to see who from where he was, but he watched and waited.

She was gorgeous in a petite kind of way. Blake liked his women tall, leggy, busty and blonde. Or with at least two of those attributes.

This one was tiny, maybe five one, five two with slender almost skinny legs. Nice knees, *nice knees*! What the hell! Blake thought when had he ever looked at knees? He grimaced and watched as

Reece, the swarmy loans officer he couldn't stand, walk towards her.

Sexual Harassment suit waiting to happen Blake thought, seeing for himself just how touchy-feely the loans officer actually got.

Taking the girls hand, Blake watched in annoyance, as Reece led her over to his desk, making sure to brush against her as he pulled out her chair.

Blake's phone buzzed in his pocket, and he fished it out to read the text message from his friend Becca. Dinner tonight she'd invited. He read the address. Good, he thought, walking distance.

Another tinkle of laughter brought his attention back to the desk. Reece was now standing over the girl, breathing down her neck by the looks of things and the girl was looking a little uncomfortable and leaning away. Her flower fell onto the desk and Reece, the swarmy bastard, picked it up and tucked it behind her ear.

For God's sake! Blake thought, going to his own temporary desk and picking up the phone to call the internal line. A quick order and he watched his manager walk over to Reece, say a few words and saw Reece get up.

Satisfied, Blake went back to work.

Trinity couldn't believe it. The interview had been going so well. She'd even had her pen poised over the dotted line when some old manager guy took over the interview, declining her loan with one glance.

It didn't make sense, and it wasn't fair! Surely she had some form of recourse? She'd just been so gobsmacked that she'd simply walked out in a daze. What had happened?

***

As much as Blake liked seeing his friend, Becca, being at her house, her stomach swollen with baby number two, while baby number one was still in nappies was not his idea of dinner party bliss. He'd escaped as soon as he could, not missing the look of mischief on his dear friend's face.

He and Becca went way back, she was the only female friend he hadn't slept with. They'd been at boarding school together in France, or was it Italy? He couldn't remember, but they'd been friends. He was Godfather to baby number one, Dominick, and he did all his Godfatherly duties like be there at the Christening, buying bonds in the little boy's name and generally asking how he was once a month. Yes, he was a good Godfather.

Too early to go home, well to the flat he used while in Nottingham, Blake decided to walk around. It was barely nine o'clock, all the shoppers had gone as Nottingham still operated by the antiquated five o'clock shop closure system that was a pain for busy people like his PA when he needed him to get him something. He always grumbled about the early closing times.

People were heading out to restaurants, no doubt filling up before dancing off the excess of calories he thought, as he walked through Hockley. He could see his building in the distance and knew he only needed to walk for another fifteen minutes, and he'd be there.

A group of women dressed in a haze of fluorescent pink and white surged out of a pub and surrounded him like a swarm of angry bees.

"Oi, here's a nice one," one of them said.

Smiling tightly Blake tried to extricate himself, but two looped their arms through his stopping him.

"She's getting married next week," one with spiky black hair explained. "See?" She pointed to a blonde wearing a pink tutu and white sash and a gleaming plastic crown.

"Congratulations." Blake murmured, trying to hustle the women along up the narrow lane.

"Would you like to come for a drink? Her last hurrah and all that?" another one asked hopefully, batting her overly long false eyelashes at him.

"No thanks."

"Aww please," spiky black-haired woman pouted up at him.

"You're a nice looking bloke, tall and handsome. What colour are your eyes?" she moved in closer to look into his eyes. "Blue or green?"

Blake gritted his teeth. What was it with these northerners and harassment? Sexual harassment worked both ways.

Peeling himself away as firmly as he could he quickly walked around them and into the nearest shop. Then stopped.

He couldn't believe what he was seeing.

There were cats everywhere. He blinked just to see if the curry he'd had for dinner wasn't playing with his brain cells.

Yes, there were cats of all different sizes all different colours on the other side of the glass wall.

He turned to go, but a girl with a red rose in her hair caught and held his attention.

She'd changed. It was criminal to hide what she'd been hiding in that boxy suit she'd worn earlier at the bank.

Now, as she was bent over a cat, he could see her cute derrière and slender legs in a pair of blue faded jeans. The fabric was worn and faded where it cupped her bottom.

The door opened behind him.

"Go on in please mate, before that hen party change their minds and find me." A man, not much younger than Blake said taking off his shoes.

"Take your shoes off, or Trinity will eat you alive," the man advised. "You don't bring outside dirt near the cats."

"What is this place?" Blake asked, puzzled.

The man grinned.

"The Cat Café, I come here every chance I get," the man explained. "My girlfriend is allergic to cats, but I like to come here and chill out and watch some football if I can wrangle the remote off Trinity."

"Cat café?"

"Yes mate," the man stuck his hand out. "I'm Travis,"

"Blake."

They shook hands.

"Take your shoes off and stick 'em in there," Travis advised, pointing to a row of wooden lockers with keys, watching as Blake followed his instruction with obvious reluctance. "Use this."

After placing his shoes in the locker, he palmed the key the young man gave him, then following his example Blake put on a pair of disposable socks. Travis then pumped hand sanitiser on his hands and indicated for Blake to follow his example

"Are you ready?" Travis asked, practically bursting with excitement.

"What for exactly?"

Travis grinned, wriggling his pale eyebrow. "To fall in love of course." He pushed open the glass door.

Blake looked at the girl with the red rose in her hair and perfect, golden brown skin, he exhaled and went in.

***

Trinity watched Travis and his friend enter. Travis was a regular. He was a med student who said he 'needed to decompress' and play with the cats as he couldn't have his own at home.

"Hey, Trin,"

"Trinity," she replied automatically but without malice. "How many times do I have to tell you to call me Trinity?"

"I don't know what your mother was thinking," he replied going into his back pocket and pulling out his wallet. "Two hours please." He said pulling out a few notes and handing them to her.

"Okay. How about your friend?" She looked at the tall man with jet black hair who was staring down at her with the clearest blue eyes she'd ever seen.

"We just met," Travis revealed. "Five pounds for an hour at a time mate." He said over his shoulder as he walked off in a rush.

Blake had never seen anyone so beautiful. Her eyes were the darkest brown he'd ever seen. He couldn't see her pupils in this light, and he wondered if they would dilate with pleasure when he took her to bed. Her skin was the colour of toasted bread and her lips full, the bottom lip slightly plumper than the top.

Blake felt a pull all the way to his groin, making it tighten with awareness for her. He hadn't had an instant arousal in years.

"Welcome to The Cat Café," Trinity smiled up at the man Travis had left behind. "How long are you staying?"

Blake heard her words, but they were muffled under the now painful pressure behind the buttons on his jeans.

"Sir? Are you okay?" Trinity asked with concern. He was still staring at her, and if she knew she wasn't surrounded by people who would look out for her, she'd be calling the police. His look was scary.

"Sir?"

Blake shook his head. She'd be in his bed this week he thought.

"Sorry, I was just remembering something,"

"Must have been really important as you looked like you were in another place," Trinity said.

Your bed, Blake thought, with your slender legs wrapped around my waist, he pictured with growing excitement, but keeping his thoughts to himself, searched his pockets for his money.

"I've not seen one of those in years," Trinity said seeing the gold money clip.

"This?" Blake looked at the clip his grandpop had given him for his birthday, his twenty-second he thought it may have been. He'd never used a wallet since.

"My dad uses money clips. It's something he picked up while living in America." Trinity divulged. The man was making her nervous.

He was in the wrong place. She'd bet money, all the money in her till that he'd never intended to be here tonight. He looked so out of place. Yes, he was wearing jeans, but they had a seam. Nobody ironed jeans any more, and he was wearing a navy blazer over a white linen shirt. Those were not clothes to lounge around on the floor or the low sofas to let the cats sleep or crawl on you with.

"It was a present," he told her. "How much?" Smaller notes hid the larger notes on the inside. Not that he walked around with much cash on him.

"Twenty pounds," she said and watched in amazement as the man pulled out a crisp new twenty. "I was joking," she smiled. "How long do you want to stay?"

As long as it takes, Blake thought. What the hell was wrong with him? Since when had he developed stalkerish tendencies? "An hour?"

"Okay," she took the twenty, turned to the till then gave him his change. "Please follow the rules. They're over there," she pointed to a large blackboard. "Number one rule? Please do not pick up the cats. If they come to you and sit on you fine. The vending machines are over there," she pointed to the back of the room. "And newspapers, magazines and some books are on that shelf there." She pointed to another section of the room. "All info on the cats is on the walls, and all of them are up for adoption," she smiled at him, and Blake saw stars. "Enjoy."

When she turned away, Blake wanted to grab her shoulders and turn her back to him. He wanted to revel in her exotic gaze, but he forced himself to sit on one of the low sofas instead.

It was bloody uncomfortable he thought, folding his long frame onto the brown leather sofa without any feet so that it lay flat on the floor.

Grabbing a cushion which of course had a cat embroidered on it, he stuffed it behind his back and looked around. About eighteen people were lounging around, he noted. Travis was towards the back lying stomach down on the floor using some sort of stringy toy with a feather on the end to play with a grey, black and white cat. There was a group of girls sat on another sofa talking quietly amongst themselves, each stroking or playing with a cat. An elderly pair and others, all with cats. It was bizarre.

Blake had never seen anything like it. He glanced around the room again. It was a cosy place, made to look like a living room. The walls were painted in soft earth tones, and the walls had shelves going up and down, it looked as though a game of Tetris was being played. A few cats were lying high up their paws hanging over the edge. There was a sizeable tree-like thing in the centre of the room, with holes and ledges and curved branches wide enough for the cats to lay down on and watch the goings on from up above.

He was trying to get comfortable and was thinking about moving when a ginger cat decided to smooth itself against his leg. When he didn't react, the cat looked at him and did it again and again.

Blake wasn't sure what he was supposed to do. The rules listed on the blackboard said nothing about cats rubbing against you.

"Would you like me to introduce you?"

Blake took his time to look up. From his vantage point, he could see the surprising fullness of her breasts.

"Excuse me?"

"Would you like me to introduce you?" Trinity offered again folding down easily to sit beside him. "Come here, baby."

Blake swung round to her. "What?"

She giggled, "Not you," she leaned forward offering her hand and making kissing noises at the cat. "William here,"

He was such an idiot, Blake thought, watching the way her lips puckered and he steeled himself against his arousal that was making him hot, hard and heavy. "No, I'm okay thanks." Blake choked just as the cat walked off to the group of girls instead. "How about a cup of coffee?"

He got up quickly and offered her his hand for assistance when she took it he felt a zing up his arm and noticing her slight gasp, knew she had felt it too.

"Come on, follow me," she walked ahead of him but said over her shoulder. "You didn't plan to come here tonight did you?" She asked conversationally as they stepped over Travis who was now propped up against a bean bag with a cat lying on his chest. They both appeared to be sleeping.

"I was accosted by a hen party group," Blake revealed honestly, "and thought it safer to come in here."

They'd reached the machines.

"Ah, so you didn't expect to be spending the evening with the cats and me?"

"With you? Maybe. With cats? No." He offered his hand. "I'm Blake."

"Trinity," She said. "Trinity Peters."

She was looking up at him with a playful twinkle in her eye. He wanted to scoop her up and press her against the machine and kiss her silly.

"This is a novel experience."

She tipped her head to one side as though trying to solve some problem, then turned to the machine. "What would you like?"

He looked at the red and chrome machine that looked as though it could transform into a lorry or something. He hadn't drunk his coffee out of a vending machine in years. "Black. No sugar." He instructed taking change out of his pocket.

"This one will be on me," she winked at him before rapidly pressing several buttons, and they both watched as the machine went through the elaborate mechanics of making a simple cup of coffee. She handed him the paper cup. "Careful it's hot."

"Thank you." Blake didn't want her to go. "Tell me about this place. Have you worked here long?"

She indicated a small table and chairs and sat down. A tabby cat immediately jumped onto her lap. Blake watched mesmerised as she stroked the cat behind the ears and the cat closed its eyes in heavenly bliss. Her touch looked so gentle, her fingers long and elegant topped off with short unvarnished nails.

She tipped her head to the side before she spoke. "I own it."

He nodded. "What made you think of a cat café? It's a risky novelty don't you think?" Her dark eyes flashed at him, and he realised he'd offended her. "But a great novelty." He tagged on quickly.

"I used to live in Japan, and when I wasn't working I spent my time in a café much like this," she revealed, smiling as she looked down at the cat. "Do you like cats?" She asked.

Blake shrugged. "I don't know," he answered honestly.

"Well you're not running for the hills and Soldier there has been eye-balling you since you walked in."

"Soldier?"

She pointed to a black cat he hadn't noticed that was lying on one of the shelves on the wall. It's intent yellow gaze trained unblinking on him.

"He's been here the longest, and he doesn't interact very much." She gasped. "Oh my!"

The cat choose that moment to jump down, flex the nails on his front paws on the sisal rug and roll his back into a long slow stretch and then yawn widely.

"Well he's made a liar out of me haven't you Soldier" She bent down to him, but the cat on her lap took exception and gurgled in displeasure.

Blake watched fascinated as the cat walked up to him and sat down, it's white-tipped tail slowly swishing from side to side. He was not going to let a cat jump onto his lap Blake thought.

"He wants you to pet him," Trinity encouraged. "Like this." She demonstrated by stroking the tabby cat on her lap between the ears.

Resigned, and because the damned cat was daring him, Blake reached down and touched the cats head. The cat, Soldier, nudged its head into his fingers. Blake smiled and did it again.

"See," Trinity said, "they make us happy." She gently placed her cat on the floor and stood up to see to a customer.

Blake took a moment to pet the cat and checking the time, thought he'd stay a few more minutes before heading home. He picked up a newspaper he'd already read today and moved to sit on a normal height wicker chair.

The cat 'Soldier' sat by his feet and levelled him with a stare. Blake looked around. What was he supposed to do?

Trinity watched the sexy man, Blake, from the corner of her eye. He looked so out of place, but there was a glimmer of hope for him as she smothered a smile and watched as he chucked Soldier under his chin before turning to his newspaper, only to keep glancing at the cat who was patiently waiting for some more attention.

Soldier, was one of her first cats. He was mainly black but had two white front paws and another bit of white on his tail. He'd been through a lot if the raggedy right ear and permanent bend in his tail was anything to go by. Aside from coming off his perch for meals and toilet he rarely moved, much less take over a human.

"Thanks, Trin," Travis said coming over to lean on the counter.

"Trinity." She answered automatically. "For what?"

"I lost one today," Travis pushed his hands into his jeans pockets and looked at her. His hazel eyes shadowed with grief. "My first."

"Oh Travis, I'm so sorry."

"They say you'll always remember the first patient you lose and it's true. I worked so hard trying to keep her Trinity," he breathed in deep and Trinity came around the counter and hugged him close rubbing his back as he struggled to compose himself.

"I know you did Travis." She soothed.

He pulled away, a touch of red creeping up his neck.

"Sorry," he gave her a small smile and raked a hand through his reddish brown hair. "The girlfriend wasn't in, and I came straight here."

"That's what we're here for."

"You're brilliant you know that don't you?"

"Absolutely."

They smiled at each other.

"If I weren't already attached I'd ask you out," he revealed, honestly.

He'd said it many times before. "But you are," Trinity answered, "and I'm happy as I am. A mad cat lady."

He looked at her then nodded. "I'd best be going," he squeezed her hand before turning to Blake. "I'm heading out mate. Told you you'd fall in love." He said, then he was gone.

Eleven o'clock was closing time. Trinity had tried staying open later as the cats were most active at night, but some drunks had come in, falling all over the cats and disrespecting their space. It was safer to close. In Japan they were able to stay open until the wee hours of the morning, it was so unfair she mused, wishing she could stay open longer.

The students left, leaving Blake and the elderly pair. He stood up to go. He didn't want to.

"It's a great place you have here," he told Trinity, watching as she picked up cat toys.

"Thanks. Glad you liked it." She indicated Soldier who was circling his feet. "You made a friend tonight. Care to adopt him?"

Blake looked down at the cat. "I live in London."

"They don't have cats in the big city?" She joked.

"I travel a lot,"

"Oh." She moved towards the first set of doors. "Be sure to tell your friends about us." She said as she opened the door.

Blake walked towards her. He really didn't want to leave.

"Why do you have a rose in your hair?"

Trinity touched the soft bud having forgotten about it. "My friend gave it to me this morning."

"Male or female?"

She frowned at him. "What does that matter?"

"If it were a male giving you a rose I'd think twice about asking you out to dinner tomorrow," he explained. "If it were a female I'd simply ask."

"You'll never know."

"Have dinner with me tomorrow night."

"Can't. Working."

"Another night?"

She shook her head.

Blake was not used to women saying no, and he wasn't about to beg. Not even for this golden skinned beauty with the dark eyes and perfect smile.

"I'm sorry I can't do anything in the evenings."

"Okay," Blake said tightly. "Goodnight Trinity."

"Goodnight Blake."

She watched as he went to his locker, pulled out his shoes and put them on before turning to her again, waving goodbye and walking out.

Trinity locked the door behind him.

"Phew." She said to herself as she automatically straightened the wooden bench along the window and watched him cross the street with long easy strides.

She didn't have time to date she told herself, ignoring the chasm of disappointment that nudged inside her. She had to pull extra shifts at her second job to save as much money as she could. Not getting that loan today had really upset her plans and going out with a man, no matter how gorgeous and tingly he made her feel just wasn't a priority right now.

Mr & Mrs Horncastle were getting ready to leave, and she walked over to them, helping them with their coats and making sure they didn't have a cat tucked away in their pockets. It was a 'thing' they always did and laughing away at their antics, finally locked up and pulled the blinds down over the windows.

CHAPTER TWO

He was ruled by hormones. There was no other reason as to why he found himself looking through the window at the café at ten thirty at night.

He had loads of paperwork he needed to get through so that he could head back to London tomorrow. Four days away was enough.

A few cats were cleaning themselves by the window, and again, he thought it was really a good idea to get the felines adopted by marketing them in a homely environment.

Trinity was sat on a stool balancing a laptop on her knee. She was biting the side of her lip and frowning at the screen before tapping away at the keys.

Blake felt the tightness hit his groin area again as he watched her. Her dark hair was caught in a bun type thing on top of her head, and she was wearing a pair of dark leggings and a baggy jumper that slipped off one shoulder giving a view of a satiny deep red bra strap. Blake tried to regulate his breathing.

She looked up and caught him staring, and he watched fascinated as a slow smile spread across her face, and she waved him in.

"You can't help yourself can you?" Trinity said a moment later when he had walked in still rubbing hand sanitiser over his hands.

"Guess not," Blake replied. It wasn't a normal situation for him. He didn't hang around cafés late at night so that he could speak to a girl. He wasn't a teenager even if he felt like one. "How are you?"

"I'm good thanks," she answered. "Would you like a coffee?" She was about to get off her perch, but he stopped her by placing his hand on her shoulder.

"I'll get it," he replied moving away. "Do you want anything?"

"If I have any more tea or coffee I'll start to shake." She put her laptop on the counter behind her and watched him.

Blake, he'd been in the periphery of her thoughts all day. Those blue eyes of his and the seriousness of his expressions. He didn't smile much if at all, but he did melt. Her love of cats meant she had an appreciation of body language. What Blake didn't say out loud he said with the sway of his big shoulders the subtle glance in his eye and the minuscule expressions on his facial features. She liked looking at him.

He caught her staring as he walked over.

"Care to join me on the sofa?"

She checked the time. "I'll be closing in half an hour,"

He raised an eyebrow and waited. She watched a muscle jump at his jaw. He didn't like being told no. She crossed her arms high on her chest and mimicked his expression and waited.

Well well, Blake thought smiling inside, little Trinity had spunk.

"I'll pay for half an hour."

"I don't do half hourly rates."

He fished into his pocket and took a twenty from his money clip, all the while watching her. "Keep the change." He threw the note onto the counter. It was a symbolic challenge.

Her eyes flashed angrily. "Keep your money and drink your coffee,"

Blake said the last thing for her. "And get out?" He taunted.

"You said it."

It was the sexual tension that was putting them both at odds. They were strangers, had barely spent an hour in each others company, but for some reason, they sparked off each other.

The elderly couple who had been here yesterday said their goodbyes and Blake watched as Trinity told the older gentleman to open his coat so that she could check his pockets for Demus or Gizmo.

It must have been an inside joke as the three of them were laughing.

When they had left, Trinity turned warily to him. They could have been alone as the one other person in the place was reading a hefty novel and was absent-mindedly stroking a white three-legged cat called Minty, that was burrowed into her side.

"Meow."

Blake looked down to see Soldier at his feet and hunched down to stroke the cat along his back and up his tail before standing close to Trinity again and drinking his coffee.

"He likes you," Trinity said watching them.

Blake drained his cup and searched for the bin.

"Give it to me," Trinity held out her hand for his cup.

She didn't understand what was going on. Her body was reacting to Blake in a way that had never happened before. She'd had boyfriends and a lover for over a year, but this awareness was new. She'd felt it yesterday, but today, right now, her body seemed to throb in tune to the sexual vibes he was putting out.

She didn't want to be alone with him. She needed him to go away, and she definitely didn't want to be feeling the things she was feeling. Tonight he was wearing another pair of jeans, again with a seam ironed in, a black V-necked jumper and a sports jacket over that. The jumper set off his complexion, he wasn't English as he didn't have the English paleness going on, there was a tinge of Mediterranean or something about him, but his name gave nothing away.

"What's your last name, Blake?" She asked him suddenly.

"Lawrence," he answered automatically. "Why?"

"You sort of look familiar."

He walked towards her and took her hand. "If we'd met before I can guarantee you'd remember."

Trinity pulled her hand away before she drowned in his shimmering blue gaze full of arrogant promise.

"You say that to all the girls," she joked nervously, looking around for something to do. She straightened the magazines in the stand by the door.

"Trinity, I'm off," Katie said. "Thanks for the book. I'll bring it back I promise."

"Take your time. It's a good read. See you soon." She called after the girl.

Trinity was always aware of just how vulnerable she was in the café, late at night when everyone had left. She would normally go straight to the front door and lock it and pull down the roller blinds, but she didn't want to be locked in with Blake.

"Well that's it for the night," she hinted looking over at him. He had turned her laptop around and was reading it. She closed the lid with a snap.

"How about going to get something to eat?" He asked, instead of the apology she was expecting.

The front door opened and Blake watched in irritation as a group of teenagers came inside. He wanted to talk about the website she had been on. Payday loans were not the way to go, and he wondered why she was even exploring that route when only yesterday she had been in his bank.

"Hold on," Trinity went to the door. "I'm sorry we're closed." She told the group who were now making meow noises. It wasn't the first time that they had made a nuisance of themselves.

"Can I stroke your kitty?" One of them asked, leering at her with his palm upwards and insinuating a stroking motion. He licked his fingers.

"Would you care to repeat that?" Blake growled quietly, stepping around her and shielding her with his big body.

"And so what if I do?" The teenager said, boosted by his three friends egging him on. He made a rude gesture with his middle finger and then turned to leave, swearing loudly with his friends.

Blake locked the door before turning towards her. She was so tiny, she didn't stand a chance with a group of yobs like that. It wasn't safe for her.

"Thank you," she said turning away to roll the blinds down. "But I had it in hand."

"Did you now?"

She did not appreciate his tone and told him as much.

Blake drew himself up to his full height. "You need to put some sort of buzzer on the door. It's not safe for you to be here on your own!"

"Don't you shout at me!" She told him crossing her arms in front of her. "Who are you to tell me what to do? I don't even know you!"

The cats were looking at them, some of them even meowed in distress picking up the negative energy that was going on around them. Soldier and Demus walked around their ankles weaving in and out between the two of them.

"You're upsetting the cats," Trinity accused.

"No, you're the one shouting."

Blake caught her arm and swung her towards him when she turned to walk off. Before she could do anything, his lips were covering hers in a brutal kiss that had her head snapping back. She pushed against his shoulders, but then a single sweep of his tongue had her opening her mouth and letting him in.

His hair was super soft under her fingers, and she played with the strands at his nape.

Blake shifted, gentling the kiss to sip at her full lips. He soothed the tiny bruise he'd made with his tongue in apology.

Trinity tasted of ambrosia Blake thought as he shifted her still closer, tucking her small frame into his and moulding her against him. She was small, but she fitted him perfectly.

"Hmm," she murmured as her tongue danced against his, and she plastered herself against him. She wanted to wrap her legs around him and push against his heavy arousal.

Blake, sensing her need, picked her up with ease, and she clung to him, now able to rock her sex against his as he walked over to the counter and sat her on it, not once leaving her lips.

Trinity made an impatient sound as she tried to reach his skin. She pushed his jacket off his shoulders and swept her hands over his forearms. They were hot and muscular with wiry hair that tickled her palms.

Blake released her mouth then to sweep down her neck, he nibbled the back of her ear, sucked on the lobe as his hands swept up beneath her jumper.

He unsnapped her bra and pushed his hands up to cup her breasts.

"Trinity," he breathed, he'd never wanted to have sex with someone as badly as he wanted to have her at this very moment. "Trinity?" He said again, pushing her jumper and bra out of his way as he skipped kisses across her smooth chest, finally settling on her dark, cocoa tipped nipples, first one and then the other.

Trinity leaned back, offering more of herself as she held his head to her.

"My God you're beautiful," he told her as he sucked a brown nipple deep into his mouth before moving up to claim another deep kiss and sweep her up again. She was in his arms when he moved and stepped on a cat.

"Meow!"

"Oh no! Put me down, Blake!" Trinity wriggled out of his arms, and Blake reluctantly set her onto her feet.

She was already on the floor, soothing the cat, a white, black and orange one he hadn't seen before.

Getting his breathing under control, he asked. "Is it all right?"

"I think so. Gizmo always gets underfoot. He's partially sighted." She explained hugging the cat to her.

Blake knew the moment had gone, but not wanting to leave the fog of arousal just yet reached for her hand but she moved away.

"I think you'd better go now," Trinity said quietly.

"Me or the cat?" Blake asked watching as she buried her face into the cat's fur, very much like she had buried her face in his neck only a moment ago.

"You." She mumbled.

"Are we going to talk about what just happened?"

"Why?"

"Because I want more of it,"

"Not bloody likely,"

"Why don't you put the cat down and talk to my face," he challenged tightly. "Scared?"

"Not bloody likely," she repeated but put the cat down, tugged off her bra via the sleeves of her jumper before pulling it down.

Blake noticed she'd put her bra in her back pocket and his penis twitched.

"You're not going to be one of those men who's going to dissect what we just did to death are you?" Trinity asked as she walked past him, opened a drawer and pulled out a lint roller. She started to roll the gadget up and down her legs.

After that statement, nothing would make Blake talk about what just happened. "What are you doing?"

"Getting rid of the fur,"

"I know that but why?"

She sighed and looked at him.

Blake's heart skipped a beat. Her lips were swollen from his kisses her hair was all tousled and simply knowing she wasn't wearing a bra made his arousal nudge once again behind the zipper of his jeans. He wanted to press her delicate hands against it and lose himself.

"I would like to take you to dinner." His voice sounded aggressive and gritty even to him.

"So you've said," she dismissed, bending to use the roller again.

"And?" He was not going to beg.

"and I told you I can't make dinner," she gasped. "Oh my goodness. I'm going to be late!" She flung the roller back in the drawer. "You need to go." She grabbed his hand and was pulling him over to the first door.

"Late for what?"

"Huh?"

"You said you're going to be late. For what?"

"Work."

He was confused. "But you're already closed."

"Not this work," she pulled his shoes from the locker and pressed them against his chest. "Here, put these on. I need you to go."

Blake took the shoes but didn't move.

"You're being as cooperative as a brick wall right now," she said. "But I need you to go so that I can lock up and get out of here."

"Where are you going?"

"Not far."

He waited, one dark silky eyebrow-raising ever so slightly and Trinity gave in.

"I work in the office of a taxi service. I should be starting in ten minutes." She revealed reluctantly.

"But it's almost midnight."

"Yes, I know. Will you please put those on!" She all but sat him down and was about to take off his disposable socks herself when she thought better of it.

Blake smiled.

"I'll go if you have dinner with me tomorrow night," Blake said, pressing his advantage.

"No."

"We need to talk about all this."

"I don't have anyone to look after the café."

That wasn't a no, he thought.

"Breakfast tomorrow."

She sighed dramatically, and Blake held his breath. Why did he want to spend time with this fiery woman who was nothing like his usual type.

"Fine," she answered resentfully if the stubborn set of her chin was anything to go by.

Blake slipped his loafers on and walked to the door. He dipped his head for a quick kiss before she could object. "Lock the door behind me." He stepped out and turned to watch as she locked the door.

She didn't look at him. Not once and Blake fought the urge to swear.

***

Trinity raced around, securing the cats, saying goodnight to them all, before dashing upstairs to grab her handbag, pet Mercy, who was watching TV and went outside.

Blake was leaning against a car watching her.

"I thought you'd left."

He shrugged. "I'll walk you."

"Thanks, but it's not far."

"Then I won't be put out too much will I?"

Trinity didn't like his attitude but remained silent as she crossed the narrow lane. It could get a little hairy walking the streets at this time. Most people were drunk and tripping over themselves, causing trouble, acting outrageously or throwing up in doorways. Normally two out of the three if not all of the above.

The taxi office was on the next street. A road used as the main artery through Hockley and ran alongside the tramlines.

"Made it," She looked up at him, feeling somewhat breathless. "Thank you."

He nodded, looking around seeing groups of men talking and smoking with teenagers and twenty-somethings stumbling about worse for wear. This was no place for her. He reached for her hand stopping her.

"I've got to go," Trinity breathed, afraid of what she was feeling. Afraid of what he was making her feel. It was too much all at once.

He looked down at her, his blue gaze intent on her face but she had the distinct impression he wasn't really in the moment with her.

"Bye Blake." She tugged free and went up the narrow stairs to where she took bookings and where patrons were able to wait on cars.

The drivers hung out in the room that was at street level.

"Hi ladies," she greeted the two other women who had headsets on. "Sorry, I'm late." Trinity stashed her handbag under the table as they didn't have a proper desk and she wiped the small leather padded earpiece with a smear of antibacterial gel she kept beside the computer, before plunking the device on her head and started taking calls.

***

Blake could not believe Trinity worked in such a place. She was obviously smart and ran her own business, why was she here?

Looking across the street, he noticed a fast food restaurant open and that it had seating. He crossed the street, preparing to wait for her. She should not be walking these streets alone. Why was she working another job he thought to himself, as he stepped inside the restaurant, only for his nostrils to be assaulted and tantalised by the smell of hot cooking oil and fried chicken.

"What can I get you mate?" The young Asian man with a heavy Pakistani accent asked.

"Coffee?"

"No coffee."

Blake looked around. He could really do with a Bacardi over ice, but that wasn't going to happen, so he settled on a Coke instead and ordered a tray of chips.

"Would you like cheese on them?" The man asked.

"Cheese on chips?" Blake had never heard of such a thing.

"It's the best thing. I'll give you the cheese for free mate." The chef smothered grated cheddar cheese over Blake's chips and handed him a small brown plastic tray with coke already on it.

After paying, Blake found a spot by the window where he was just about able to see the top of Trinity's head. Two other women were beside her. She was in a fishbowl, he thought, not liking how open and insecure the place was with people walking up and down.

The cheese on chips was good, so good in fact that Blake thought about ordering another tray but then thoughts of clogged arteries immediately vetoed that idea, and he sipped his drink while he thought about the night.

Remembering the website he had seen her on, Blake fished into his pocket for his phone and, regardless of the time, called the branch manager at home.

He wasn't happy with what he was told and now found himself in a predicament he didn't know how to get out of. The manager had declined her loan when Blake had asked what the amount was, he almost laughed. The amount was a pittance, and almost as much as he would spend in a single weekend in Paris.

He would give her the money.

"Not your type of place is it my friend?" The Asian man came and sat at his table.

"No, I'm waiting for someone," Blake glanced across at the taxi office.

"Who?" The Asian man was peering out of the window too, trying to fathom who the well-dressed man who looked completely out of place could be waiting for. He'd already been here an hour.

Blake turned to face his inquisitor. "She works over there."

"Oh you mean, one of the girls. Which one? It's not that I'm nosy or anything," his accent was heavy, but there were distinct traces of East Midlander like words creeping out. Blake relaxed as the chef chatted on. "There's fat Lorraine, she's a big one. I send her a box of chicken when she's on. You like Lorraine?"

The man tried to look fierce, and Blake held up his hands laughing. "No, Trinity."

"Ah, sexy black cat woman,"

"That's her,"

"She's well nice. I got my Lu-Lu from her. Best cat I've ever had. I swear she speaks to me in my native language, Urdu."

"Smart cat." Blake drawled.

He stuck out his hand. "Mohamed, but you can call me Mo."

"Blake."

They shook hands.

"Trinity." Mo laughed looking at him. "You don't look like Trinity's type."

"What's her type?" Blake shifted so that he could talk to the chef and watch Trinity in a single glance.

"I don't know really. Come to think of it I've not really seen her with anyone more than once. You going out with her then?"

Blake had never had such a weird conversation especially this late, or should he say early in the morning with a complete stranger.

He shrugged, preferring not to answer. The chef wasn't put off. "It must be something if you're waiting for her. You're not an axe murderer or anything like that 'cause I'm good with knives." Mo warned, leaning closer with narrowed dark eyes. "Real good."

Blake wanted to laugh. "I'm just her friend," Blake answered, watching as a group of under-dressed girls stumbled up the stairs. They were loud and vulgar and flashing their breasts at the taxi drivers.

A group of partygoers came into the shop, and Mo left him to see to their orders.

From his vantage point, Blake could see one of the girls leaning out of the window. She was pulling her top up and shouting lewd comments to people below. Her friends were trying to control her without success.

It was disgusting to watch. Is this what nightlife in Britain had become? When he'd been a student, yes they got drunk, but they never got stupid.

The girl threw up, down onto the pavement below and Blake watched as Trinity got up from her desk, disappeared, but came back with a glass of water. She was holding the girl's long black hair away from her face.

But the girl shrugged her off aggressively, and Blake watched horrified as Trinity stumbled and then disappeared from view.

He was across the street in a shot and up the stairs in time to see the girl fly across the room at Trinity who was trying to defend herself.

Blake grabbed the drunken girl around the waist and pushed her into a chair.

"You stay there!" He yelled and waited for a second to see if she would stay. He turned to Trinity who was being helped up by a large woman with a shock of pink hair, who could only be Lorraine. "Are you all right?" He asked her. Skimming his eyes over her body.

She nodded. "Where did you come from?" She asked looking slightly dazed.

"Come on poppet," Lorraine guided her into a single chair away from all the people milling around. "You're way too small to be dealing with drunken freaks like that tart!" She told her. She looked over at Blake. "Stay with her while I get her a glass of water."

Blake crouched down beside her. "Are you okay?" He asked again, taking her hands.

"Yes, I wasn't expecting her to be so strong," she revealed. "How come you're here?"

"I was planning on walking you home."

She smiled, and it was the sweetest smile he had ever seen in his life.

"Thank you, bu—"

"Now don't go and spoil it," Blake advised gently, sweeping his thumb across her bottom lip before moving away as Lorraine came back with a glass of water. "I'll be just over there." He nodded towards another chair at the back of the room.

"You coming back in Trinity? It's easing off a bit now." Lorraine asked looking at the thinning crowd.

Trinity looked at the time.

"I've only got another half hour anyway," she stood up and turned to Blake who was watching the exchange with interest. "Can you wait for me?"

He nodded and watched as she and Lorraine opened a glass door to the side and went inside.

***

The area eventually emptied, everyone, including the drunk girl who had pushed Trinity was gone, and the office door opened. Blake noted the look of relief on Trinity's face when she spotted him.

She walked over.

"Thanks for waiting,"

"No problem. Let's go."

She led the way down the stairs. "I just need to nip over there." She'd already started to cross the street.

Blake couldn't believe he was walking around Nottingham City Centre at four o'clock in the morning trailing behind a woman as though she held some sort of secret he needed to get his hands on.

"Dinner." She called out over her shoulder as she walked into the very shop he'd spent most of the night in.

"Ah, I see you found her," Mo called out spying Blake. "Wait, Trinity," he gave her an extra box of fried chicken.

"Thanks, Mo." She told him before leaving the shop. "I think this is for you." She indicated the red and white striped plastic bag and Blake took it from her.

They walked on and Trinity, not wanting to break the silence, kept her mouth shut even though she had a million questions to ask him. They reached her café in no time, and she searched her handbag for her keys.

"You live here too?" Blake asked as she unlocked the door and stepped over the threshold.

"Yep. Are you coming in?" She asked, holding the door open for him.

"If you want me to."

Blake closed the door behind him, watching the gentle sway of her bottom as she climbed the steps ahead of him.

"It's the least I could do with you rescuing and waiting for me like that." She turned on the narrow stairs and caught him looking at her behind. "You're not an axe murderer or anything are you?"

What was it with these Midlanders and axe murderers? He thought dryly. "It's a little late to be thinking like that don't you think?" He drawled, with a small smile. "I've already locked myself in with you."

"Soldier likes you." She said in the way of an explanation and continued up the steps.

Blake noticed the naked bulb in the ceiling was flashing intermittently. "That needs changing," he said as she led him into her space.

"That's the third bulb in two months," she advised. "Make yourself at home." She invited as she went over to her TV and switched the channel over. She had a sophisticated security camera system set up, and she was able to see the front and back entrances as well as see what the cats were doing all in living colour.

"Have you ever had any trouble?" Blake asked, peering at the different screens.

"No, but it's an old building, and there's an adjoining warehouse that is empty and had a couple of squatters in it a few months ago." She moved around him, toed off her shoes and went to the kitchenette, coming back with a plate.

"Sit."

"You like ordering me around don't you?" Blake asked with a slight twist of his lips.

"For some reason, I don't think it happens very often to you." She sat across from him at the tiny table and delved into the bags.

"I've already had cheesy chips tonight."

"Oh yum. Divine," she smacked her lips. "Mo makes the best food." Trinity pulled out the box of chicken. "I don't see you as a cheesy chip kind of guy,"

"Oh yeah," he said with a glint in his eye. "You know what I'm going to ask now don't you?"

She bit into a chicken leg and chewed for a moment before answering. "What kind of man do I see you as?" She volunteered, fluttering her eyelashes with exaggerated innocence.

Blake caught her hand with the chicken and pulled her hand towards him. He took a bite, all the while holding her gaze as he chewed the tender meat.

"You're a great kisser." She revealed seriously, as though he hadn't just done one of the most erotic things in her life.

He laughed out loud, not expecting her to say that.

"Thank you." He chuckled.

She tipped her head to one side in that adorable way he was beginning to like, Blake thought and relaxed into the chair as she continued to look at him.

"Your clothes say one thing but your body another," Trinity went on.

"Oh?" He was captivated, completely caught up in the moment.

"Yeah," she sighed. "Your jeans have seams."

Blake looked down at his jeans, He'd never noticed the seams before. That would be Malcolm his elderly housekeeper's doing.

"Go on," he encouraged.

"You don't smile very much, but when you do I get—"

He leaned closer, completely captivated. "You get?" he encouraged softly, watching as her tongue quickly licked away a drop of ketchup from the corner of her mouth.

"Eat your chicken it's getting cold." She told him instead.

He leaned back into his chair. "Spoilsport."

They both laughed at each other.

CHAPTER THREE

Trinity did a rubbish job of smothering her yawn and blinking several times.

"I'd best be going." Blake stood up to go, getting the hint. He himself should have been tired, but he felt as though he could run a marathon or two. "Thanks for dinner, or maybe it was breakfast?"

She looked at him, did he dare see an invitation in her sleepy gaze?

"You can stay if you like," Trinity offered quietly, before quickly picking up the remnants of their take-out and walking to her kitchenette where she dropped the boxes into the metal rubbish bin with efficient swiftness.

Blake watched and waited for her to turn to him. They'd laughed and teased over their food, and there was no denying the sexual undercurrents as they talked, but she was now ignoring him.

When she turned on the taps to wash their plates, he walked over and leaned against the cupboard, watching her closely.

"What are you saying?" He asked eventually, afraid yet excited about her answer.

Trinity exhaled before turning to look at him with wide overly bright eyes. She tried to pull in some much-needed air.

Blake stepped closer still and turned off the taps. He smiled gently as he reached for a blue chequered hand towel and dried her fingers one by one with the rough cotton.

When he finished, he dropped the towel beside the sink and laced his fingers through hers, captivated by their differences. Dark and light, small and strong. He tugged her forward and kissed her knuckles.

Trinity felt a pool of heat all the way to the juncture of her thighs. He was barely touching her, yet she felt his magnetic pull and couldn't stop herself from reaching up with her other hand, wrapping it around his nape and pulling him down to her.

She kissed him, a tentative brushing of lips as she explored the soft curves of his mouth.

Blake let her do whatever she wanted to do. He kept his hands at his side even though he wanted to explore every dip and curve of her lush body. He wanted to walk her to any flat surface, the wall, the floor or her bed but he didn't want to rush this moment for either of them.

Trinity, feeling a little braver, ran her hands under Blake's jumper touching the smooth skin that was hot under her fingertips. His body felt beautiful, strong and athletic. She ran her fingers up and over his wide chest, noting the scattering of hair and with a knowing smile pinched his nipples. Hearing his breath hitch, she pinched them again.

Blake couldn't help a moan from escaping. With everything he had, he kept his hands to his side as she touched him. He wanted to explode. He'd never been so aroused in his life. He'd never wanted to slam into a woman, her, as much as he needed to right now. He gritted his teeth as she pulled at the hem of his jumper and whipped it over his head.

Her look almost undid him.

"You're beautiful Blake," she whispered in awe, her lovely brown eyes wide as she took in his strong shoulders and narrow waist.

Trinity traced his muscles with her fingers. Smoothing them down the centre of his chest, up and over the tight knots of muscle and following the line of dark hair as it narrowed and disappeared into the white elasticated band of his briefs.

Flashing him another look, Trinity tugged at his belt, releasing the buckle and snapping open the row of buttons. His ridge of arousal was huge, and Trinity grabbed him feeling the length and breadth of him.

Blake broke.

Taking over, he yanked her to him and slammed his mouth

over hers as he picked her up, wrapping her slender legs around his waist as he kissed her.

She made a sound deep in her throat as they kissed and he frantically got rid of her jeans to smooth his fingers along her damp panties. She was so wet for him.

He pulled the moist lace to the side and swept his fingers along her swollen lips. She was so ready for him.

With a desperation he hadn't felt in years he searched for his pockets for the condom he knew was there but was unwilling to release her to find.

"Trinity? I need—" he spoke against her lips, "help," he kissed her neck. "Condom. Pockets." His vocabulary had gone to hell.

Trinity pushed off him and dropped to her knees. She frantically searched his jeans that had now dropped down his legs. Oh my, she thought, distracted by the tantalising ridge that was level with her gaze and laying heavy and throbbing to one side, the smooth tip nosing out of the top of his white cotton boxers.

She grasped him through his underpants again and rubbed her face against him, breathing in his musky male scent, before reaching in and pulling his arousal free.

Her first thought before she kissed the smooth head was how beautiful he was. Her second thought, as he jumped and twitched in her hand, was how amazing he was going to make her feel.

Grasping her hair, he gently pulled her away and shook his head as she pouted up at him. "Next time," he promised. "I need to be inside you right now."

Blake shrugged out of his jeans and knelt on the floor, finding the condom and watching her watch him, with dark eyes heavy with promise. He rolled it on.

Trinity, unable to wait a moment longer, rained kisses over his neck and chest as she pushed him against the fridge. A part of her realised they were still in the kitchen. Another part of her- the part ruled only by sex-didn't care. Now with concentrated slowness she smiled and climbed over his massive thighs, kissing him deeply as he massaged her bottom before pushing her panties to the side and pushing her down onto him.

She gasped in his mouth as she took him deep inside her. He was wide, stretching her inner walls in a way she had never felt before.

The feeling was unexplainable, and she wriggled her hips, feeling more of his fullness as she picked up a rhythm that had him grabbing her hips as she slammed over him again and again.

Blake had never felt like this in his entire life. He had never let a woman take control of him this way either. She took everything he had with greedy abandon, and he didn't have long to wait before her head rolled back and she arched her back as ripples of pleasure went through her.

That was the signal he'd been waiting for. In a sudden shift of bodies he got rid of her panties and flipped her over spreading his hands under her smooth bottom and pushing into her over and over as he felt her ripple against him once again before he finally let himself go. It was unbelievable.

***

Trinity woke to tiny nails digging into her head.

"Mercy," she mumbled sleepily, reaching up to move the cat. "Stop that right now." She scolded tiredly, trying to move but finding herself pressed into the mattress by something heavy laying across her thighs.

She opened her eyes, afraid to see what she knew she was going to see. Blake was sleeping beside her, his arms and legs wrapped around her clamping her to his side as though afraid she might try to escape.

Mercy was above their heads, walking back and forth along the pillows impatiently and giving her a haughty look that made Trinity feel like a slut.

What had she done? She thought as she slowly tried to lift Blake's arm from over her chest.

He shifted in his sleep and cupped her breast, sweeping his thumb across her nipple back and forth, and she slammed her legs together, squeezing them tight as she fought against her arousal. She needed to get up.

They'd only had the one condom, and once that had been used, Blake used his tongue, his mouth, his fingers to make her come time and time again. She'd fallen apart in shameful abandon in his arms. Her bedroom had been bright with sunlight by the time they'd finally fallen asleep.

She moved her whole body out from under him inch by inch. She didn't want to wake him, she didn't want to talk, she just wanted to shower and have a nice cup of tea and think.

***

Blake opened his eyes to see a cloud with vivid blue holes next to his face. He blinked and looked again. A fluffy white cat was staring at him in the most unnerving way.

Sitting up and looking around, he smiled with satisfaction. Last night, or rather this morning, had been incredible. He'd had the best sex of his life.

Where was she?

There wasn't a sound in the flat at all, so he stood up, stretched his arms high over his head then pulled on his briefs and jeans and looked around.

The flat was empty.

Her flat was tiny, neat but cosy, he noticed as he walked around the bright yellow living room he hadn't paid any attention to last night.

There was a selection of framed photos on the wall, Trinity with a girl who had to be a younger relative, sister or cousin he thought, as their smiles were identical. Another photo showed Trinity between two people Blake presumed to be her parents on her graduation day. Her cap was slightly askew, and she was beaming. There was another of her with a tall man with wet looking curls down to his shoulders and wearing some sort of 70s costume.

Blake passed the bulging two seater sofa in pretty blue and yellow flowers to push the matching curtains aside, intending to look out of the single sash window, or so he thought.

The window had some sort of yellowing plastic sheeting nailed into the wooden window frame to keep out any draughts no doubt, he thought, as he looked down into the street, already busy with people hurrying along, their open umbrellas a blurred kaleidoscope of pattern and colour.

He used the bathroom and tried to use her shower, but the trickle of water that came out of the pipe was so unsatisfying he gave up. Then he used his finger to brush his teeth. She had a half bottle of mouthwash, and he rinsed his mouth before pulling on his clothes again and turning on the TV to look at the CCTV.

There she was sitting cross-legged on the floor surrounded by her cats. She was stroking one and then the other as they vied for her attention, but Blake could see her mind was on something else as her shoulders were slumped and she wasn't smiling. She looked dejected, not like the loved up satisfied woman he expected to see, he thought frowning.

Turning off the TV, he searched and found her comb and tidied his hair. A shave would have to wait, he thought, as he rubbed the itchy bristles on his face before carefully navigating the narrow stairwell, absently noting the dampness of the walls as he moved.

"Good morning," he said, stepping into the room and then he stopped on the threshold as he was wearing his shoes. "Shall I take these off?" He enquired, looking at his shoes.

"No, it's okay. Just stay where you are," she told him, getting up from the floor.

Blake had never had a problem with the morning after scenario as he'd never spent the whole night with a woman before, now he knew why. She was looking at him nervously and wringing her hands. Was he expected to declare undying love? Were they about to dissect what had happened? Was she about to cling and start making demands just because they'd had sex? Amazing sex. But still sex. Blake reasoned, but she did none of those. The silence pulled taut between them.

Trinity eventually walked over to the vending machine,

pressed a few buttons and walked back towards him with a cup of coffee in her hand. She held it out to him, being careful not to touch his fingers as he took the cup.

"I've got a lot to do today." She told him dismissively, turning her back and walking away from him.

Blake could not believe what he was hearing. She was kicking him out! She had his bitc mark on her neck, and she was kicking him out! He felt a wave of anger ripple through him.

"That's it?" Blake seethed. "You shag the life out of me, give me a cup of coffee and send me on my way?"

She shrugged.

Blake looked at her on the far side of the room, surrounded by cats, looking gorgeous in tight grey jeans and a black long sleeved t-shirt with The Cat Café written across her breasts in shiny pink flamboyant lettering. She was kicking him out. He couldn't believe she was kicking him out. This was not how he envisioned his morning. He'd wanted to assuage his morning ache for her, taste her one more time. Kiss her. Touch her. Not this!

Before he could say anything he might regret, he gulped down the coffee, wincing as it scalded the roof of his mouth, tossed the cup onto the nearest surface, which just happened to be where Soldier was sitting looking at him hopefully. But he tightened his heart and, with one last scathing glance at Trinity, closed the door.

***

Trinity listened for the front door to open and close and watched when Blake walked past the window. He did not look inside.

She breathed a sigh of relief.

She had never in all her years behaved as she did with him this morning. She was so embarrassed, doing things to a relative stranger. Hell, he was a stranger! She didn't even know where he lived if he was married. My God! What if he was married?

She didn't like herself right now and to distract herself went about finding something for herself to eat. She still had another hour before the café opened and she was not going to think about the one night stand she'd just had.

CHAPTER FOUR

Blake stood under the torrent of water in his shower, appreciating for the first time how fortunate he was compared to that ridiculous trickle Trinity had.

Trinity, he thought angrily. He'd been dismissed, he still couldn't believe it. Him, Baldassario Blake Carmello De Laurentis had been dismissed by a slip of a woman who lived and breathed cats.

She was mad, had to be deluded to kick him out of her bed. Women played all kinds of tricks just to get in it, Blake mused arrogantly as he washed every last trace of her from his skin before walking out of his wet room, hearing the water automatically switch off with satisfaction. He liked the trappings of wealth. He didn't need to drink his coffee from a vending machine or spend time in a café!

Yes, this was his life. The only reason he wasn't living in the penthouse was because his father, Baldassario Carmello De Laurentis the Third used it and Blake didn't go into his father's space, even if the man was in another country.

Yesterday and the day before was an aberration. Blake didn't need to see Trinity again. His bank had finished all dealings with her. Her loan had been declined. She would need to look elsewhere for the tuppence she wanted. He was done with her. Finished.

Blake stopped rubbing his hair with the towel as he looked out across the city remembering the website she'd been on just last night. Payday loan companies were loan sharks in sheep's clothing. The disgrace of the banking industry. If she went that route, she'd never repay her loan. She'd drown in debt.

One last visit, Blake told himself. It was his duty as a man placed in the highest regard with his peers to make sure she made the right decision. He'd see her one last time before leaving the East Midlands and heading back to the good life. Then again, he thought, remembering the way she'd looked at him as though he were a slug leaving a trail of slime across her floor, he owed her nothing. Nothing at all.

***

"What's that?"

"Hmm," Trinity looked up to see Travis looking at her with a quizzical expression on his face. "What?"

"The love bite. Aren't you a bit old to be getting love bites?"

Trinity touched the small bruise on her neck. Two days and it hadn't even begun to fade.

"It's a good job, I'm not the jealous type." He told her laughing as he swung away to play *Roll the Ball* with Demus.

Trinity shook her head. It had been two days. Two days of her watching the door. She'd even caught herself hoping that her phone would ring, but then scolded herself as he didn't even have her mobile number. They were strangers.

He'd be that guy she'd fondly remember in years to come as the one who gave her the multiple orgasms. She'd remember him forever.

"Why are you here again Travis?" She asked the young doctor.

Travis looked over. "Mel was in."

"And?"

"I preferred to be here," he dodged. "What's going on with the expansion you want to do?" He asked switching the subject.

Trinity noted the change of subject but followed his lead. He didn't want to talk about his home life.

"I didn't get the loan from the bank,"

"That's rubbish Trin, this place has potential." Travis looked around, and Trinity followed his gaze.

It was early evening, and the place was filled. Two humans to one cat, Trinity counted. All paying for more than an hour.

Saturday was adoption day, and fourteen of her cats were due to leave. The rescue centre would be dropping off more cats on

Sunday afternoon.

Her business was booming. There was no reason to decline her loan. Ah well, she thought moving on from her depressing thoughts, onwards and upwards. She'd find a way to get the money to put the down-payment on the place next door. But she was not going to her father.

She didn't want to move premises completely as she was central enough for every student, resident, office worker and passers-by to drop in. She'd already made a name for herself and worked hard with her brand. Moving right now was not an option.

After her last customer had left she locked the door and pulled down the blinds. She had a shift at the taxi office tonight so went upstairs and had a quick shower, noting the water was running even slower than usual and changed into a pair of leggings and a baggy sweatshirt. She pulled her hair into one, made herself a cup of tea and sat with Mercy for a bit before heading out.

***

Blake couldn't sleep. He knew what he wanted to do but had forced all thoughts of her from his head. She meant nothing, that night was hot, but he could have many more like that with other women.

He threw back the sheet and checked his phone for the time. After midnight.

Walking to his floor to ceiling windows he looked down at the city sprawled below. He was central to everything and able to walk anywhere with no real hardship.

The streets were crowded again, and he slid open a door and stepped out onto the balcony to look out, the wooden flooring was numbingly cold on his bare feet.

Girls hobbled along on platform heels screaming and laughing loudly with boys. The Friday night mating ritual, Blake thought shaking his head. They'd be drinking for another couple of hours, getting completely inebriated and then trying to find a way home.

Taxis.

Blake looked in the direction of the taxi office where Trinity worked. He didn't even know if she worked there every night.

Friday nights would be even worse than it was earlier in the week when she'd been tackled by that drunken girl.

Closing the door, Blake knew he was going to see if she was working. She didn't need to know he was there. He just needed to make sure she was safe. He couldn't sleep anyway so he may as well he reasoned, pulling on a pair of grey flannel bottoms, trainers and a navy coloured sweatshirt and shutting the door behind him.

***

"Hey, you're back my friend!" Mo, the chef at the chicken place, said as Blake walked in. "You want cheesy chips?"

Blake laughed. "Please,"

"You stay there, let me just serve this little ruffian and get to you." Mo teased a man old enough to be his grandfather.

Blake laughed and sat at his usual spot.

She was there. He could see the top of her head. She'd changed her hair. It was high up on her head, and he was able to see the long sweep of her neck. She was laughing.

"Here you go mate," Mo placed a can of coke, and a large tray of cheesy chips in front of him and Blake mentally reminded himself to run an extra two miles tomorrow morning just to burn the meal off.

"Thanks,"

Mo looked over his shoulder. "I like that you're looking out for Trinity, she's a nice girl."

"Hmm," Blake said non-committally avoiding the all too knowing gaze from him.

"What?" The young man looked at him sharply. "You're not going out?"

"I don't really know," Blake replied honestly, looking over the street.

"Lorraine changed her status to 'It's complicated.' last night. I mean really? What's complicated. I make you chicken, you make me babies. What's so complicated about that?" Mo said in all seriousness.

Blake choked back his laugh. "You and Lorraine?" Blake said remembering Trinity's colleague.

Mo smiled widely. "She's a whole lot of woman. For weeks I've been trying to get with her. She smiles, she laughs, she eats my chicken, I put her in a taxi, what else?"

"Maybe she needs it spelt out to her?" Blake suggested, spearing a fat chip smothered with cheese onto his plastic fork.

Mo flashed his hands. "It's complicated," he mumbled again. "I am a businessman. I work hard. I make money I make people happy with my food, and still, I get nothing."

Blake didn't know what to say. None of his friends ever had this kind of trouble when it came to women. They all wanted the same thing. The men, a beautiful woman, who turned a blind eye if the husband had a mistress and the women a monthly allowance and exotic holidays. They didn't change status making announcements for all to see.

It was getting later, all the taxis were out dropping people home, and the office was getting full. Nobody wanted to wait outside in the cold.

Blake didn't like it. He knew it was a disaster waiting to happen.

"What time does the office close?" Blake asked Mo.

"It's twenty-four hours. Always so much trouble, but they bring me business. The police have to come out sometimes."

"That bad?"

"Yeah," Mo confirmed. "There was this one stupid boy who thought to lock himself in with the ladies, Trinity wasn't working there at the time, but my Lorraine was. He was getting too, and she had to sit on him until the police came and rescued him." He finished proudly as he got up to serve another group of loud clubbers.

Blake had visions of Trinity being accosted and even worse. She wouldn't stand a chance against a fly much less a man intent on injuring her. She weighed nothing.

Blake couldn't finish the chips and slid the paper tray in the bin before Mo saw, then he waited.

The crowds grew faster than the taxis could carry them away. It was practically another party going and spilling into the street.

A girl was shouting at full volume, and the crowd turned to see what was going on.

The girl, dressed in a short black clingy dress and gold accessories was crying, walking barefoot and holding her heels in her hand.

"How could you do that to me?" She screeched at a man in his early twenties who was walking a few steps behind her.

The girl stumbled up the stairs all the while shouting abuse and crying.

"I'm going outside," Blake called out to Mo, who was putting another load of heavily floured chicken into the oil. Mo waved him off.

Blake crossed the street and shouldered his way through the crowd.

Kids were sitting on the steps, and it took him twice as long to reach the lounge upstairs.

The girl and her boyfriend were having a raging shouting match, and the crowd was watching and laughing as the drama unfolded.

Why was there no security at this place? Blake thought, not for the first time.

The girl raised her hand to slap her boyfriend, but he caught her hand in his. They stood nose to nose. Neither giving in.

Before Blake could even step in, Trinity flew out of the office and was telling the two off.

Blake stepped out of her vision and watched from behind a fake bamboo plant. If she needed him, he was there, but it looked as though she knew the warring pair.

"Steph? How many times do I have to tell you? You don't get physical. He is bigger and stronger, if he hits you back, it will hurt."

"But he was dancing with another girl," the girl said in her defence.

"So, he's hot," Trinity said. "He chose you to be with. It was only dancing."

Blake watched as Trinity turned to the boy with her hands on her hips.

"Callum, do you fancy this other girl?"

"No."

"So why do we have to go through this every week? Kiss and make up," Trinity ordered. "Now." She told them, folding her hands across her chest.

Blake wanted to smile, she was magnificent. The smallest in the room but she commanded and got the utmost respect.

The young couple kissed and then turned to Trinity sheepishly.

"Come on then," she told them holding out her arms before being engulfed in a three-way hug. "No more drama guys," She warned before turning back to her office but paused with her hand on the handle and said. "I'm leaving in half an hour, and it's been a long night."

Blake slipped out, walked across the street, paid Mo and waited in the doorway of a charity shop.

***

Blake didn't have long to wait. Trinity walked past him with her head bent low.

"Trinity?" He called out.

Trinity stopped and turned, seeing Blake saunter out of a doorway and walk casually towards her.

She refused to acknowledge the glimmer of excitement just seeing him did to her body and turned back to walk home.

He caught up with her.

"Can we talk?"

"I'm too tired."

"I've got some things I need to say,"

"It'll have to wait."

"Please," Blake begged.

She stopped then at the very top of May Hill Lane. Her shop was exactly thirty-seven steps away she knew. She'd counted them one night.

"If you've come for a what the Americans call a booty call, you're out of luck. I'm keeping you as the one-night stand memory." She walked away, counting her steps.

Eight before he next spoke.

"I've never had a one night stand in my life," Blake all but roared to her back.

Fourteen.

"Are you married?" Trinity swung round to ask.

"What! No."

She continued walking.

Blake did not appreciate the view of her back, as sexy as it was, as she walked away from him. "I want to talk to you about the loan,"

Twenty-two.

She swung back to him, not expecting him to be so close and took a step back.

Twenty-three.

"What are you talking about?"

"You can't go to a payday lender for money," he stated solemnly.

"Who said I was?"

"You were on a website the other night."

Trinity thought back remembering the night. "It's none of your business."

"They charge almost seven hundred per cent interest. You'd never be able to pay it back!"

Trinity flicked him a look and walked to her door. "I don't see why you care what I do."

"We are lovers," Blake stated bluntly.

"For a night," she said warily taking her keys out of her pocket. "For a few hours." She amended on a whisper.

"The best hours of my life," he told her gruffly, stepping close enough to feel her body heat.

"You are not coming inside, and I am not sleeping with you."

She pressed her hands against his chest holding him off. She had to look way up just to capture his gaze.

"Wait to be asked, Trinity."

Trinity gasped, spun around, fumbled with her keys and then stepped inside as soon as the door opened. He was looking at her in a way she hadn't seen before.

She held onto the door, using it as a shield against his blatant sexiness. He was really a gorgeous man, masculine angles, dark hair and vivid blue eyes, she thought, pressing her thighs together and hoping he didn't notice the way he affected her.

She'd never seen him look so casual, grey sweat bottoms and top and a pair of white trainers. The way he was looking at her was an invitation to explore, all of him. If she invited him in, he would come and their one night stand would become two.

"You'll do what I said?" He asked quietly, Trinity was looking at him as though she wanted to eat him alive, he didn't even bother to hide his arousal.

"Huh?"

He sighed, she wasn't making it easy for him. "No payday loans. In fact, don't go to any lender who calls money anything other than money. It's a, and you will be the loser," he stated softly. "Okay?"

"Yes okay."

"I'm leaving tomorrow." He told her, reaching forward to cup her face gently with one hand.

She nodded, feeling the backs of her eyes begin to sting and she nudged her head into his palm, pressing a kiss at the base of his thumb.

"Oh,"

"I'll always remember you," he promised gruffly, sliding his thumb across her bottom lip.

"You too—I mean me too."

Blake leaned in and kissed her. It was meant to be a goodbye kiss, but somehow he was inside the hall. The door had slammed shut, and they were upstairs in her flat.

***

Trinity worked flat out. The adoptions went without a hitch, and she was given sixteen more cats from the shelter.

The week of transition was always difficult for the cats, especially for those who already considered the café home. They could become very territorial with the new cats and spats would break out.

Remembering her promise to Blake, she didn't apply for any loans and made do with pulling extra shifts at the taxi office. She had very few choices when it came to extra work, what with the café being open for a large chunk of the day. It left the taxi office, bar work and cleaning jobs.

She needed another income that was easy and didn't tax her brain.

***

Blake was bored. London was home, he travelled to Italy less and less because London was the place that excited him. Except the excitement had evaded him these past few weeks.

He wrenched his mind back to the screen on his laptop when it had begun to wander again, up north to be precise. The Midlands.

He thought about Trinity when he was in bed, suffering from a raging hard-on that only thirty minutes of breath-stealing cold showers could alleviate. He'd be catching a damn cold at this rate if he kept this up he thought to himself, slumping in his chair to spin around to the windows.

"I see you're working hard,"

Blake spun back to face the room at the sound of his grandfather.

"Lunch?" Blake inquired, ready to leave the confines of his office.

"Humph, it's barely ten o'clock, and you're talking about lunch? What's going on and why haven't you been to see me?"

"Time," Blake replied warily.

"Humph, when had that ever stopped you?" the old man who

was the older version of Blake scolded. "You know I don't like wearing suits but to come down here, I have to dig them out. I'm not a part of this rat race any more; it's for you to take over."

"Yes, Grandpop I know."

"What's the matter?" The old man sat in the chair opposite. This had once been his office, but when he married Annalise, he gave up everything, retired fully and packed away his suits. "Have you lost all our money?"

"Of course not,"

"Bank about to be bailed out by the government like that other one?"

"No, the bank is fine," Blake stood up and moved around the desk to sit beside his grandfather.

"Got a girl pregnant?"

Blake laughed, he had too. Five years ago his grandpop wouldn't even be having this conversation with him. Marrying Annalise and he became a real person. Human.

"Me and Annalise wouldn't mind having some babies around you know. Getting a woman pregnant isn't the end of the world."

"I haven't got anyone pregnant."

"Sure?"

Blake sighed. "Grandpop I can assure you there aren't any little De Laurentis's about to be born."

"Pity," the old man looked at him slyly. "Some girl has caught your eye, hasn't she? I can tell."

"In Nottingham," Blake admitted warily.

"Oh yeah, what's she like?"

"She likes cats," Blake smiled. "She has about twenty."

"Twenty cats!"

"Yeah and they all live downstairs, although she had this cute fluffy white one who lives upstairs." Blake babbled looking off into the distance as he remembered waking up to the fluffy white cat staring at him. "Some of them might be gone by now though," he went on. "They get adopted every week. I'm hoping Soldier went to a good home."

Grandpop was looking at him with his mouth open, but Blake

missed the look.

It was a pleasant visit, and Blake was grateful for the distraction.

"Did you go and check that building I told you to?"

"What building?" Blake asked.

"The one I sent you to Nottingham to look at?"

"No,"

"Why not?"

Blake sighed. "Do we really need another building?"

"No, but Annalise needs a reason to see her family."

"Why does she need a reason to see her family?"

"She married me against their wishes."

Blake flashed his grandfather a quizzical look. "Isn't she like seventy?"

"Seventy-six," he clarified. "She looks good doesn't she?" Grandpop enthused, winking at Blake. "She's from Derby. When we met up again, it fractured her family as it was her brother who had lied all those years ago. He ripped up my letters and told her I'd moved on."

"Bastard."

"That's what I called him. I'd moved on only after I'd waited for almost ten years."

"I'm glad you found her again Grandpop,"

His grandfather smiled.

"Yes my son, I need a project for her. She misses her family. Will you help?"

"I'll check it out."

"Will you visit your girlfriend?"

"She's not my girlfriend."

"But you miss her?"

"Grandpop, we spent a night, well two together," he wasn't the least bit embarrassed about talking to his grandfather like this.

"And you don't plan on going back?"

"I didn't plan to, no."

"Why not?"

"Well because, well," Blake sighed running a hand through his hair. "Just because."

"I sent you to an expensive boarding school, and you come out with that?"

"We said our goodbyes. It ended."

"Oh well, you look all the better for it, don't you?" Grandpop pointed out before standing and walking to the door. "Annalise told me to tell you dinner tomorrow night, she's making a pappardelle, and you will tell her how perfect it is." He stressed.

Blake took the hint but didn't even try to hide his grimace. Annalise could not cook. "Yes, Grandpop."

"Bye son, see you tomorrow."

***

It was Sunday, and Trinity was walking through town. She opened an hour later on a Sunday, and she usually spent the time catching up on her sleep, but today she decided to go for a walk by the canal as although chilly, it wasn't raining and the sun was playing nice.

It's wasn't too far, and she liked to look at the narrow boats and talk to the owners who were usually sat on chairs reading newspapers or listening to the radio. Enjoying a simpler life, they said. She did envy them their simpler lives sometimes though, like now.

"Hey, Trinity! Trinity Peters!" Someone shouted behind her, and she turned to see Reece, the guy from the bank running towards her in full running gear.

"Hi," she said.

"Hi, what are you doing this side of town?" He asked, fiddling with his watch as he ran on the spot then stopped, taking deep breaths as he looked down at her.

"Taking a walk, clearing my head, figuring out life," she listed despondently. She was tired. Tired of slogging away knowing she really didn't need to, but knowing she had to.

"Sorry about the loan thingy," Reece apologised. "It was the damnedest thing."

"What do you mean?"

"Everything was fine, you'd been approved, and then my boss took over. I later heard the big fish from London had told him to decline it."

"But why?"

"God only knows. Want to go get a bite to eat?" He offered.

"Thank you but no."

"I'm really sorry about that," he started running on the spot again.

"Don't worry about it."

"Please don't hold it against me. I tried my best."

"It's okay Reece," she soothed. "Things happen for a reason."

"Okay," he did something to his watch again. "See you around. You look great by the way."

"Bye."

She watched him run off, all the while wondering why someone who didn't know her or her background would interfere with her life.

Later that evening Michelle the florist came by. She also lived above her shop.

"You look exhausted kiddo, still at that damned taxi office?"

"Yeah."

"I get you needing another job, but why that place?" She asked.

"It's handy, you know that,"

"You can work with me,"

"Doing what?"

"I do a bit of cleaning two days a week."

"What's the hourly rate?"

Michelle told her and Trinity had to keep from rubbing her hands together. If she did that she wouldn't have to work at the taxi office at all.

They talked about it some more and Michelle promised to get her more information before the week was out.

Trinity went to bed that night feeling more positive than she had done in days. She didn't cry. She would never cry over a man, but she just couldn't pick herself up. She missed him.

He'd been in her life a total of fourteen physical hours. She'd actually counted them, yes she was that sad, and yes she missed him.

So he wasn't married, that was great, but maybe he had lied about that and she was now the other woman, the thought shamed her.

Switching on her laptop, she typed his name into the search engine. Everyone had something online these days, she thought clicking on all the Blake Lawrences. He was not any of them. She went to images and again he wasn't there. She put her name in, and her café, some of her cats, her website, her social networks and several articles all came up. Her image was everywhere. Where was his?

She'd been duped by him again. She closed the laptop angry with herself. This is what you get when you sleep with a man you know nothing about. She wasn't the kind to do one night stands. She'd only ever shared her body with one other man beside Blake. This was not her, and it was eating her up. She'd gone against her principles, her moral code, her Sunday sermons, her everything.

It was time to move on and forget him.

***

Trinity enjoyed the cleaning job. The ladies that she worked with were great fun, and she was able to work her own hours.

Tonight she wasn't in the office block but doing a couple of residential flats not far from May Hill.

All of them were empty, and the cleaning agency had a long-running contract for them. Trinity thought her boss was maybe pulling a fast one, as she was sure the flat owners didn't want the cleaners in late at night. But she wasn't about to ask any questions. She was grateful for the money.

Trinity had four flats to do, and she went through them easily enough, flicking her duster all the while dancing to her playlist via her headphones.

About to polish a large table, Trinity shook the can only to realise it was empty and she danced over to her supply bucket to look for another one. Unfortunately, there wasn't one.

Walking down to the car park to replenish her supplies, Trinity was temporarily blinded when a car swept past, and she squinted against the glare, before opening the back of the cleaning van to find a new can of polish. Picking up a clean packet of cloths as well, Trinity slammed the van door shut and headed back to the steps.

The car park was brightly lit. The crude walls painted brilliant white, but it was still an eerie place, and Trinity hurried on and was about to put her headphones on when familiar laughter caught her attention. She looked over her shoulder and froze. Blake was there, helping a stunningly lovely woman out of a car.

Trinity wanted to be sick. She wanted to move, run, hide, anything but stay where she was, lit by bright light and fighting waves of nausea as she watched him holding the woman close around the waist.

The can of polish slipped from her fingers, and she watched in horror as it rolled clank, clank, clank down the concrete steps almost in slow motion.

She went after it, inadvertently kicking it under a car in her haste.

Freaking out and dashing behind the vehicle she went down on her knees trying to reach the can that had rolled to a stop by the rear wheel, just out of her reach. She'd need to crawl under the vehicle to extract it she thought in dismay, or just leave it. It was only a can of polish.

"Trinity?"

Oh God, no, no, no! She thought frantically, her embarrassment complete. She had no choice but to face him.

"Hi," she said breezily, getting up and dusting off her knees.

"What are you doing?"

"I—I—couldn't find the polish," she explained feebly, feeling the heat in her cheeks.

They stood staring at each other until Trinity dropped her gaze, noticing his black tuxedo and how gorgeous he looked in it. The seam in his trousers was razor sharp, and his shoes were so shiny the light bounced off them. His dark hair had some sort of product in it, as it was expertly sculpted away from his forehead and his eyes were sparkling. He looked gorgeous, she thought. Drop dead gorgeous. But he didn't look that way for her.

"I need to go," Trinity gulped past the acidic lump in her throat as she ran past him and dashed up the steps to race to the front door.

"Wait!" He shouted, following her.

"No, I—," her humiliation was complete when the front door wouldn't open, and Blake caught her around the waist.

"What are you doing?" Blake asked, pulling her away from the door.

"I don't know," she sniffed, struggling against him.

"I see you have your hands full, darling." His companion said, walking up the stairs towards the bank of elevators.

"Call the lift for me Leigh." He ordered over his shoulder.

"I'm not going anywhere with you," Trinity stated, finally gathering her wits around her and digging in her heels.

Blake simply rearranged her in his arms and threw her over his shoulder instead.

"Of all the outrageous things ever done to me this is it, Blake Lawrence, if that's even your name."

Blake ignored her, knowing he had lied and that he had some explaining to do. But not today. They went into the lift Leigh had called. He smiled his thanks when she called for another one for herself.

Blake strode down the corridor, used his card to open the door and then dumped Trinity unceremoniously on the sofa.

"What are you doing in my building?" Blake asked standing over her, looking at her through narrowed eyes.

Had she found out who he was and was planning on doing something underhanded? Stalking? It had happened more than once. He was a wealthy man. A target for manipulative, greedy women. He'd found a woman—a past lover—naked in his bed once. Had Trinity developed stalker tendencies too?

Trinity sat up and shook her head slightly. She still felt sick, but she would be damned if she would be ill in front of him. She pushed her hair out of her face and looked up at him.

"I work here,"

Blake frowned down at her. "Doing what?"

"I clean a couple of the flats."

"At night?" He asked in disbelief. Who would let a cleaning crew into their home at night? She was lying.

"Yes,"

"and you so happened to be working in my building?"

"I didn't know you lived here. You said you lived in London." She defended, standing up.

"Sit down." He ordered.

"I don't want to sit down," Trinity countered. "I'd like to leave now."

"Sit down!" He shouted.

Trinity edged towards the door, aware that she was in a flat with a man she didn't really know and no one knew where she was. He grabbed her arm to stop her from leaving.

"Please don't hurt me," she begged, pulling away from him.

Blake frowned, taken aback. "Why would I hurt you?"

Trinity purposely looked down at his hand that was still gripping her upper arm. Blake snapped his fingers off her as though she'd grown spikes.

"I'm sorry. I don't mean to frighten you," he turned away. "Would you like a drink?" He offered, going to the kitchen.

"No thank you."

"Trinity," he came back with two glasses of water and handed her one. "I didn't mean to scare you. I was surprised to find you in the place I least expected that's all." He apologised, pulling at his bow tie and loosening the top buttons of his shirt.

She took a sip of the water, noticing for the first time that she was still wearing her yellow rubber gloves. She pulled them off and stuck them in her back pockets.

"Please have a seat,"

"No thanks, I'd best be going. I left my things in the flat downstairs."

"Stay a while and talk to me. How have you been?"

"Fine."

"How are the cats?"

"Soldier is still with me. Nobody wants a cat with a torn ear and a crooked tail. The rescue centre will take him back soon."

"Then what will happen to him?"

"I don't know." She did know, but she didn't want to say it out loud. She was still hoping he would be adopted or she would just keep him.

Blake was silent, thinking.

"I was coming to see you," he finally said into the silence.

"Why? We said our goodbyes."

"I want to see you again."

"Sorry but I don't think that's a good idea."

"Why not?"

"Because we don't know each other."

"I already know every bit of your gorgeous body,"

"Stop it," she crossed her arms over chest. "I don't know anything about you. Any of the normal stuff."

"Like what?"

She looked at him, standing there looking model perfect in his tux and shiny shoes.

"How long have you been in Nottingham?" She asked suddenly.

"Three days," he answered without thinking and was about to expand when she turned her back and started towards the door.

"I was planning on coming to see you when I had finished my business," he explained, trailing behind her.

"That's very gracious of you. I've got to go now."

"I don't think I like you working in empty homes,"

"It's none of your business," she opened the door. "See you around," she looked at him. "Darling."

She shut the door in his face.

CHAPTER FIVE

Blake was waiting by the van in the underground car park when Trinity finished work later that night.

She wasn't surprised to see him, knowing him well enough to know he didn't like to leave things unsaid. Funny she knew that about him but nothing else. Not even his phone number.

"Can we talk?"

She looked at her phone for the time. It was a little after three. She sighed tiredly.

"It won't take long," he persuaded, with a half smile.

He'd changed out of the tuxedo, she noticed, and was now wearing clothes she was more comfortable with seeing him in. Navy flannel tracksuit bottoms and a white long sleeved t-shirt. His arms looked tanned, sexy and strong where he'd pushed up the sleeves. He was wearing his trainers again.

She nodded, spoke to her work colleagues who had been watching them curiously and then walked with him to the elevators.

"How long have you lived here?" She asked just for something to say.

"About two years on and off. I don't use it often as I'm not usually this far up north if I can help it."

"Don't you like the Midlands?"

"It's not London."

Her mouth twitched into a smile.

"You're a city boy," she said without malice.

He winked at her. "Unashamedly."

Trinity felt a little flutter in her stomach, and she dipped her head to look at the floor.

They reached his floor, and he led the way down the corridor to his flat.

Once inside she looked around properly for the first time.

It was a large open plan space with a fantastic view of the city and some of the hills bathed in shadows in the not so near distance.

"Nice place."

"It's functional," he said, shrugging. "Would you like a drink?"

"Have you got any tea?"

He shrugged, turning to the kitchen to search through his cupboards. He was a coffee man. He didn't believe in any other hot drink.

"It's okay if you haven't. I'll just have water."

"Sorry. I'll get some stocked for you."

She looked at him. "Why would you do that?"

"What?"

"Stock teabags for me?"

He walked towards her, stopping just a hairsbreadth away. She could feel his body heat as it radiated from him.

"I came here for you."

"No, you didn't."

"I had business to get out of the way first," he admitted. "But I did come here for you."

"We'd said goodbye," she reminded him.

The last time they had been together, they had made love the entire night, slowly, knowing it was for the last time. They'd made memories that would last her a lifetime. Memories she'd keep as a secret to cherish close to her heart when she was married to some other man.

"I know, but I can't stop thinking about you." His look was layered with sweet accusation.

She smiled daintily knowing he really didn't want to admit his feelings. She helped him out. "I know. I can't stop thinking about you either."

"What are we going to do about it, Trinity?" His voice had dipped to a gravelly softness that had her clenching her thighs together.

She shrugged, definitely not wanting to make any sort of

commitment first. She took a step back needing the distance.

"I think we should talk about it tomorrow, after," he suggested, stepping closer as he looked at her from her toes all the way up to her lips where they stayed for a moment before he looked into her dark eyes. "After I've made love to you." Blake captured her hands and pulled her close so that she was standing flush against him and bent to kiss her.

She moaned against him and relaxed into his hard body, feeling his heavy arousal against her stomach as she reached her arms around his neck, holding on as her knees turned to liquid.

"Blake?" She whispered his name against his mouth. "Blake we need to stop,"

"No."

"We can't," Trinity pressed.

Blake trailed kisses down her neck and tucked his hands under her shirt to feel her warm skin.

"Blake we really shouldn't," she pulled away, stepping back to put some distance between them. It was the hardest thing she had ever done.

Blake was so aroused he could barely think straight, all he knew, all he saw was Trinity, standing steps away, her gorgeous breasts heaving and her mouth swollen with his kisses.

With every effort, he calmed himself down.

"What's the matter?" He asked.

Trinity walked to the sofa, slipped off her canvas slip-on shoes, sat down and curled her feet under herself.

She looked so cute in the large black leather sofa, and Blake smiled even though he knew they weren't going to be having sex any time soon, he thought with regret.

"The first time we met you told me your first name," she started. "The second time we met I asked for your surname," she listed.

Where was she going with this, Blake thought, as he flung himself into the single chair opposite her, it was going to be a long night at this rate. "And?"

"And that's all I know," she replied. "I know you work in

London, I don't know what you do, what kind of business you're in or anything. We've never even been out. You're wearing a tux. And what about the woman you were with tonight?"

Blake sighed internally. He didn't talk about himself. The women he went out with knew better than to ask him anything. Then again, the women he went out with knew who he was. Who he really was, he tacked on without guilt. He liked this anonymity. It was, refreshing and he didn't want it to end.

"What do you want to know?" He asked reluctantly managing to ignore her reference to dating. "No wait," he put up a hand when she was about to speak. "Leigh is simply a friend, a neighbour," he clarified. "We were at the same place that's all. A charity thing." And that was all he was going to say on the subject.

"Have you slept with her?" the question slipped out, and she saw his eyes flash with annoyance, but she didn't care.

"Since you?" he asked. "No."

She nodded into the silence.

"How about we talk tomorrow?" He suggested before she could ask anything else that really wasn't any of her business. "Come to bed and tomorrow we talk."

Her smile slipped off her face, and Blake saw a flicker of hurt in her dark eyes.

"How about I go home now." She shot back angrily.

Blake frowned over at her. He was not ready to talk just because *she* said so. He did not operate like that.

"Go home or come to bed," he said tightly. "You decide." He was angry and frustrated. All he wanted was to sink into her and enjoy the pleasure only she could bring him. It had been weeks!

What the hell! He thought looking at her sharply. She wasn't the only one who could give him pleasure. She can't be.

"I'd best be going then." Trinity pushed her feet into her canvas shoes and walked dejectedly to the door.

Blake wasn't listening. To him, she was the booty call, the shag, the woman up north available to sleep with whenever he happened to snap his fingers. She wasn't like that. She valued herself more than that.

"Trinity?" Blake said, catching her at the door.

She turned hopeful brown eyes the colour of dark rum up at him.

"Yes?"

"I'll walk you home, and tomorrow we'll go out. Together. Somewhere nice."

The smile she bestowed on him made his toes curl.

***

Bright and early the next morning Blake pressed the intercom to Trinity's flat and waited. He was taking her out to breakfast knowing she would have to be back before lunch to open the café.

When the door opened, he was expecting to see her all dressed up and ready. She wasn't.

"I'm sorry I overslept," she rushed in explanation, opening the door wider and letting him in. "You can wait upstairs, or you can put the socks on," she indicated the box of disposable socks by the door. "And talk to me while I finish sorting the cats out."

Blake found himself looking longingly up the dark stairwell but knew it was the wrong decision, she'd hold it against him if he chose to stay upstairs when last night all she wanted to do was 'talk'.

"I'll help." He swapped his shoes for the socks and followed her through the café to the back of the building, stopping on the threshold to wrinkle his nose in distaste.

"I've just got to finish the trays, and I'll be all yours." She explained, turning on the hose.

"Why don't you have help?" He asked this would be the perfect job for a student or someone who liked working with animals.

"Can't afford it just yet. I'm barely making the rent as it is."

"Then why do you want the loan?"

She looked at him then, frowning. "I told you about the loan?"

Blake realised his mistake. "In passing," he improvised quickly.

"Oh," she turned back to the trays.

Blake could see that she was thinking over their past conversations and held his breath.

"I want to expand into the other shop next door," she explained, turning off the hose and stacking the wet trays against the wall to dry. "Then sell cat merchandise and cakes. It'll be more of a café."

"You'll need help for that," Blake stated, watching as she picked up another stack of dry trays and lined them up on the floor. When she reached for a large bag of kitty litter, he moved in to help.

"Fill five please," she advised.

"Why only five?"

"Some cats prefer different textures," she explained.

To Blake, kitty litter was kitty litter; he didn't even know they sold different textures.

Once the job was finished, they washed and dried their hands and Trinity locked the door. When she used her foot to push the cat flap, Blake turned to her looking puzzled.

"Once the flap had locked, and the cats had nowhere to go and do their business," she explained wrinkling her nose, remembering the day with a shudder. "Let's just say, I've never made that mistake again."

"Coffee?" Blake asked going to the machine. He'd developed a taste for her vending machine coffee, he thought dryly.

"No thanks. Stay here I'm just going to have a quick shower."

Coffee in hand, Blake sat down at the small table and looked around.

He noticed the new cats but he also recognised Demus, Gizmo the partially blind cat and looking up on the wall there was Soldier.

He smiled at the cat and looked around before copying the kissing noises he'd heard Trinity do, and called the cat down.

Soldier, made an answering trilling sound deep in his throat before jumping down to him.

Before he knew it, Blake was kneeling on the floor stroking the cat's silky fur. He liked how Soldier's soft, pliant body undulated under his hand in pleasure from the top of his head all the way to the tip of his tail.

Blake heard and felt the deep vibrations of the funny sound, purring, as Soldier curled and danced sensuously against his hand. The movement reminded him of Trinity when he smoothed his hands along her legs when they'd made love.

Watching the TV screen upstairs, Trinity smiled in amusement as Blake made himself comfortable on the floor. Soldier, had chosen Blake to be his human and Blake, poor Blake, was caught.

Trinity quickly pulled on a pair of indigo coloured jeans and a black v-necked jumper before yanking on a pair of low heeled ankle boots.

She was currently growing out the relaxer from her hair so, because the ends were so fragile, added a dollop of hair moisturiser and smoothed it through her delicate strands before brushing it all up into a loose bun.

Earrings, eye-liner, mascara and lip gloss and she was ready. Their first date. She could barely contain her excitement as she practically bounced down the stairs to him.

***

It had been a great morning.

They'd gone to an American style diner and had stacked pancakes with maple syrup. They'd talked about the café and Blake, after a while, opened up and talked about himself.

He was an only child. He didn't like his father very much but got all excited when he talked about his grandfather who he called grandpop.

He worked in accounts and travelled around overseeing the different branches here and overseas.

He'd never been married. Was thirty-one. Didn't have any children and, when asked about his favourite colour, reluctantly admitted he was partial to pink.

Trinity had laughed, and when he looked at her sternly, she admitted men wearing pink was a real turn on. His blue gaze had heated faster than butter in a microwave at her admission.

***

Trinity wasn't doing any extra hours that night so had invited him round to dinner. She could only cook one dish, Spaghetti Bolognese, but it was very good. She made it with red wine and was quite proud of her single culinary achievement.

Her front door buzzed and she checked the camera, seeing him standing looking directly at the camera. His look was smouldering, and she felt the heat all the way through her body. She knew how she wanted the night to end and with a smile let him in.

***

"What's this one called?" Blake asked after dinner as he watched the white cloud with four legs walk across the back of the sofa near his head.

"That's Mercy,"

"She's beautiful." Blake reached up and scratched the cat under her chin. He smiled when she stretched her neck, twisting it this way and that as she allowed him to scratch her.

"Someone had dumped a box of kittens outside my door a few months back," Trinity explained as she quickly washed the dishes. "She was the only survivor."

"Someone actually left kittens here? Outside?"

Trinity turned to him, drying her hands. "It's not the first time," she sat beside him, and the cat jumped down to walk on Blake's legs. "It must have been horrible for the poor darling, in a small dirty box and her brothers and sisters all dead around her."

Blake found himself stroking Mercy's head as she rhythmically kneaded his thigh one paw at a time. "The poor thing," he said. "She lucked out with you though didn't she?"

"How do you mean?"

"Cat-lover extraordinaire," he smiled and inched closer to her. "No one could ever love her as much as you." He finished, looking between her and the cat.

Trinity followed Blake's fingers and stroked the cat who was now purring loudly, then she suddenly jumped off his knee, turned to look at Trinity before leaving the room with a flick of her fluffy tail.

Trinity laughed. "I think you're only allowed to stroke her now."

Blake took her hand. "How about you?" He asked. "How much stroking do you like?"

Their eyes met and the air crackled with awareness.

"Depends where," she whispered, seeing Blake's pupils dilate at the invitation of her words.

He took her hand and pulled her onto his lap, rearranging her so that she was facing him.

"Oh my," she said, feeling how hard he was, as she rocked against him.

"You like that?"

"Maybe," she teased.

Blake leaned forward and captured her bottom lip with his teeth, gently nipping at the fullness before sucking on it gently.

She tasted of tomatoes and a hint of basil. Her taste spoke to the Italian in him, and he found it somewhat comforting.

Not wanting to rush, he nibbled along her jaw, down the side of her neck and back again.

"No more bites," she warned, moving to give him better access to her neck.

"Why not?" He swirled his tongue where he'd previously left his mark.

"Too many questions from too many people."

He didn't like that and broke their connection.

"Like who?" He asked darkly.

"Travis, Michelle the florist across the street," she listed. "And Mo of course. He doesn't miss a thing." She laughed, but Blake wasn't laughing.

"Travis?"

Noting Blake's stern look, she pushed off his knee and stood over him.

"You know Travis?" She explained. "You came in with him the first time we met,"

"I know who he is," Blake gritted coldly. "I also remember you hugged him that night too."

Trinity felt her fog of arousal dissipate like mist on a summers morning.

"So?" She couldn't believe his attitude and walked to the bathroom to wash her hands. "I hug everyone."

"You've never hugged me," Blake followed her, crowding into the small space to also wash his hands.

She turned to him with her hands on her hips. "You're jealous."

Blake drew himself up to his full height as he looked down at her.

"Don't be ridiculous," he scathed. "I've never been jealous in my life!"

"So why would me hugging my friend, cause an argument between us?"

"I'm not jealous."

She noticed he hadn't given a reason. She stepped closer and pushed her small hands under his jumper, skimming her fingers up and down the deep ridge of his spine. She hugged him close, laying her head on his chest and hearing his heartbeat.

"I thought you were going to stroke me?" She encouraged when his hands remained rigid at his side.

Spreading her fingers up and around to his chest she tweaked his nipples. He moaned just like she knew he would. He was as responsive there as she was.

"We're having an argument," he said through gritted teeth as he looked above her head.

"You're the one having the argument, I'm just listening to you make an idiot of yourself," She pushed his jumper up and grazed one nipple with her teeth before stepping away.

With a smile, she turned her back, threw him a look over her shoulder and pulled off her own jumper as she walked into the living room.

She squealed when he picked her up swinging her in the air as he sat with her on the sofa again. Again chest to chest.

"You're a tease, do you know that?" He said as he kissed her deeply, not really expecting her to answer.

Trinity moved to her knees and opened his jeans to wrap her hands around his semi-erect length. She stroked the tip, making tiny circles around the smooth head as he grew in her hands.

Blake quickly got rid of her clothes and swung her around, pulling her nipple into his mouth as he spread her legs, wide, revealing her golden folds to his hungry gaze. She was so beautiful, glistening and ready for him as he dipped his head to taste her. It had been weeks since he'd tasted her and he closed his eyes, breathing in her familiar scent as he stroked her with his tongue.

When she was all but sobbing in his arms and begging for release, he donned a condom and surged into her.

She screamed and came apart as he entered. She sobbed and clung and came again as he controlled their pace, refusing to give in to her hands now pulling frantically at his bottom urging him to move faster.

When she came again and all but fainted he let go, finally giving in to the most intense orgasm he'd had in his life.

CHAPTER SIX

They'd settled into a routine. Blake travelled during the week, coming back when he could or staying in whichever city he was in at the time, but he always stayed at the weekends.

At first, he was frustrated she was so busy, always working, if not with her cats she was cleaning offices.

He'd tried convincing her to give the cleaning job up, but when she said she'd go back to the taxi office instead, he let the subject drop. That taxi job was just too dangerous.

She only cleaned two nights a week and was able to be home by two o'clock at the latest, where he would run a bath for her, and they would eat a light meal.

Before him she never ate a proper meal, snacks and copious cups of tea got her through the day. Now he found himself sending her a text message while in the middle of a meeting, reminding her to have something to eat and demanding photographic evidence of her meals.

A month turned into two, and tonight Trinity had a surprise for him.

Usually, he could read her like a book, but whatever she had planned she was keeping it to herself, he thought nervously.

He ordered take-out and had it set up upstairs for when the last of the customers downstairs had left.

He usually went down at that point, locking the door while she pulled down the blinds.

Together they said goodnight to the cats.

He found it all very frustrating, her being downstairs in the mock living room while he had to wait in the real living room. She needed to hire someone, and when he'd broached the subject again, she had slammed it down. She liked what she did.

"What did you order?" Trinity asked as she came out of the

shower, a sky blue towel wrapped around her slim frame. "And don't you be getting any ideas?" she said, seeing his heated gaze slide over her.

"You are such a spoilsport sometimes." He answered as he shared out their food. "All of your favourites."

She peered over his arm. "Hmm satay chicken. Did you remember the crispy seaweed?"

"Of course."

"Good man." She patted his cheek before going to the sofa.

"Aren't you getting dressed?" Blake asked as he sat beside her, balancing his meal on the arm of the sofa. They seldom used the table.

"Not much point, you'll only be taking everything off again." She replied deadpan and he laughed.

They ate in silence, Mercy sat at Blake's feet as she always did. Trinity was surplus to requirements nowadays it seemed. Blake fed the cat and played with the cat and Mercy followed him around completely lovestruck.

The last time Trinity had picked Mercy up, she had swiped at her, hitting her chin with her paw, but at least Trinity took comfort that the cat hadn't used her claws.

After their meal, Trinity got up and went to the bedroom. She came back with a little dark pink chequered box tied with a white ribbon, balancing it on the palm of her hand.

Blake saw it, and his mind raced. No, it wasn't a leap year, and it wasn't February. She would not be proposing. He eyed the box suspiciously. "What is it?"

"I got you a little something."

Blake leaned forward as she sat beside him, practically bouncing with excitement as she looked at him expectantly.

Blake tried to smile and lifted the box, untying the ribbon and looking inside. Relief leapt through him, but then another horror quickly followed. A key.

"It's for the front door," Trinity explained, now unsure of her gesture due to his lack of response. "I thought—I thought that now maybe you can—"

"You want me to move in with you?" Blake asked. "Here?"

"No!" she exclaimed quickly with a nervous laugh. "We haven't known each other long enough for that," she clarified. "It's so you don't have to go through the café looking for me," she explained. "You can come straight up."

Blake was looking at the key as though it was a serpent she had given him.

She'd overstepped his invisible boundary, she realised too late fighting the hurt. They'd been so happy. She considered them a couple. Didn't he?

"It's okay if you don't want it," she went to grab it from him, but he moved his hand out of her reach before looking at her and smiling.

"Come here," he ordered quietly.

"You're not mad?" she asked blinking rapidly against the tears that were threatening.

He pulled her into his side, kissing her forehead tenderly and tucking her head under his chin.

"Why would I be mad?"

"You don't look too happy,"

"You took me by surprise that's all," he explained. "I don't like surprises. Thank you."

Trinity heard his words but recognised he was only saying what he thought she needed to hear.

She yawned indelicately and stretched her arms over her head before getting up and walking to the bedroom.

"I'm off to bed," she said, trying to inject some normality into her voice when she was really crumbling inside.

"I'll be there shortly," he answered, very much aware they had just broken their ritual. They locked up, checked the CCTV and went to bed, normally together.

***

"Hello,"

Trinity felt Blake's arms snake around her waist as he turned her around, smoothed her body against his and dipped his head for a kiss.

"Hmm, hello," Trinity melted into him, reached for another kiss before stepping away to look at him. "You went home I see?" she said, noticing his casual soft jeans and plain jumper. She hadn't seen him in six days.

Blake looked down at himself before looking at her. "That thing you call a shower is ridiculous."

"The water pressure goes up and down. The other tenant has been having the same problem as well."

"It needs sorting out," he looked around. "Ten minutes until closing," he stated with a crafty wink.

Trinity felt herself blush. She didn't see much of him during the week as he worked in different cities and couldn't always make it back, but when he was here, they spent every waking moment making love.

"Are you going upstairs?" she asked.

"No, I'll stick around down here and play with Soldier."

When her last customer had left, Trinity locked the door and went about tidying up. She'd actually started putting the cat toys away and stowing the day's newspapers in the back before he'd arrived. Once they were alone, she quickly vacuumed the sisal rug and, handing Blake a packet of natural antibacterial wipes, instructed him to wipe the chairs while she sprayed animal-friendly disinfectant on the tables and mopped the floor.

When they were finished, they sat on the floor. Some cats joined them, others curled up to sleep now that playtime was over and a few were busying licking every last human scent from their fur.

Soldier, jumped off his favourite perch and stepped onto Blake.

"I think he's missed you," Trinity said as she stroked Theo and Ben, the two brothers that had come in from the rescue centre. Theo was a huge vocal, energetic black and white and Ben a laid back tabby. They couldn't have been more different.

"We're hoping these two will be adopted together," she said, as she made herself comfortable on a bean bag beside Blake who was on the floor, leaning against a chair with his legs stretched out, and soldier curled up in a tight ball on his thighs.

"What will happen if there is only interest in one?" Blake asked.

"I don't know, it's never happened before, but most cat lovers—hell pet lovers in general—are sensitive to siblings, so I'm hoping they'll be okay.

Theo attempted to step onto Blake's legs, and Soldier opened one eye and growled at him, flicking his tail with a rough thump.

Trinity laughed. "I think you've been adopted, Blake. You're definitely his human."

Blake tickled Soldier under his chin. "That's fine with me buddy, us soldiers stick together,"

"Have you ever thought about closing earlier?" Blake asked sometime later, aware that she worked long exhausting hours and she had circles under her eyes.

"Cats are more active at night," she answered. "They interact better."

Blake looked around, seeing the harsh fluorescent lights.

"You need to trick them into thinking it's later,"

"And how do I do that?"

"Softer lights for one," he advised. "Maybe wall lights or a few spotlights on a dimmer switch and toning down the atmosphere."

Trinity followed his gaze, yes it could work she admitted, looking at the harsh old fashioned fluorescent tubes on the ceiling.

"Hmm, might be something to think about,"

"I'll call an electrician to take a look."

"No, you won't."

He looked at her sharply. "Why not?"

"Changing the lighting will cost money, and I can't afford it right now."

"I'll take care of it."

"No, you won't."

"It's not a problem."

She laughed. "Blake I know you work with figures, but you don't own a bank. I'll take care of it when I can." She finished.

Blake felt a spasm of regret. He should have told her. He should have told her long ago, but now he was caught in a lie, not really a lie, more like an omission he reasoned, but still, he needed to make it right.

"Trinity?" he edged picking up her hand and smoothing his fingers over her knuckles.

"Hmm?" she stretched her arms over her head and rolled her shoulders as she yawned. "Have you eaten? Shall we order some cheesy chips from Mo?"

She knew he liked the chips and they had them at least once a week.

"You look exhausted," he jumped on the excuse to avoid making his confession. "I'll go and pick them up. You take a shower and get ready for me,"

She sent him a flirtatious look. "All ready for you huh?"

He pulled her close nudging her neck with his lips. "I'll lock up down here," he stood up pulling her with him and planting another kiss on her full lips.

"Sure?"

"Trinity," he sighed. "Let go a little," he urged. "I can lock up. Let's say goodnight to the cats."

One by one they both said goodnight to the cats. Each feline got a stroke or a tickle under the chin.

Trinity left Blake to turn the radio down low, switch off the lights and lock all the doors before going to pick up their dinner from Mo.

Halfway through her shower, the water turned stone cold, so gasping she quickly rinsed off and towelled herself roughly to warm up again.

She had never been so happy, she thought as she 'got ready for him' sweeping shea butter body lotion over her legs and massaging it in before pulling on a white vest and fleecy leopard print shorts, just as she heard the door slam downstairs.

"Honey I'm home," Blake called out as he walked into the flat.

"I can't believe you just said that," Trinity laughed. "And where do you think you're going with all that food?" she asked eyeing all the bags he was holding. "I sent you out for a single tray of chips."

"Mo said something about sending you a *Lorraine Special*. You're supposed to know what that means."

Trinity laughed. "I'm not eating all that, and neither are you if we're going to live past fifty." She told him sternly but ruined the effect by looking in the bag and pouncing on the deep fried garlic mushrooms. "Bless him!"

CHAPTER SEVEN

"How long are you staying this time?" Trinity asked Blake as they snuggled on the sofa, too stuffed with Mo's food to move.

"I'm going tomorrow,"

"Oh,"

"I'll be back as soon as I can." He promised, and he would move mountains to get through all the work that was waiting for him.

He had a quarterly board meeting in London and then he had to fly over to Italy to repeat everything that was said at the London meeting to the Italian board members, who were mostly family and who were more interested in the profits than how the bank was actually run.

"Oh," she said again, not even trying to hide her disappointment.

"Going to miss me?"

"You know I will."

"I'll miss this place too."

Trinity noticed his play on words, he'd said it before, he wouldn't miss her, but he would miss Mercy, or Soldier, he'd miss the vending machine coffee even Mo's cheesy chips! But he had never once said he would miss her.

Biting her lip, she rode the tide of upset and disappointment. She was getting in too deep, and it seemed a bit one-sided. But when he was here, it was magical. He was so attentive and caring and the way he made love to her, oh my, she bit down on the inside of her mouth just to distract herself.

"Ouch!" she explained, using her tongue to soothe the bite.

"What?"

"Nothing."

Blake sat up and turned to face her, his all-knowing blue gaze trained on her face. "What?" he repeated patiently.

"I bit my tongue that's all. I'm such an idiot,"

"Let me see?"

"Why?"

"So that I can kiss it better."

"You just want an excuse to kiss me."

"Since when do I need an excuse?" he asked, reaching up to wrap his hand behind her neck.

She giggled and even to her own ears she sounded like a seductress calling to all sailors.

He smiled and stroked his tongue over her lips.

"You taste of garlic and mushroom and," he cupped her head. "Is that—"

"Cheese maybe?" she suggested, desperate for him to kiss her properly.

"Now you've gone and spoilt my game," he chided, resisting the pull of her hands as she grabbed his t-shirt.

"Come here, Blake Lawrence."

"What do I get?"

"A little bit of my something something?"

"Something something huh?"

"Yeah," she pulled him off the sofa and led him to the bedroom.

"Something something."

***

Trinity worked just as hard as she always did. In a month she had re-homed all her cats except Soldier and Gizmo, and she knew they would be permanent residents in the café now as she could never send them back to the rescue centre.

Things had changed slightly with her relationship with Blake, he wasn't withdrawn, she just knew *Key Gate*—as she now called it—played a part in his change.

He used the key, and more than once she'd been pleasantly surprised to find him upstairs, only coming into the café when the last of the customers had left. It meant a lot to her that he cared so much about her safety.

"Hey, Trin,"

"Trinity," she said when Travis walked in. "I think you'll be asking to buy shares here soon," she teased.

"I know I know, but I can't help myself. Seeing your beautiful smile three times a week is getting me through these dark exhausting days of med school."

She rolled her eyes at him. "How long are you staying this time?" she asked walking over to the till. She had to harden her heart as she really wanted to let him have a free session, but her bottom line couldn't allow it.

"Two hours please."

"Two hours!"

He shrugged. "Things are getting a little difficult at home," he explained, his mouth turning down on one side.

"I'm sorry."

He breathed in deeply before leaning his elbows onto the counter as he looked at her.

"I think it may have run its course,"

"But didn't she follow you here from Durham?"

"I never asked her to come."

"But you never told her not to did you?"

He shrugged again. "Guilty. It was just easier to have someone familiar with me."

He turned to survey the café and all the cats lazing about or playing with the customers.

"I love this place," he said almost to himself. "How's it going with Blake?" he asked turning to her.

She smiled. "Good."

"Been out anywhere nice lately?"

"No, I've been working."

His hazel eyes became watchful. "You're my friend, and I like you," he edged, taking a deep breath. "Tell me to mind my own business if you want but don't you think it's strange that he always comes here? You never go any place with him. Have you met any of his friends?"

"I can't go anywhere Travis, I'm always here."

He dipped his head.

"If you ever need a couple of extra hours on a Sunday I'll take over."

"You'd do that for me?"

"Sure. It's no hardship. I love it here."

"Thank you," she reached out and hugged him over the counter then watched as he walked away, pulling a thick medical book from his rucksack before sinking into a bean bag. Before long he had Gizmo lying on his chest.

Blake watched the conversation from upstairs. Trinity had always said Travis was just a friend, but Trinity never saw the heated looks Travis sent her way when she wasn't looking.

***

"I'm going to get my hair braided soon," Trinity said as they curled up in bed later that night. His front to her back and their legs a twist of limbs.

"Okay," Blake replied sleepily, stroking a bare breast with his thumb.

"Do you like braids? I've not done it in years."

"Braids being plaits?"

"Yeah, you can have different lengths, colours and thickness. I'm thinking long and dark brown, maybe a light brown at the front?"

"Sounds good," Blake cuddled her closer enjoying her warm smoothness and her delicate scent of shea butter and vanilla as he drifted off into sleep.

"Travis said he'll help out on Sunday so we can go somewhere together."

Blake's eyes snapped open, all sleepiness gone. "Why?"

"So that I can get a day off," she explained.

"What does he get out of it?" Blake asked tightly. "Are you paying him?"

"No, well I don't think so. He never said anything about taking any money, he just thought I should have a day off, and he offered."

Blake shifted and pulled her down so that she was flat on her back and he could see her face. "I've been telling you to get some help for weeks, and you ignored me. But suddenly wonder boy offers and it's okay!" He blazed. "Nobody ever offers something for nothing Trinity. Know that."

"Of course they do, Blake," she scoffed. "I do it all the time."

"That's you, you're not very worldly."

She pushed at his shoulders and moved so that he wasn't leaning over her in that domineering, arrogant way.

"What do you mean I'm not worldly? I travelled and back-packed most of Asia! By myself, I might add!"

"That's not what I meant. You live your life in a tiny bubble not venturing out of it."

"That's an awful thing to say!"

"You're twenty-four, and you've buried yourself in the wilderness with a bunch of cats."

She was hurt. All this time she thought Blake knew her better than this.

"My life has purpose," she moved away completely, and he let her. "I have my business, I have my degree, and I have a boyfriend who I thought liked me the way I am."

Trinity watched in the dim glow of the street light outside as Blake's face shuttered. She scrambled back over what she had said. Boyfriend. They had never defined their relationship.

"I'll be going to London for a few days," Blake said coldly, as though she hadn't spoken. "When I get back, we'll talk about getting you an assistant for a few hours each day, and you can tell Travis thanks but no thanks."

"I don't want, need or can afford an assistant!"

"We'll talk about it when I get back." He repeated tightly, wrapping an arm around her waist and dragging her close.

Trinity allowed him to mould her body against his when he drifted off into sleep. But she didn't close her eyes. Instead, she thought about what he'd said and his presumptions about her business. She didn't like it, and tomorrow she was going to tell him so.

Usually, he would make love to her in the mornings, he said

thinking of her beneath him and leaving her sated and smiling always got him through the hours until he got back to her. This morning he'd just left.

***

Trinity spent the next few days settling her new cats. She spoke to Blake every night. He kept insisting that they would talk when he got back whenever she tried to speak to him about the assistant and spending time together, but he kept the calls brief, and she was coming to the realisation that maybe their affair had run its course.

She loved him, had never told him, but she did. She knew he was pulling away and she wasn't going to be one of those pathetic women who clung on for dear life. She had a life before Blake, and she could easily go back to it.

Travis had been right about one thing though, and she knew she had been guilty of burying her head in the sand. Why had Blake never introduced her to his friends, his granddad or arranged to take her with him on one of his trips? They'd had a couple of breakfasts out together but nothing more.

She was going to end it before he did, that way at least she'd be saving her pride and leaving with her dignity and her heart in one piece.

***

"Murrow," Trinity looked down at Soldier, he'd been extra quiet lately, and she picked him up.

"What's the matter big fella?" she asked the cat, stroking his tattered ear. He had a black nose so she couldn't tell if he had a temperature, but it looked moist, and there wasn't any gooey stuff coming from his eyes, always a tell-tale sign of a cat feeling under the weather.

"Are you missing him too?" she asked, giving him a cuddle before putting him down, watching closely as he ambled stiffly to a wigwam styled cat bed. He wanted to be left alone.

Trinity made a note to call the vet out. She had a friend, Stevie, who had a practice, and gave his services to her for free. They'd

85

started the foundation veterinary classes together when they were teenagers, but because she couldn't stomach all the blood and gore had to pull out, Stevie had stayed on and was now running a thriving practice.

CHAPTER EIGHT

From inside Trinity watched an old lady with a halo of white curls stop at the café window and smile at the cats that were sunning themselves.

Trinity had thought it a good idea to showcase her felines and had taken inspiration from that 50's song about the doggy in the window.

A row of friendly kitty grass in dainty white pots, several scratching posts and differently sized cat trees were placed in the window, and she was on to a winner.

She had yet to see someone look at the cats and not come in if only to satisfy their curiosity and gladly add a donation in the bright orange bucket she now kept by the door.

She was happy. Well almost. When Blake had rung this morning, she'd looked at her mobile, flashing and playing that stupid ring tone that announced that it was him and let it ring out. It was time to distance herself. It was going to be hard. But she could do it.

"Hello?" The old lady was hovering just inside the second door, and Trinity walked over.

"Hi, which one of my babies gave you an irresistible you-just can't-help-your-self look?" Trinity asked with a gentle smile.

Trinity was short, but this lady was shorter and reminded Trinity of Mrs Claus.

"It was that black, ginger and brown one lying on the tree. What a beautiful cat." The old lady looked over at the window, and Trinity noticed it was Gizmo playing the starring role.

"That's Gizmo," she told her. "Would you like to come in and I'll introduce you properly?"

"Oh, that's all right dear, I've got another appointment soon, but I like what you're doing." The lady reached into her purse and pulled out a fifty-pound note. "This is for the rescue centre."

Trinity gasped at the size of the note. "No that's too much. You've given me a fifty." She pushed the note back into the lady's hand.

The lady shook her head, and her curls bounced around her head as she laughed. "I am so sorry. I do that all the time. I'm just glad you told me about it." She was looking down into her purse and pulling at her paper money nervously.

"Excuse me?" Trinity began wanting to soothe her before the old lady worked herself into a tizz. "Would you like to come in for a cup of tea?" she offered.

The old lady looked at her, her surprisingly smooth face creasing in pleasure. "That would be lovely dear."

"I've just got one request though?"

"Oh?"

"Can I ask you to take off your shoes and put on these socks for me? I don't allow outside shoes inside."

"That's fine dear. What's your name?"

"I'm Trinity. Trinity Peters, and you are?"

"Leonora Botticelli. Pleased to meet you."

Trinity helped Leonora with the disposable socks and held her hand as she sat her down at the table before pressing several buttons to instruct the vending machine to make two cups of tea.

"Mrs Botticelli?"

"Please call me Leonora,"

"Leonora, you really shouldn't be walking around with so much cash on you, it isn't safe."

"My husband tells me all the time, God rest his soul. But I'm so frightened of banks."

"Maybe you should get yourself a debit card?" Trinity suggested. "It's just like cash and the money comes straight from your account. Very easy." She explained, but the woman, Leonora, wasn't listening, she was busy looking around her.

"What a lovely place this is."

"Thank you," Trinity answered with a small smile.

"How many cats do you have?"

"Today eighteen. Twelve have already got homes to go to on Saturday."

Trinity took a moment to look at her, unobserved. Leonora's eyes were brown behind the glasses, and she was wearing a coral coloured lipstick and white plastic earrings shaped like bunches of grapes. Her coat was olive green and cut in a timeless three button style. Trinity noted the quality.

"The new owners come and pick up the cats on a Saturday between one, and three and I get new cats on Sunday evenings," Trinity explained.

"Very efficient," Leonora said. "I'd best be going."

She stood up to go with surprising swiftness, Trinity thought watching Leonora as she straightened her coat and fluffed her hair.

"Thank you for not robbing me Trinity Peters."

"My pleasure. If you need anything, I'm here all the time. I live just upstairs."

Leonora turned to her then, her eyes dark but clear like a Scottish Loch in winter, but then the look was replaced by a twinkle and Trinity thought maybe the lights had flickered again.

"I'll let myself out. Bye kitty cat," Leonora said to the cat that had circled her ankles, and she bent down and stroked it. "Thank you for the tea Trinity," she said again as she looked at her with a small knowing smile on her face. "And for settling my mind."

Puzzled, Trinity watched her replace her shoes and, turning with a bright smile, waved as she let herself out.

Leonora became as regular as Travis, the only difference being she came along just after lunch and left before teatime.

Trinity looked forward to seeing the old lady who carried an olde worlde sophistication about her. Her clothes were understated but well made and from the way that she talked Trinity knew the older woman was well travelled and she also found her interesting to talk to. They became firm friends in the days that followed.

***

Blake still called, and Trinity answered one in four calls. She was a glutton for punishment she knew, but she needed to hear his voice at least once for the week.

Her heart was breaking, as she knew it would, but she also knew she had to harden it too. They'd known each other for such a short time. He hadn't moved in, or anything and they hadn't merged bank accounts. She had nothing at his flat, and he'd only had the toothbrush she had bought him at her place. He didn't even have a change of clothes.

The writing was on the wall, only she'd been too stupid and lovestruck to see it.

"What's the matter Trinity dear?" Leonora asked from where she was sat in a comfortable chair with two cats Gizmo and Leon the new white and light brown male that epitomised scaredy cat on her knee.

Trinity sighed and tried to smile.

"Come on, I've seen everything and done everything. I don't like seeing you without that smile of yours." Leonora encouraged as she lifted her elbow to stop Leon from burrowing his head under her arm.

"Man troubles," Trinity revealed, picking up Naomi, a beautiful minky coloured cat with four white paws and white fur on her chin that went down her chest. She was unusually beautiful.

"Oh?"

Trinity shrugged. "I'm going to break it off with someone I really like."

Leonora stopped stroking the cats and looked at her with brown eyes clouding in concern. "If you like him why break up?"

"He doesn't treat me right."

"Men can be pretty dense at most things. What hasn't he done?" Leonora pressed as she resumed her strokes along one cat's back and then the other.

"I know it sounds stupid," Trinity whispered, looking around

90

to see if any of her customers could hear their conversation. "But he's gone all cold and distracted."

"He just might be busy?"

"No, it's not that," Trinity answered with a confidence she really didn't feel. "He says he's not married or anything like that, but I think he's lying about something," she looked at her friend. "Something isn't right."

"Come over here Trinity," Leonora ordered. "I'm straining my ears,"

With Naomi in her arms, Trinity walked over to Leonora and pulled out a bean bag, she sat down wriggling her bottom to get comfortable.

"Why do you think he's lying?" Leonora asked.

"I've not met any of his family,"

"I see," Leonora looked off into the distance. "How long have you been seeing each other? It could be early days yet."

"No, it's almost two months."

"Hmm,"

"It's not going to work," Trinity admitted more to herself before looking imploringly at Leonora. "To me, it's all about family Leonora."

"Has he met yours?"

"Well no, but that's because my mum is a lecturer in Birmingham and my dad lives in America now. He's a musician, with a band and comes here every now and again."

"Hmm,"

Trinity had been expecting something a little more than a simple hmm.

"Maybe his family is overseas?" Leonora suggested.

"If that was the case, why wouldn't he say?" she shook her head. "No Leonora it's more than that. He's hiding something, and whatever it is I don't want to get hurt."

"Of course you don't Pet."

They were both lost in their own thoughts for a moment. Naomi, the cat, uncurled herself to rearrange her lithe body on Trinity's lap, only to change her mind and go into her first position again.

"I don't know what to say, Trinity. Do you like him?"

"I think he's the most amazing man," Trinity sniffed trying to hold back the tears. "When he's here it's just so magical. He's never had a pet before, but he loves the cats. Mercy and Soldier adore him, and he's become important to me." She looked at Leonora and scrubbed at her eyes. "He's going to break my heart, Leonora."

"Ah Pet, I'm sorry," Leonora reached out and touched Trinity's shoulder giving it a comforting squeeze. "It'll work out. Give him a chance to explain things—"

"No I can't, when I gave him a key, he all but froze, and when I called him my boyfriend he practically ran for the hills."

"You jest,"

Trinity giggled. "Well no, but he froze me out and left the next morning. I've not seen him since."

"I'm sorry Pet. Give him a chance. You're a nice girl, he'll be realising he's onto a good thing."

"I doubt it." Trinity gently moved Naomi off her lap and stood up. "I don't like subterfuge Leonora, honesty is very important to me." She picked up a calico cushion with purple piping and fluffed it before replacing it on the sofa. "I'd better see to that girl over there, she seems to be playing a little too enthusiastically with the cats.

***

Trinity was at her all day appointment with the hairdresser, getting her hair braided. Leonora had volunteered to watch the café and Travis was taking over later in the evening.

This had been the first time in months that she had some time for herself. She only wished she could get at least one day off. Then she scolded herself, her business was just getting off the ground, everyone knew the first two years could make or break a business. She was one year in and was staying in for a lifetime.

It was later in the evening, almost closing when Trinity finally got back to the café. She'd called Leonora throughout the day and was happy that all was well. Leonora had asked if Trinity could use a regular volunteer as she liked to be busy and she loved the cats. Trinity jumped at the chance and said they would discuss what worked best for both of them later.

Travis whistled when she walked in.

"You look great," he grinned, looking at her hair now plaited in hundreds of braids that swept down her back.

"Thank you. How's it been going?"

"Fine, I've put the money in the pouch in there and yeah everything's been fine."

"Thank you for doing this for me."

They hugged, and she walked him out, waving as she locked the door behind him.

Trinity took comfort in her routine as she rolled down the blinds, tidied up and said goodnight to the cats.

Five weeks Blake had been gone. Five weeks. The last two he hadn't even called.

CHAPTER NINE

Half an hour before opening, Trinity went in search of company and found it with Michelle who was rearranging some bright orange calla lilies in a bucket and placing it on a wooden stand at the front of her shop. Just looking at the bright colours made Trinity think of warmer climes.

"I hear your building is up for sale?" Michelle said as Trinity approached.

"Again?" Trinity turned to look at the building. It was old, but it had potential with three floors of equally huge space. It must have been an impressive place in its day. Now it looked tired with only two out of the seven shops occupied, her café and the vintage clothing shop on the corner. But it was a solid building. Unfortunately, it wasn't a listed building. "I thought the council had decided to keep it?"

"They can't afford to keep it, not with all the cuts and whatnot they have going on," Michelle used her fingers and fluffed at the delicate white gypsophila she had left over from a wedding bouquet. "I've not seen that young man of yours lately?"

"Me neither," Trinity answered, ignoring the sting in her heart.

"Trouble in paradise?" Michelle straightened to face her.

"Let's just say," Trinity began. "Like you, I'll be concentrating on my business for the foreseeable future." Michelle had gone through a nasty divorce, where her ex had stolen her money and her best friend.

"I'm sorry," Michelle picked out several yellow and cream roses and made a quick, yet very pretty bouquet. "Here," she gave the stems to Trinity to hold, then dipping into the pockets of her apron pulled out some green florist string and a pair of scissors. She tied the bouquet. "To cheer you up."

"Thanks. Oh, look." Trinity said, watching as an elderly couple peered into the empty shop windows across the street.

"Might be buyers," Michelle wondered out loud.

"She looks like a creative type," Trinity observed, noting the floaty skirt and many bangles the lady was wearing. The man beside her was just smiling indulgently as he listened to her talk with obvious enthusiasm, her arms sweeping and waving around as she talked. "He looks as though he would give her the world," Trinity observed wistfully.

"Isn't it sweet to watch." Michelle mused with a small smile. "There's hope for you yet kiddo."

"We'll see. Someone for me." Trinity quickly said goodbye and crossed the street to let the first of her customers in.

***

Later that night, while watching TV, the screen switched over, and she saw Blake open the front door. She hadn't been expecting him. In fact, she had turned off her phone just so she wouldn't be tempted to talk to him. She'd gone three weeks without speaking to him. Now she watched with a mixture of bubbling excitement and laden regret as he climbed the narrow stairs.

"Hi," he said wearily as he opened the door and stepped inside.

Everything was scrambling inside of Trinity in erotic chaos as she turned to look at him. She hated that he was still so gorgeous to look at. She hated that he stayed by the door, leaning against it looking all sexy and manly. She wanted to hate him but knew that she never would.

He'd been home and changed, she noted. He hadn't been in any great rush to see her. His hair was damp from his shower, and he was wearing his soft, casual clothes. The clothes he'd put on tomorrow as he left again. No no no, she argued with herself. He wasn't staying. He. Was. Not. Staying.

Trinity dipped her head as she hugged Mercy closer, hearing his footsteps as he walked across the laminated floor.

"I know you're upset with me,"

She heard him say. What could she say to that? Forgiven was a word she wasn't likely to use any time soon.

"I've missed you, little lady."

From beneath her lashes, Trinity saw his strong, tanned fingers pull gently on Mercy's ears, the cat flattened them and moved her head away with an abrupt hiss. For once the cat was staying loyal and refused to acknowledge him. Good girl, Trinity thought stroking the cat between her ears.

Trinity heard Blake make an impatient huffing sound and he picked up the cat and put her gently on the floor before scooping Trinity up and sitting her on his knee as he sat down.

"I've missed you," he said, nudging his head into her neck and breathing deeply.

The evidence of just how much he had missed her was obvious, beneath her bottom and with stiff offence, she scrambled off him.

"Where have you been Blake?" she asked.

"Working."

"I know that Blake but where?"

"Do we have to do this now?" he raked a hand through his hair. "I'm tired and just want to hold you. It's been weeks Trinity."

His voice had dipped to a persuasive purr, and he took her hand sweeping his thumb over her knuckles.

"I've had a long day and was just going off to bed," she pulled her hand away and stood up. "Maybe you should go."

"You don't mean that," Blake said gruffly, standing beside her and reaching for her hands again, but she tucked them behind her back.

"I do Blake."

His look was steady and serious as he looked at her. She'd never seen him look like this before, she looked closer. He'd lost weight, and his face appeared drawn and slightly gaunt.

"I need to tell you something," he said suddenly.

Blake had been hoping to put off this conversation until tomorrow but no such luck. She had barely talked to him at all over the phone and had ignored his e-mails. Then to his frustration, she'd turned off her phone entirely. He knew she had every right to be mad at him and had almost told her the truth over the phone, but this conversation needed to be said face to face.

It was all on him. The past weeks had been hellish, what with the hostile takeover attempt that had come out of nowhere making him have to fly all over Europe and North America as he scrabbled and rallied and soothed the shareholders. Then, to make matters worse, his little stint in a hospital had locked him down completely, when all he wanted to do was get back to her.

"You're really married?" A swift darkness whipped around her like a cloak and Trinity reached for the table to steady herself. She'd known something was off. She'd known he'd been lying to her. All the signs were there.

"No!" Blake turned his back and ran his fingers through his dark hair again before turning back to her. Her eyes were over-bright, and he knew with aching regret that she was holding back the tears.

He'd been desperate to get back to her and didn't realise how much she really meant to him, until he was laid up in that damn hospital bed, drenched in sweat fighting Malaria. The doctors thought he may have been bitten while in Brazil last year and the parasite had lain inactive until now.

He was tired but happy to finally see her, to be with her. But seeing her beautiful mouth tremble and her lovely dark eyes fill with tears he knew he had to tell her the truth. Now. He owed her that much.

"I'm not married Trinity," he moved to the sofa. "Please sit down,"

He waited for her to do so, knowing she wanted to be anywhere but with him right now. This was all his fault. His deception and unreasonable possessiveness. She was just so trusting and naive; he had a duty to look out for her and protect her.

He retook her hand and threaded his fingers through hers.

"My real name is Baldassario Blake Carmello De Laurentis, officially there is a fourth that's supposed to be tagged on the end, but I never use it," he looked at her knowing his name meant nothing to her. It gave him hope as he went on.

"I first saw you in the bank, with a red rose in your lapel."

Trinity frowned as she remembered her appointment with Reece the loans officer, all those months ago when Michelle had given her the rose for luck.

"You didn't see me. I was looking down and didn't like the way Reece was pawing you. I knew, even then, that I wanted you. I wanted to protect you from sleazebags like him. So sent one of the managers to interrupt."

"That doesn't make any sense," Trinity said as she remembered that day.

"Then I saw you later that night you still had the rose but now in your hair, and I came into your shop."

"With Travis," she remembered.

"Yes,"

"Hold on a minute," she turned to him fully with one knee up on the sofa. "Go back to the bank. You sent a manager to turn down my loan?" she felt a wave of heat creep up her neck, it was not out of embarrassment. "How could you!"

"I own the bank. Well my family does."

"You own the bank?" She repeated, incredulous. "You're not an accountant?"

"I have several degrees. Accounting is one of them," he answered on a chuckle.

"Don't you dare laugh!" she shifted away and moved to the other side of the room. "You've lied to me all this time? You own a bank, told that horrible man to decline my loan, just because you wanted to get into my knickers!"

"I did not tell him to decline your loan! He did that on his own."

"Oh well that's okay then," she scoffed looking at the ceiling and turning her back before swinging quickly back to him in anger. "What are you doing with me? Having a bit of fun until you swan back to your offices in Canary Wharf and laugh about your little dalliance with a black girl up north where no-one need know."

"No!" he shouted fiercely. "It was not like that!" he reached for her, grabbing her narrow shoulders as he challenged her to look at him. "You know me, Trinity, this is me. I'm only guilty of not wanting to share you."

She didn't try to hold back the tears any more. She was just so hurt.

"You lied to me. You think I'm after your money. That I'm a gold digger." She whispered through her tears, completely devastated by his lack of trust. "I think I would like my key back now."

Blake rocked back on his heels. "Trinity no," he urged her closer and hugged her tight. "I'm not letting you do this to us."

"Everything we had, Blake," she pulled away, and when he went to hold her again, she held out her arms warning him off. "Everything we had was based on—why did you even lie like that?"

"I don't know," he admitted, his blue gaze imploring her to understand.

"Not good enough," she spied the keyring she had given him just a few weeks ago and picked it up. She'd spent so much time choosing between the wooden Robin Hood or the wooden Great Oak key rings. Settling on the Great Oak as she'd seen the tree in Sherwood Forest and remembered how magnificent it was and how humble it had made her feel. He must have been laughing himself silly when she presented the basic keyring to him.

"Look at me," Trinity looked down at herself, seeing her simple leggings and white vest, but it wasn't her clothing she was referring to. "Everything you see is everything I've given you, freely, and with all my heart." She whispered as she pulled a tissue from its box on the table and dabbed at her tears. "I'm so open; it's no wonder you took me for a fool like this."

"Trinity stop,"

"It's no wonder you don't have a change of clothes here," she went on as though he hadn't spoken, "you don't want the bloody cat hair on your suits."

"Have you finished?" he asked quietly, folding his arms across his chest.

"I can't believe you lied to me." She sniffed.

"So I lied," Blake said losing his temper. "Get over it!"

Trinity gasped at his outburst. She was the one who was wronged here. She hadn't lied. "No! I want you to leave."

"I'm not going anywhere," Blake replied. "We are good together, and I'm not going to let you wreck it."

"Tough." She took a deep breath that was so cleansing she felt as though she was on a mountain top in Vienna. "You're so selfish, all you do is take. It's all about you and how you feel. Did you even think, even once, about telling me sooner?" She put a finger to her chin and looked at the ceiling in a classic theatrical ponder. "How about the time when I was thinking about going to the payday loan people."

"I told you not to."

"Yes, you did. Thank you," she finished sarcastically. "My God you own a bank!"

He shrugged as though it was no big deal.

"Did you think I'd ask you for money or something?" She was on a roll now. "Did you think I'd want to move in with you? It's no wonder you were horrified that day I gave you the key, looking back on it now, you must have been appalled when you thought I wanted you to live with me here. I was so stupid! You hid me away as though I was your dirty little—"

"Don't you say it!" He thundered.

"Secret." She finished, cutting her eyes at him. Her Jamaican grandmother would have been proud of the look. "Your dirty little secret."

"Why are you even thinking like this?" Blake challenged, he was too tired to even think straight. He'd flown straight over from New York, and jet lag was rapidly catching up with him. "I'm sorry okay. Sorry!"

"What do you want from me Blake?" she asked on a sniff.

"I want to go back to how we were," he began looking at the door. "I want to come through that door, and I want you to walk up to me—no run—I want you to run up to me and jump into my arms. I want to make love to you by the door and on the floor and then in our bed. I want to hold you all night and then I want to wake up to you in the morning. That's what I want."

His words inflamed her imagination, she had done those things in the past. They had done those things in the past. It was a shared memory all in vivid candy colour.

"Please Trinity," he breathed tortuously holding her gaze with his. "I'm sorry."

She hadn't been aware of him walking towards her, holding her hands as he was doing now.

"We'll start over," he promised, moving closer to wipe the tears from her eyes with his thumbs. "I'll buy you flowers,"

"I already have flowers," she stated, looking at the yellow roses in the vase.

Blake followed her gaze and stilled.

"Who gave you flowers?" he asked none too gently.

"Are you really going to ask me that?"

"I just did."

"You don't have that right," she cut in. "But it was Michelle from across the street. She gave me the flowers because she thought they would cheer me up." She went to the bouquet and pulled out a bright rose, it was just beginning to open, and she dipped her nose to the soft petals and breathed in the barely-there scent. "She gave them because she's my friend and she cares about my feelings."

"So you want me to give you flowers?"

"I wouldn't presume you would do anything for me, Blake. You never have before." She moved a delicate shoulder and replaced the flower in the case.

"Travis did come over that Sunday, the Sunday I wanted us to do something together, but guess what?" She didn't wait for him to answer. "You weren't here. So I went out and had lunch in town by myself, because my boyfriend—and yes I'll use that word—because that's how I saw you, my boyfriend was off in the country somewhere! You didn't even ring me. That's how much you value my feelings."

"I tried to get back, but we missed the slot."

"Slot?"

"I was stuck in Rome." He replied with tight reluctance.

She shook her head, and a tear slipped down her cheek. "Unbelievable. You weren't even in the country."

"I'm sorry."

"Doesn't matter any more Blake. Our relationship was one-sided." She still held the key in her hand, and she looked down at it. "You need to leave now,"

"Don't do this Trinity,"

"It's for the best."

"For whom?"

"I need to think about me now Blake. Me and my business."

"Can I stay tonight?"

She hadn't been expecting that.

"I—I— don't think that's—"

"I just need to hold you, Trinity," he coaxed. "Just for tonight."

"No sex?"

"If that's what you want."

Mercy took that moment to stroll in, her tail high as she weaved between Trinity's feet and looked up at her. Trinity picked her up.

"And tomorrow you go away?" Trinity asked, hiding behind the cat.

"If that's what you want." He repeated.

Blake walked to her and tilted her chin up to him. "Please give me this night." He asked quietly, his blue gaze awash with sadness and regret.

He had never sounded so earnest.

She'd give him this one night only because she needed it too. Another goodbye.

"Okay."

***

Trinity took her time getting ready for bed. Tonight she would not be undressing in front of him like she usually did. Tonight she would turn out the lights and go to sleep being held by him knowing that their heartbeats would be perfectly in sync.

As she got ready for bed, she remembered discovering their quirk.

They'd been curled up together in those first weeks, breathing heavily from the rapid but satisfying lovemaking session they'd just had. Trinity had laid her head on his chest, her ear over his heart as she played with his chest hairs trying to compose herself. She hadn't been able to differentiate her heartbeat from his. It was freaky at first, and she had pulled away, but then listened again.

Their hearts really did beat at the same time. He was bigger and heavier, yet they were the same.

When she told him to listen, he hadn't taken it seriously and had fallen asleep. She had spent half the night listening, waiting for one of their rhythms to change. When she'd held her breath, her heart raced for a moment, but then settled and beat to his same tune. She'd seen it as a sign. Hearts beating as one and all that malarkey, what a fool she was.

With a vest and long fleecy pyjama bottoms, Trinity got into her side of the bed, and Blake pulled her close.

"Relax," he urged, already enjoying the heavy fog of a promised sleep. Trinity was in his arms. Finally. He kissed the nape of her neck. "Trinity?"

"Yes?"

"I like your hair."

"I thought you didn't notice,"

"I noticed."

They settled into the silence. Trinity could hear Mercy licking herself from the cat bed in the corner of the room.

"Trinity?"

"Yes, Blake?"

"I missed you."

She stayed silent.

"Trinity?"

"Go to sleep Blake,"

"I can't, knowing you're still mad at me. I'm sorry for hurting you."

"So am I Blake."

He kissed her nape again, wrapped his arm beneath her breasts and threw a leg over hers before finally settling into sleep.

***

Trinity couldn't breathe, Blake's arm was heavy on her chest, and she moved it lower.

He moaned in his sleep and pushed his erection into her bottom. She turned to face him.

This would be the last time she would see him like this, and she let the tears fall as she traced his face, his eyes and nose. She smoothed a finger over his thick silky eyebrows, and she memorised the outline of his lips and skimmed the laugh lines bracketing his mouth. She'd miss his mouth and all the things he could do with it.

She grew warm remembering the places his tongue had traced, and her nipples peaked.

She couldn't help the sob that escaped from her throat, and she moved closer, wrapping her legs around his and sliding her arms up and over his naked shoulders. She breathed him in deeply, committing his masculine scent to memory and feeling the bristly roughness along his jaw as she kissed the strong column of his throat.

One last night, she wanted one last night, and with her tongue stroking the soft seam of his lips, she coaxed him awake.

When she woke late the next morning, he had already gone.

CHAPTER TEN

"What's the matter, Pet?" Leonora asked as soon as Trinity came downstairs.

"He came back,"

"Your boyfriend?"

Trinity nodded. She was a mess. After waking up, seeing him gone, and knowing it was for the best, she'd cried her eyes out. Her eyes were still red and swollen even after all the cold water she'd splashed on them.

She couldn't believe he'd lied to her about who he was. What hurt the most was that his lie was so unnecessary. Maybe it would have been better if he had been married she thought, not for the first time, only to immediately dismiss the thought. Again.

She'd asked herself all sorts of questions and still came up with nothing. She didn't understand why he hadn't merely told her who he was. Wealth, status, colour, none of those things mattered to her. It was what was on the inside, honesty and integrity, that's what she valued above all else.

He thought she'd be after his money. Was that the kind of people who were always around him? If that was the case, she could understand his caution in the early days, but he had been around her for weeks. She wasn't a complicated person, had never wanted to be. She was just a girl who now lived an uncomplicated life and loved cats.

Leonora went to get her a cup of tea and came back with one for herself as well.

"Come and sit down Trinity and tell me what happened."

Between tears and laughter that Blake could be so underhanded, she told Leonora everything, even that he had stayed over.

She could talk to Leonora and had developed a closeness Trinity hadn't really had with her own mother.

Several weeks ago, they had come to an arrangement where Leonora would come at lunchtime and stay until four o'clock every day. She wouldn't accept payment and said coming into the café was a joy and that it kept her out of trouble.

"My God Leonora, his initials are on top of a building in Canary Wharf!" Trinity exclaimed, again realising the magnitude of his deceit. It was just too much for her right now.

"Does it really matter Trinity?" Leonora interjected softly.

"It does to me,"

"But why?"

"Honesty is important to me. I was brought up to be honest in all things, even if I got a good telling off for it."

"And well done you," Leonora drawled dryly, pursing her lips.

Trinity looked at her sharply, not appreciating her tone.

"I don't mean it like that so you can stop throwing daggers," Leonora advised on a smile. "I mean honesty is a good trait, but think about his life and the people around him. Maybe being around you he was able to be himself, and he wanted to hold onto that for as long as possible?"

Trinity hadn't thought of that and mulled it over, picking up the young silver Bengal cat that had few manners and tried to swipe at her chin as she held him close.

"But why take so long to tell me?"

Leonora shrugged, her plastic triangle earring bounced against her neck. "Maybe he didn't want it to end? People in the banking industry are cut throat savages. You were probably a breath of fresh air, and you knocked him off his feet. So much so, he didn't want it to end."

Leonora made it sound so damned romantic.

"But you'll have to ask him," Leonora added.

"I can't," admitted Trinity.

"Why not? And put the poor cat down, you're strangling it."

Trinity looked at the Bengal she was holding too tightly and gave it a soothing stroke of apology before setting it on its feet, watching as it sauntered off with a sleekness his leopard ancestors would be proud of. "Last night was our last night together."

"Oh dear." Leonora reached across the table and took Trinity's hand. "You'll have to give him another chance."

Trinity pulled away, finished her tea before saying. "What's the point? He never treated me like a girlfriend, even if he did hide who he was. The only thing I had of his was his toothbrush," she laughed remembering the time she'd used it just because she was missing him so much. "His toothbrush!"

"How do you mean?"

"The one time I called him my boyfriend you would have thought I'd committed one of the deadly sins." She remembered her feelings of panic when he'd frozen, unable to hide his horror. "I had to be so careful how I referred to our relationship even then Leonora. I was hiding a part of myself when I really wanted to climb up to the roof and declare my love for him!" A tear slipped down her face and she dashed it away. "I was so happy, but so cautious as well. I don't want to feel like that Leonora, I deserve better."

"You love him?"

Trinity blinked back the tears and nodded. "But I'll get over it," she added with gusto. "I'm going to start dating. I'm going to find me a man who will introduce me to his family the first chance he gets. Family is important.

"I want a boyfriend who will hold my hand and cherish me and who will never ever take me for granted. Blake took me for granted Leonora, and I will never let another man do that to me!" She finished, walking to the back door saying. "I'm going to see about the litter trays."

***

Later that day, Leonora shooed her out of the shop, and Trinity took herself off to do some window shopping. She needed to think and was grateful for the time to wander mindlessly through Victoria Centre even though it was being renovated and was a bit dusty and chaotic.

She went into Smiths with the intent of buying herself a good book, a steamy romance with a happy ending, reasoning that if she couldn't have a happy ending at least, it would be nice to read about one she mused as, disconcerted, she stopped, finding herself in the newspaper aisle.

She picked up one of the daily financials and leafed through it.

"You're not allowed to read the papers here." A lanky teenaged boy, called Bradley if his name tag was correct said.

"Sorry."

She refolded the paper and went in search of the romances, finding a promising paperback with a bare-chested man wearing tight leather trousers holding a woman in a sexy clinch with tumbling hair and heaving breasts. That would do.

She paid for her items and found herself a seat at the back of an independent coffee shop.

Ordering a hot chocolate, she spread the paper out and went through it page by page. Telling herself off every time she turned a page expecting to see Blake. No, that wasn't his name. She couldn't even remember what it was.

And then he was there, standing with a group of equally dark-suited men that looked as though they held the world's finances in their hands. They probably did, she mused peering closer. He didn't look too happy she thought, he looked tired and distracted and his usually warm eyes chilly as they stared at the camera. She read the article, realising from the date he'd actually been in New York just yesterday morning.

He'd come straight to her.

Taking out her phone, and looking at the spellings of his name she typed it into her search engine and went straight to images. There he was. In different forms of business wear, but that was him behind a glass desk with the Barclays building in the background. It was him walking out of number ten, the Prime Ministers house. It was him holding a tall blonde Trinity had just seen on the cover of Vogue. They were all him. Pages and pages of a man called Baldassario Blake Carmello De Laurentis.

***

When she got back, Leonora was at the shop entrance talking to a man who was doing something to it.

"What's going on?" Trinity asked. Noticing the screwdriver the man was holding.

"Got an order to put a buzzer in Miss." He answered.

"Stop right there," she turned to them both. "Who ordered this?"

The man stopped, fished into his pocket and pulled out a crushed work order he then handed to her.

"It's signed De Laurentis," she mumbled more to herself.

"I do all the maintenance work over at the bank," he explained. "If you don't mind I'd like to get on?"

Trinity followed Leonora inside.

"Why is he doing this?" Trinity asked.

Leonora shrugged briskly. "Maybe he wants to make sure you're safe. It's not a bad thing, seeing you're on your own most nights and any old body could walk in." Leonora reasoned, watching as Trinity looked at the paper in her hand and then walked back to the front door to talk to the maintenance man.

"What are you doing?" Leonora asked as Trinity stomped back, went into a locked drawer below the counter and pulled out a cheque book.

"He can keep his money, Leonora." She filled it in and snapped it out of the book with a quick flick of her wrist. Then with brisk efficiency, wrote a short note, folded them together, pushed them into an envelope and handed it to the maintenance man.

"I've never taken anything from him before why would I even start now?" she said to Leonora, who remained surprisingly quiet.

An hour later, Michelle came over with a huge bouquet of balloons attached to a white Teddy that looked like Mercy, she said it had been ordered specially, and no, she was not going to take it back she stated seeing Trinity's angry glare.

When Leonora left for the day, Trinity did something she had never done before, she closed the shop.

***

She spent the evening catching up with her friend Felicity and then because 'Fliss' as she was called, had a spare ticket for an ice hockey game, she went to that as well, cheering on Marcin, Fliss's boyfriend as he brought the Nottingham Outlaws to victory.

It was after midnight when Marcin walked her home, and with a kiss and a wave she let herself in, opened the door to the café where she peeked on the cats before climbing tiredly up the stairs.

The light bulb was flashing again and, opening her door, she turned the switch off before going inside.

It was only later when she was in bed that she realised Blake must have taken the key as it wasn't on the table where she had left it last night.

CHAPTER ELEVEN

Blake slept for a solid sixteen hours and woke feeling heavy-lidded and hungry.

He looked in the fridge knowing he wouldn't find anything there and, taking a quick shower, knew where he was going to go.

"Hey! Where have you been my friend?" Mo exclaimed as he put another basket of chips into the hot bubbling oil.

"Overseas Mo," Blake explained as he waited behind a young couple who were holding hands in the line.

Mo quickly dealt with them and without Blake actually ordering anything, accepted the tray laden with his favourite cheesy chips and a can of pop and walked to the nearest table.

"I've not seen Trinity in ages, my friend."

"Me neither," Blake said as he forked a hot thick chip into his mouth.

"What's up? She hasn't changed her status to single has she?" Mo frowned as he pulled out his phone and scrolled through it. "No, she still has 'In A Relationship' on it,"

"Let me see," Blake asked, he hadn't even known Trinity had a Social Networking page.

There was a picture of them with their heads together, but his was turned slightly away, so if you didn't know him you would never know who he was. She was smiling up into the camera and her eyes were sparkling. She looked happy and in love.

"You two broken up?" Mo asked, not looking too pleased.

"It was my fault," Blake admitted. "I didn't tell her the whole truth Mo, and now I'm—"

"Sat here in the middle of the night eating chips with me when you should be working on how to get her back?" Mo summarised. "My friend, Trinity is like gold, she's worth more than any money I have in my account, and I can tell you, my friend, I have a lot." Mo boasted.

Blake laughed at the irony. Trinity was worth more than all the money he had too, and he had lots of it.

While eating his meal, Blake told Mo who he was and watched closely for a change in the Asian man's attitude. Mo didn't even blink.

"To me, you're just some bloke who likes my food," Mo shrugged. "I'll still use my knives on you if you don't make this right though. Trinity is a good girl. Do you know how rare that is?" Mo didn't wait for him to answer. "It won't be long before some other bloke will go sniffing around her and then what will you do?" Mo stood up to serve a customer.

Blake finished his meal, deep in thought. When he was ready to go, Mo gave him a bag of the infamous *Lorraine Special* and all but told him to do right by his friend.

Blake walked over to May Hill Lane, it was late, the café would be closed, but she would be upstairs, probably cursing the hot water as she tried to have a shower, Blake mused as at the top of the lane stopped, watching frozen as Trinity walked up the other end of the street with a man Blake had never seen before.

He held his breath, for the first time in his life, afraid of what he would do if she let the man into her flat.

She didn't, but she did kiss his cheek before closing the door.

It was time to be proactive. He couldn't lose her if this were what it was going to feel like, this feeling of gurgling sickness in his stomach. She was different from all the other women he had known in his life. Mo was right, Trinity was pure gold. Worth more than all the money he already had.

CHAPTER TWELVE

"Why is he doing this Leonora?" Trinity asked several days later when the shop was finally quiet, and they were able to talk.

Leonora smiled at her "Doing what Pet?"

"Look at this," Trinity showed her the Thank You card from the cat rescue centre. "It's thanking me for the donation. I didn't make a donation, he did, but in my name."

"Very clever I must say,"

"Whose side are you on? Anyone would think you know him." Trinity accused as she looked down at the card.

"It's not like you can send it back now can you?" Leonora pointed out, knowing Trinity had been sending the flowers and other personal gifts back as soon as they had been delivered.

Then Blake had gotten creative. He'd bought a whole elaborate bookcase that doubled as a cat tree and stuffed it with cat-related books for the café. It was sheer coincidence that the delivery had arrived on the one afternoon she had been getting her braids re-done.

Then another huge cat tree she remembered talking to him about one night had arrived and been installed in the window the morning she'd gone for a walk.

"He's not playing fair,"

"Maybe, you should talk to him," Leonora suggested as she wrote in the book they used to log the cats who were leaving for adoption.

Trinity bit her lip. She hadn't seen Blake since that night, and she missed him. She watched the news and read the financials just to see what he was up to. Leonora had hugged her when she had found her crying over a picture of him on her iPad.

"Go and talk to him Trinity," Leonora urged. "He's obviously trying."

"He's just buying stuff, using his money to—"

Leonora held up her hand like a lollipop lady on a Friday afternoon. "Stop. He's using what he can," she advised. "So what if he's using his money?"

"He's never used it on me before, why start now?"

"Now you're just being stubborn," Leonora scolded. "Life is too short for game playing Trinity." She went on. "I'll stay here an extra hour, you go upstairs, make yourself pretty and go and see him."

"He might not even be in Nottingham."

"You'll never know unless you go and find out."

Trinity looked at her phone, she could ring him she thought.

"Go and see him in person Trinity, at least that way, you can look into his eyes and see if he really cares."

Trinity wavered. "He'll probably be at the bank,"

"So? Don't you know where it is?"

"Yes,"

"So stop making excuses."

"Fine."

***

Blake pulled on a suit and raced across town, thankful for the tip-off from Michelle. Luckily, Trinity had told her where she was going.

Everyone was surprised to see him march into the branch and were panicking, thinking something was up.

He spoke to the manager, and before long a wave of relief swept through the office, and things went almost back to normal, even though he could appreciate his being there would always make them edgy. So many changes and redundancies were going on in the financial sector, people naturally thought their jobs were at risk.

Blake watched as Trinity entered and, with a smidgen of annoyance saw Reece scramble out from behind his desk to talk to her. When she spoke, he watched as Reece looked up at the mezzanine before escorting Trinity to the stairs.

She looked sensational, he thought as he watched. No boxy suit this time. She was wearing skin-tight black jeans that did amazing things to her legs, black over the knee boots and a heavy white v necked jumper that skimmed her hips. Her braids were arranged into an artful updo, with a few strands dangling over one shoulder and down her back.

He moved to the wide desk that the manager had quickly vacated and pretended to look at something on the laptop screen he'd insisted the manager leave behind.

"Can I talk to you?" Trinity said as she walked across to him.

No, she didn't walk, Blake thought, she stalked, much like her feline friends when they are about to pounce on some small unsuspecting mouse. Only he wasn't a mouse.

"Of course, would you like a seat?" Blake gestured to the leather chair opposite his desk.

"What is this?" Trinity held out the card.

"I don't know," Blake relaxed into his chair and laced his fingers behind his head. "What is it?"

"It's a Thank You card from the rescue centre,"

"That was nice of them. But what has that got to do with me?"

"Stop it Bla—er—Baldess—"

"Blake will do," he advised, hiding his smile when she stumbled over his name, it was so cute. She looked so flustered for getting it wrong too. He was going to take great pleasure in teaching her how to let the letters roll off her tongue. He was going to take great pleasure in one day making love to her while wearing those boots. He was—

"Are you even listening to me?"

Blake blinked and looked at her. God, she was beautiful. Her dark skin smooth, cool and glowing. He'd had the pleasure of watching her rub body lotion over her body more than once and had massaged the shea butter into her skin himself.

She didn't need cosmetics, but today she was wearing a deep red lipstick, and her eyelashes looked darker than usual.

"I said—"

Blake stood up and walked around the desk.

Trinity stood up too, but then stopped, her hands on the arms of the chair as she stared at him wide-eyed.

She had never seen him like this in person. A charcoal grey suit moulded his broad shoulders, a crisp white shirt set off his tanned skin, and a pink paisley tie was knotted at his throat. Pink, he liked pink she remembered.

"I'm still me," he said quietly.

"What?" she was still gaping at him.

"It's only a suit," he shrugged. "It's still me underneath."

Trinity mentally shook herself. It was still him. The problem was he looked so damn bloody sexy in the suit, maybe even more so than in his jeans, or tux or even the flannel sweat bottoms that rode low on his hips. Trinity grew warm.

"I've never seen you dressed like this before, it threw me for a moment," she answered honestly as she pulled herself together and faced him. "You can't keep buying me things."

"Why not? You said I'd never treated you like a girlfriend. Now I'm treating you like a girlfriend."

"But I'm not your girlfriend. Not any more."

He picked up her hand, weaving his fingers through hers and swinging their hands between them.

"I'm sorry for not telling you," he began quietly, looking down at their entwined fingers. "It's just that I was a coward," he admitted. "I'm a very rich man Trinity. My family portraits go back for generations." He looked at her then, his blue eyes shadowed with sadness. "Women see my money before they see me and for once—with you—you saw only me. A regular man."

Trinity fought the wedge of emotion in her throat, and she swallowed it down.

"I didn't want that to end," he went on kissing her knuckles. "Funny really, as once I did tell you, it ended anyway." He dropped her hand with regret and went back to his chair.

They stared at each other. Trinity could hear her own heartbeat and wondered if his was still beating in tune with hers.

"How's Soldier?"

Trinity started at the abrupt change of subject.

"He had to go to the vets a few weeks ago as he was feeling a bit under the weather,"

"Is he all right?"

"Stevie, the vet, says it's just old age. Apparently, Soldier is about eighteen years old."

"That old?"

"I'll never be able to get him adopted now and I'm not sending him back."

"I'll take him." Blake offered, leaning forward and resting his arms on the desk.

"You don't have room in your life for a cat," she dismissed.

"I'll make a home for him."

"It's not that simple Blake. Cats are a responsibility. They may be independent, but they still need love and attention."

"I've got plenty of that."

She looked at him sharply, her lips curling downwards.

"No. He's mine." She stood up to go. "Please stop sending me presents Blake. Please." She asked in earnest. "It isn't fair to me, and I'm trying to move on."

"Was the guy I saw you with the other night the one you're planning to move on with?" He charged suddenly. He hadn't intended to bring that up but hearing her talk about moving on, already, made an electrical volt charge through him.

"What guy?" She asked in confusion knitting her brow. "Have you been spying on me?"

"I went to get some food and Mo had sent some for you, I was dropping it off when I saw you with him," he said tightly, feeling that electrical charge now wrap tightly around him.

"Jealous Blake?" She taunted, crossing her arms with a small knowing smile.

It was the wrong thing to say. Before she knew it, he was around the desk and in his arms as he kissed her. Hard.

She moaned against his mouth as she tore her lips from his and pushed him away.

"What are you doing?" she touched two fingers to her lips

aware of his imprint.

"Reminding *you* that you are mine."

"You're a bloody savage."

"But your bloody savage Trinity."

"I'm going now."

He nodded, watching as she picked her bag up from the floor.

"No more grand gestures Blake, please."

She'd reached the stairs when he next spoke.

"That last night, we didn't use anything."

She swung back to him, one foot already on the second step down. "What?"

"Our last night together we didn't use any protection."

"How can you be so careless!" She yelled stomping back to him as she remembered and scrambled with the dates in her head.

"I was asleep. This is on you."

"So now you think I'm strapping myself to a rich man for the next eighteen years!" she accused.

"I can't help being rich Trinity. But you can strap yourself to me for the rest of your life. I'm yours." He finished quietly, his mouth curving into an easy smile.

She gasped as she saw the love, open and raw coming from him. She all but ran down the stairs and out of the building.

CHAPTER THIRTEEN

"What are you doing here so early Travis?" Trinity asked him as he came inside, still rubbing the antibacterial gel between his fingers with quick efficiency.

"I swear I spend most of my life rubbing this stuff into my hands," he complained.

Leonora and Trinity laughed at the disgruntled look he was sending them.

"I've been sent home,"

"Why, what did you do?"

"I've been sent home to sleep," he swept them both a speculative look.

"If you haven't realised Travis my boy, we don't have any beds here," Leonora pointed out.

"Actually she's moving out today, and I want to give her time to pack up." He explained in a guilty rush.

"Your girlfriend?"

"She's allergic to cats Leonora. What am I doing with a woman who's allergic to cats?"

"What indeed. Come on and have a cup of coffee with us son."

"Thanks"

They chatted for a while, catching up on his antics at the hospital, Trinity looked at him, all animated and passionate as he talked. He'd make someone a brilliant boyfriend. But not her, a man with dark hair and blue eyes was still stealing her dreams.

"So Trin?" he asked. "What plans do you have for this place now?" he glanced around.

"Trinity," she corrected raising an eyebrow at him. "If it were up to me Travis, I'd expand into all three empty shops."

"More cats?"

"Not necessarily, but I'd have a vet at the far end and run a cattery as well and of course expand the living room space and probably offer cooked chicken and treats that the customers can buy to offer the cats. There's a cat café in Japan that does that, and it works very well."

"You know what I was thinking Trinity?" Leonora asked.

"What's that?"

"You should move the day the new cats come from Sunday to Monday, just to free up a day for you and the cats have a day to settle, what with Monday being a quiet day anyway."

"Hmm, that's something to think about. Ah to have a Sunday to myself," Trinity sighed in pleasure at the thought.

"It can be done," Leonora said.

"We could try it this weekend. How many cats are going?" She asked Leonora who seemed to know more about the business these days than she did, but she didn't mind as it was a relief being able to share and talk about her worries and aspirations. She only wished Leonora would take some form of payment so she wouldn't feel so guilty.

"All but Gizmo, Soldier and that feisty one Miss Quaint," Leonora answered.

They all turned to look at Miss Quaint. A beautiful white and brown cat with big yellow eyes, but boy what a temper. She couldn't go to a home with children or with another cat that was for sure.

"Okay, I'm going to ring Pam at the rescue centre and see if we can rearrange the drop off day." She got up, but stopped and kissed her friend on the cheek as she passed. "Good idea Leonora."

***

"I'll be going now Pet," Leonora called out to Trinity who was at the back. "All the cats have gone, so it's a quiet night."

"Thanks Leonora, how did I ever manage without you.?" Trinity asked with a smile as she came from the back where she was checking the levels of dry food.

"Make sure to put the buzzer on, and I'll see you on Monday Pet."

"Thanks, Leonora."

Trinity watched her friend leave and moved to tidy up. The café was strangely quiet, and she clicked on the buzzer before mopping the floor.

Sometime later she jumped when the bell sounded, and she looked over and saw Blake standing there.

She was tempted to leave him outside, she really was, they hadn't seen each other since the afternoon at his bank, and she just wanted to breathe in his vicinity even if she didn't want to hear what he had to say. She pushed the button under the counter and let him in. He was holding a leather cat carrier.

"Hi," he smiled and reached over and kissed her on the cheek.

She all but melted as his familiar woodsy scent washed over her.

"Hi," She wasn't sure what the dynamic of their relationship was. She'd never been friends with an ex before. "What are you doing with that?" she asked, indicating the carrier he'd now put on the floor.

"I'd like to take Soldier, home," he said looking almost afraid of her answer.

"Soldier?"

"Hmm hmm."

Upon hearing his name Soldier jumped down from his perch and brushed against Blake's legs, meowing all the while, as though to say 'I'm ready.'

"I've missed you too buddy." Blake picked him up.

"You're not supposed to pick up the cats Blake, you know that."

"No-ones here Trinity."

He held the cat close and all but turned him over as though holding a baby, Trinity noticed and Soldier loved it, already closing his eyes and purring loudly as Blake scratched his chest. Soldier was one cat who loved his chest scratched.

"How can you take him home Bla—Bala—"

"My family and friends call me Sarrio," he explained watchfully, not wanting to remind her of his deception, but knowing he had no choice. She was struggling with his identity.

"Or Blake."

"Sarrio?" she tried it out, liking the way it flowed. He looked like a Sarrio, but to her he was Blake. The man who'd tipped her life upside down and still kept her off balance.

"How about I try it out for a couple of weeks and see how it goes?" he persuaded with a smile. "I'll be good to him I promise."

"I know you will," she acknowledged. For someone who had never had a pet, he was great with the cats. Although that night he had tried to teach Mercy to jump into his arms would stay with her forever. She had never laughed so much in her life. "You'll be here? In Nottingham?"

"No place I'd rather be." His words held a wealth of meaning and the blue glance he levelled her way even more so.

"You're a city boy," she pointed out somewhat breathlessly. "You even said."

"That was then," he looked around. "Place is looking good. Nice tree."

She laughed, seeing the new cat tree that fitted perfectly in the window. It's fake branches spreading along at the perfect height for people on the pavement to see the cats.

"Thanks for that." She tipped her head up and smiled up at him cheekily. "The cats were already on it, so I couldn't send it back." They shared what could only be called a 'moment' and she sighed. "Would—would you like a coffee?"

"No thanks. I want to get him home and settled before it gets late."

"Oh." She didn't bother to hide her disappointment.

"Another time," Blake promised. He picked up the carrier, and placed it on the counter, gently turning and placing Soldier in it, who surprisingly, seemed eager to leave. "Okay?"

She nodded.

Blake leaned forward and sipped at her lips in the gentlest of kisses.

Trinity closed her eyes and felt him. Felt everything about him, everything he didn't say out loud.

"I'll see you soon," he said gruffly, as, with another kiss, he turned to go.

"You have food for him?" Trinity asked. "A bed?"

"I went shopping this morning."

"Here," she walked over to the wigwam Soldier favoured and handed it to him. "This is his favourite bed. Having it will help him settle." She didn't know why but she was fighting the tears. Soldier leaving with Blake held a significance she couldn't explain.

"Thank you,"

"Can you manage to carry it all?"

He smiled indulgently down at her.

"I can manage," he assured her with amusement picking up the carrier. "See you around babes. Hold the door for me?"

Trinity walked ahead and held the door open.

"Bye Soldier," she told the cat poking her fingers through the wires on the carrier gate to rub his black nose. "Bye Blake."

He winked and kissed her once, twice, before turning to go.

CHAPTER FOURTEEN

Trinity picked up her mobile phone and answered without looking to see who the caller was. She was busy reading the romance novel she'd recently bought and was at the part where the hero was about to declare his love, the heroine was being unfairly stubborn, but the ribbons on her bodice were already undone.

"Trinity?

"Hmm,"

"Trinity it's Blake,"

"Oh sorry," she put the book face down on the floor. "Hi."

"Everything okay? You sound strange."

"Just being silly, I'm reading—," she began and then laughed at herself. "What can I do for you Blake?"

"It's Soldier,"

She sat up and swung her legs off the sofa, Mercy meowed at the sudden movement and jumped to the floor, flicking her fluffy white tail and strutting off.

"You're such a diva,"

"Excuse me?"

She laughed again. "Sorry it's Mercy," she explained candidly. "What's up with Soldier?"

"I don't know."

"What's he doing?"

"Looking at me as though I'm supposed to know what's wrong with him."

"Has he got a temperature?"

"How am I supposed to know that?"

"Look at his nose."

Trinity heard a sound and waited.

"It looks the same to me."

"Has he been eating?"

"His bowl is empty."

"Drinking?"

"I topped up his water this afternoon."

"Then what makes you think something is wrong with him?"

"I just know."

She could hear the worry in Blake's voice.

"I can come over." She volunteered.

"Would you please?"

"Sure. I'll be right there. Give me fifteen minutes." She advised, going into her room to change out of her pyjamas and into jeans, hoodie and trainers.

She wasn't the least bit surprised when he met her halfway and smiled her thanks. It wasn't late, and the pub crawlers hadn't yet taken over the streets, but still, it was nice that he cared so much.

He was wearing the exact same clothes that she was, she noticed.

They entered his building and rode the elevator in silence. Blake was looking straight ahead with his hands stuffed in the pouch of his top.

They were in *No Man's Land* Trinity accepted, a place between emotional lands of heartache, lies and sex. Great sex. Were they going to have sex tonight? Coming here was like an endorsement to sleep with him she knew.

Blake unlocked the door and invited her in. Two table lamps were on, but the rest of his flat was shadowed.

Of course she had been here before, but she could count the number of times on one hand.

"Where is he?" she asked, looking for the cat.

"Have a seat. I'll call him."

Blake stood beside her chair. Then he got down on bended knee and called the cat, making sweet kissing noises.

Trinity watched and waited.

"Why don't you just take me to him Blake?" she asked, about to get up.

"No, he's coming."

Trinity turned to see Soldier walking towards him. Cats never rushed unless it was something they wanted. Soldier obviously didn't want or need anything.

He ambled over, and Trinity noted his brand new collar. It wasn't a standard collar, oh no, Soldier had what looked like a designer leather collar with a blinged out ring type thing on it.

Trinity reached out and gently picked up the cat.

"Hello big boy," she cuddled him close. "Remember me?"

It had been a week since Blake had taken him home.

"What's the matter? Feeling poorly?" She asked the cat gently stroking his chest the way he liked.

"He's been very quiet," Blake said.

"Everything is new to him. It'll take him some time to settle in," she looked at Blake, startled that he was so close and looking at her with an intent blue gaze she couldn't decipher. "What is it, Blake? He'll be okay. He's old, but he's healthy. Stevie says—"

She continued to fondle the cat's chest until her little finger caught in the metal ring in his collar under his chin, and she bent to see what it was. She had never been a fan of animals wearing hardware no matter how cute or blingy.

A ring. A ring with a large shiny stone attached.

She stared at it, not knowing what to think but Blake moved and still on his knees took her free hand.

"Trinity Peters? Will you marry me?"

Trinity thought she'd misheard him, but turned his words over in her head. His lovely eyes were swirling with a mixture of love and hope.

"He's not poorly?"

Blake smiled nervously. "He's not poorly."

She dipped her head and hid her face in Soldier's fur.

"Trinity?" Blake said apprehensively, for the second time in his life he was scared. The first time had been the time he had climbed her stairs knowing he was about to confess his sins. He was only ever scared of what her reaction was going to be. He couldn't live without her.

"What about Mercy?"

He frowned at her for a moment not understanding, then he smiled a slow cat-got-the-cream kind of smile. "Come with me."

He took her hand and, still holding the cat, led her to the spare bedroom.

There, bedside Soldier's wigwam was a pink princess cat bed with a frilly sequinned canopy.

"Now will you marry me?"

Trinity was overwhelmed. She hadn't been expecting this, and with tears in her eyes and Soldier at her shoulder she nodded.

***

"I didn't even have any lipstick on," Trinity pointed out much later as they lay sated and relaxed in bed.

"Huh?" Blake pulled her even closer and nudged the back of her neck with his chin.

"You proposed and I didn't even have any lipstick on," she repeated. "What am I going to tell our grandchildren when they ask?"

Usually talks like this never happened in his life. Women he bedded knew better and even an assumption, a hint, of a tomorrow with him was quickly extinguished. But Blake could actually picture his grandchildren. He was sitting in a deck chair, Trinity beside him as they watched their golden skinned treasures with masses of curly hair playing on the grass at their home in Italy.

"You can tell them granddad was so romantic involving the cat like that and I'll tell them that it took months to train Soldier to walk in on cue."

"Months!" she laughed, "You've only had him a week."

"Months in cat years," he clarified, smoothing his hand down her flat stomach. "Thank you."

"For what?"

"For putting me out of my misery and saying yes. I love you, you know."

"I know you do. I've really missed you."

"Missed you too,"

"I need to tell you something else," Blake began quietly. "Not bad," he went on quickly when she tensed beside him, and he swept his hand up and down her smooth skin from hip to thigh until he felt her relax. "I was in hospital." He began, telling her about the ten days he'd spent fighting Malaria and how he couldn't reach her. He kissed away her sobs when he finished, then made gentle love to her.

***

"We're going to have to tell the parents," Trinity said much later. "We're going to have to meet the parents."

"Not a problem on my side. They're visiting Annalise's family in Derbyshire somewhere and will be up here for the foreseeable future."

"You mean your grandparents?"

"My father is in Italy. He'll hear about it. Eventually." Blake tagged on.

Trinity bit her lip, she knew they weren't on the best of terms, but she at least wanted to meet him before they got married.

"Why?" Blake asked when she told him.

"Seems like the right thing to do," she turned in his arms and faced him. "But it's okay you know best. Your grandparents sound lovely."

"Annalise was the love of my grandpop's life. Finding her, marrying her has changed him completely. He used to be a workaholic, a heart attack waiting to happen because he refused to slow down. When Annalise came along, he hung up his suits the same day and pursued her and married her before she could catch her breath. I bet he'll even tell you about it."

"That's so romantic. You love him very much."

"I love him very much," Blake repeated. "What about your family? Will I be told off for not asking for your hand?"

Trinity giggled. "My mum is easy, she's just down the road. Although she's not going to be pleased, I'm marrying a banker."

"Why not?"

"Let's just say when the economy collapsed and the whole

double-dip recession thing, her swear words were interspersed with bankers and words that rhymed with it. It was her favourite topic for months, being an Economics lecturer you see."

Blake groaned.

"But she'll love you," she soothed, stroking his chest. "As for my dad, we'll have to track him down in America somewhere."

"We're getting married as soon as possible," Blake warned. "None of this six-month engagement stuff. I want you wearing my ring before the year is out."

Trinity gasped. "But we're already in October, the middle of, in fact."

"We'll have a Christmas wedding."

"What's the rush?"

Blake flipped her onto her back and pushed her legs apart with his thigh as he looked down at her.

"I don't want anything to change your mind." He said with sudden seriousness.

Trinity felt a sliver of apprehension at his words. "What do you mean? I'm not going to change my mind."

He kissed her gently, dipping and stroking his tongue against her bottom lip.

"Promise me."

"I promise."

He smiled, kissed her again and smoothed a hand up her stomach to fondle her breast.

"I love you, Trinity." He said as he moved to pull her nipple into his mouth and made love to her very slowly, deep into the night.

***

When they next woke it was bright outside. Trinity couldn't see what the weather was doing as, from her spot on the bed all she could see from the large windows was the sky, and it looked as grey and uninspiring as it always did at this time of the year.

"Morning babes," Blake said as he woke stretching under the covers.

"Hmmm."

He laughed. Trinity never spoke in the mornings until she had brushed her teeth.

He kissed her nose. "There's a new toothbrush in the cabinet under the sink I think." He advised, watching indulgently as Trinity bolted naked out of bed and went to the adjacent bathroom closing the door behind her.

Blake sat up and smiled. They were getting married. She was going to be his. He couldn't be any happier. He just needed to broach the subject of her moving down to London very gently, but not today. Today was about loving and celebration.

The door opened and, brushing her teeth, she waved her ring-less fingers at him.

"What?" he asked watching with amusement the picture she made now wrapped in a white towel, leaning against the door jam, and trying to talk around the red toothbrush in her mouth.

She again pointed to her finger and walked around rolling her shoulders sensuously. She looked like a cat.

"The cat!" he confirmed and laughed when she put her thumbs up.

Blake got out of bed, pulled on a clean pair of white underpants and opened the bedroom door to call the cat.

Soldier walked in minus his collar. Blake and Trinity looked at each other horrified.

With a squeal, Trinity quickly rinsed her mouth, pulled on one of Blake's t-shirts and followed him. She found him searching the flat.

"I can't believe we left the ring on him last night," he said as he looked in all the corners.

"It's got to be here," Trinity said looking under the leather sofa. "Don't worry we'll find it."

"Don't worry. I don't think the insurance includes lost by cat!"

"Why are you panicking?"

Blake turned to her and told her how much it was worth.

Trinity blanched. "And you want me to wear a ring that cost more than a small terraced house?" She asked, wide-eyed. "Are you insane?"

"I liked it,"

"Oh well, that's all right then." She rolled her eyes before renewing her search. "Just how rich are you?"

Blake stopped and turned to her, seeing the open curiosity and not the pound signs generally associated with that question.

"Obscenely,"

"Oh Blake," she said on a sigh tinged with regret.

"Yes oh Blake," he mused, walking to her and pulling her close. "Will you help me spend it?"

"Can I buy another one of those cat bookcase things?" she asked, fluttering her eyelashes. "They like it."

He chuckled, moved his hands down and over her peachy bottom to cup it and haul her closer.

"You can buy as much as you like."

"Can we go to Jamaica to see where my great grandparents came from?"

"That would be nice," he confirmed, now distracted by the feel of her in his hands. He lifted her up, and she wrapped her legs around his waist.

"Can we go to Venice? I've wanted to go on a gondola since forever."

He smiled against her neck where he was sucking her delicate skin into his mouth. "We can go tomorrow if you like. We have our own plane." He held her against the wall and pushed inside her, capturing her sigh in his mouth as he moved.

"Oh, Blake."

"Found it!"

"Where?" Blake asked as he walked towards her wrapping a towel around his waist.

"In the wigwam. He must have been scratching and the collar came off. The ring was between the cushion and the base," she picked up the cat. "Are you a restless sleeper Soldier?"

Soldier looked at her and blinked. Trinity blinked back slowly knowing it was cat speak for hello I-am-aware-of-you.

She put him down and looked at the ring in her hand, completely unimpressed that it should cost so much. The stone, a diamond, she corrected, was shaped like a teardrop and the colour seemed a little off.

Blake took it from her, picked her up and sat down on the bed with her on his lap.

"It's a yellow diamond," he explained naming the carats, he smiled at her non-reaction.

"It's very pretty,"

"I thought the yellow would look lovely with your complexion." He pushed it onto her ring finger and felt a piece of himself fall into place. "I was right." He kissed her knuckles and watched as she held up her hand, turning it this way and that as the diamond splashed and danced light around the room. The cat tracked the sparkle.

"It's very pretty," she said again. "Thank you, but I can't wear it."

Blake stilled, "And why not?"

"Don't get all grumpy on me matey," she challenged playfully, tapping his nose. "The stone will catch on everything, and I'll be terrified I'll lose it. Please don't be mad." She tagged on nervously when he didn't speak, and she smoothed her fingers against his frown lines. "I'll wear it on special occasions." She offered into the silence.

Blake eventually caught her fingers. "Not to worry. Come on we need to tell everyone the news." He said, spilling her gently unto the bed and then pulling her up to go into his bedroom.

Trinity could tell Blake was distracted as she took a long, blisteringly hot shower and got dressed as they were going to make some telephone calls and then see to the cats at the café. It was going to be a long day.

CHAPTER FIFTEEN

Blake came with her to the café and went straight upstairs to see Mercy.

Blake had it bad, Trinity smiled remembering his conversation with her mother and his grandparents that morning. He was so happy. She was so happy.

"How come Mercy never comes downstairs?" He asked, coming into the room.

Trinity stopped dusting and turned to him. "Because she's mine," she explained simply, handing him the duster. "Can you do the top shelf for me please? I can't reach." She asked and watched as he looked down at the duster as though he hadn't seen one before.

"You flick it around Blake," she teased, going around him and lifting his arm to sweep it over the shelf.

She felt him laughing and squealed when he pulled her around and lifted her up to reach the shelves herself.

They were still playing around when the buzzer sounded some minutes later

"That'll be him," Blake explained walking to the counter to let 'him' in.

"Him who?"

Trinity watched as a small thin man in a dark three-piece suit walk in with two huge men following closely behind. The men had on sunglasses and looked like they could be in extras in the film *Men In Black*. They were about to walk through the café when Trinity stopped them.

"Hey hey hey hey," she yelled moving forward and holding up her hand. "No outdoor shoes in the café and please use the sanitiser." She indicated the pump.

"But," the small man was about to argue, and Trinity watched as his pale cheeks tinged red and he pulled himself up.

He then carefully placed the black briefcase he was holding on the floor and bent to take off his shoes.

"And you too," she said to the stiff burly men still wearing their sunglasses.

They looked at each other then did as they were told.

Trinity turned to Blake, who was leaning against the counter looking on with amusement.

Trinity tried not to smile as they fumbled with the disposable socks and pumped sanitiser gel into their hands before entering the living room area.

"Welcome to The Cat Café," she said, watching as the two men walked the circumference of the café before standing at each exit.

"What's going on Blake?" she whispered, stepping closer to him and searching for his hand.

"Thank you for your kind welcome Miss Peters." The older man replied, picking up his briefcase. "May I proceed, Sir?" He asked Blake.

Blake walked them to the small table.

"Did you do as I requested Walter?" Blake asked.

"Certainly sir," he waited.

Trinity waited. The whole thing seemed bizarre to her. What was with all the cloak and dagger stuff? She turned to look at Blake in confusion, but he only smiled a small smile at her before nodding to the man called Walter.

With a flourish, Walter opened the briefcase to reveal row upon row of rings.

"Miss Peters? I hope you like the choices I was at liberty to make, but if you don't, I can have one made for you by tomorrow." He advised somewhat nervously.

Trinity moved closer, she'd never seen so much bling in her life. "Can I borrow your sunglasses?" She joked then noticing Blake's seriousness asked. "Why am I getting another ring?"

"Because you were right the other one is too big for day to day wear."

"So I get another one?" She asked cheekily, nudging him with her body.

Blake laughed, pulling her close for a brief hug. "You get another one."

She turned back to the case.

"There's too many to choose from," she sat down and pulled the case closer. "I don't like any of those," she said pointing to the top rows. "They look like Christmas cracker rings, only twice as big and twice as shiny," she said then looked up sheepishly. "Sorry."

Walter dipped his head in acknowledgement.

"I like this." She pointed to a narrow platinum band with three small stones. The white diamond in the centre surrounded by yellow diamonds on each side.

"Sure?"

With gloved hands, Walter pulled it out, and she put it on, holding it up for Blake to see.

"I like this," she told him again. "My husband-to-be likes yellow diamonds," she advised Walter with a smile.

Blake kissed her.

"She likes that Walter."

"Very good, Sir," Walter appeared flustered. "Beautiful choice Miss Peters and congratulations to you both."

"Thank you, Walter," Trinity giggled throwing Blake a wink.

Walter cleared his throat.

"Sir? Would you like the entire set?"

"Please."

"Very good, Sir."

A short time later they were alone and sitting on the floor Trinity comfortable in the circle of Blake's arm as she admired her new ring and he was explaining what the whole 'set' included. She immediately vetoed the tiara idea, there was no way she would wear a tiara.

***

The buzzer sounded just after lunch.

"I can't wait for you to meet Leonora, she's been a Godsend,"

Trinity said letting her friend in. It was raining, Trinity noticed as Leonora came in shaking off her umbrella.

"Sarrio!"

Blake stood up stiffly, his eyes shuttered as he stared at Leonora, then exploded in rapid Italian.

Trinity gasped and looked at him wide-eyed as she'd never heard him speak more than a few words in Italian and that was when they were making love, she was temporarily distracted until Leonora answered him in the same language.

Trinity looked between the two.

"Sarrio?" Trinity repeated. "You two know each other?" She gasped, reeling and backing away from them both shaking her head in disbelief as she looked at them both. "You lied?"

"No Trinity it wasn't like that," Leonora rushed, knowing how guilty she must look. "This isn't Sarrio's fault," she caught Trinity by the shoulders stopping her retreat. "He didn't know."

"What?"

"He didn't know," Leonora reiterated before turning to Blake with eyes filled with regret. "I'm sorry Sarrio, but we had to know,"

"Had to know what? I don't understand?" Trinity swung to him. "Blake?"

"She's my aunt. My great aunt Lenny, I never made the connection when you talked about this wonderful lady called Leonora," he seethed, glaring at his aunt. "Because we call her Lenny and *she's* supposed to be supervising the palazzo in Italy!"

"Leonora?"

Leonora sighed guiltily. "I had to see why my Sarrio was behaving all out of character," she defended, crossing her arms over her chest. "Then I met you," she beamed, softening her stance to look imploringly at Trinity under her eyelashes. "And I knew why he fell in love and was acting so strange and out of character."

"But you lied," Trinity felt the hurt all the way to her toes. "I told you everything," she whispered folding her arms around herself.

"I'm really sorry," Leonora said into the silence. "I'll go if you want me to?"

Trinity pulled herself together and looked at her friend, who actually looked as though she was now about to burst into tears. She liked Leonora and knew she was only looking out for her family. Her own mother would have probably done the same.

"Lenny huh?" Trinity said into the silence flicking a quick look over at Blake who was looking at her silently.

Leonora nodded, sending her a small, encouraging smile.

"You're not a widow?" Trinity asked, remembering their first conversation and how feeble and distracted Leonora had been.

"I am," Lenny answered truthfully. "I'm really sorry,"

"It's okay," Trinity was just too happy to hold on to any malice and hugged her close, before pulling away to wave her hand in her face. "All's forgiven. Look what I got?" She stuck out a hip and flashed her ring.

"Oh my goodness!" Leonora cried, letting her tears fall as she hugged her tight again. "You too," she ordered opening her arms out to Blake.

Blake felt the air whoosh out of him with the force of a tornado as he was hugged by Lenny. He knew Trinity was big on the whole honesty thing and could have ended their engagement before they'd even celebrated a full day! His relief was intense.

"Welcome to the family Trinity," Lenny said through her tears. "Welcome to the family."

***

"We'll have to get everyone together. One big engagement party," Lenny said, "Italy or London?" she asked. "London," she answered for herself. "Easier for everyone. Oh my goodness, we've got a wedding to plan!"

"Blake wants to get married by Christmas," Trinity explained, feeling as though she was about to lose control of her life.

"Impossible," Lenny shot Blake a look. "He has no idea how long these things take to plan."

Trinity reached for Blake's hand and squeezed it. "Leonora, we'd really like to be married before the New Year."

"Call me Lenny. Leonora makes me feel old," she insisted. "Oh, my goodness are you pregnant?"

"No, well I don't think so." Trinity looked down at her flat stomach, remembering the time they'd gone without protection. She'd know in a few days. Then she looked up at Blake who was sitting on the arm of her chair. "We'll know in a few days." She told him and he nodded, strangely quiet.

"A wedding and a baby!" Lenny was practically levitating with happiness. "Oh my goodness so much to do and plan. Trinity, I'll stay here, in your flat, while you go down to London with Blake. I'll arrange for you to meet Florence, she's my PA, then again maybe I won't." Lenny was talking a mile a minute. "We can get the engagement party out of the way first, and you can meet all the family. They are going to love you!" She gushed.

Trinity watched as Lenny pulled a smartphone from her bag and she remembered how old and confused Lenny had behaved when they'd first met. It had been an act! Trinity really should be offended but couldn't find it in her heart especially seeing how happy and animated Lenny was for them both.

"Have you even set a wedding date yet?" Lenny said pulling up a calendar.

"Why do I need to go to London?" Trinity asked instead.

"Headquarters is down there, and it'll make it easier all round," Lenny explained without looking up from her phone.

Trinity looked up at Blake who was watching them silently.

"Okay," she said.

He reached for her hand and squeezed it gently, trying to ignore the feelings of dread as he remembered another girl, years ago who had moved to London and changed beyond all recognition. He was not going to allow that to happen with Trinity, he vowed silently.

***

Lenny had talked and planned well into the night and had eventually sent them back to Blake's flat while she spent the night in Trinity's.

"You've been quiet Blake," Trinity said as they got ready for bed.

"I can't believe she lied to us both like that."

"It's kind of sweet really,"

"Sweet!"

"Yeah," Trinity divided her plaits into two halves and plaited them together forming two thick pigtails as she spoke. "She was just looking out for you and making sure I'm suitable and all that,"

"I am quite capable of finding myself a wife!" he seethed in displeasure, pulling back the sheets and getting into bed. "You let her off too easily."

"Why are you getting so upset?" she asked, walking to the bed and sitting on the edge where he lay. "She meant well and I like her."

He scrubbed his hands over his face then pulled her on top of him, shifting so that she slid into the V of his legs. "You're right. I'm sorry."

"When are we going to London?"

Never, he thought. "Tomorrow evening maybe?" He said instead.

He really didn't want to go, didn't want to soil her with the pace and fakery of the city, but knew his life was there. He would do whatever it takes to make sure she didn't change. Whatever it takes.

"Okay, I'll spend the day with Leon—Lenny," Trinity grinned catching her mistake. "And make sure everything is in place."

"Trinity, Lenny used to practically run the East Coast branches of our American banks from her bedroom in Italy. She'll have no trouble with your little café." He pointed out dryly.

Trinity fought the hurt of his words. "But it's my little café, and I want to make sure everything is in place." She repeated pushing away from him, but he held her tight.

"I'm sorry. I didn't mean that as it sounded. I know how special The Cat Café is to you."

"And don't you forget it De Laurentis," she told him sternly, then ruined the effect by kissing him.

It was a long while later when he was sleeping soundly that she thought about his words and knew she was going to have to fight her corner or she'd get lost in his world. But was she really up for a prolonged fight?

CHAPTER SIXTEEN

Blake was nervous, he knew he had a problem the second he brought Trinity to his house. She was looking around all wide eyed, not saying much, but giving him sideways glances that spoke volumes of absolutely nothing.

He was frustrated as hell and felt out of depth. Hell, he wasn't only frustrated, and out of sorts, he didn't know how to introduce her to all of this.

He didn't want her to change. He'd seen it happen so many times, country girl meets rich man and becomes the city queen from hell.

It had happened to his best friend Maxim, who had found a sweet innocent girl called Zoya in Russia.

Blake looked over at Trinity, she was dressed in her jeans and her over the knee boots he loved. She now knew just how much he loved her boots after seeing his heated look earlier today when she was pulling them on and then with a sexy look, went into the bathroom and came out wearing just her boots and his favourite pink tie. He'd lost his mind for two hours while he made love to her.

He loved her, this feisty woman with the gentle soul and love for cats. He didn't want her to change, prayed she'd never change.

"Which is our room, Blake?" Trinity asked as she chose the left-hand side of the staircase.

The staircase held pride of place opposite the front door with the stairs open and welcoming like a grandmothers hug. You just wanted to smile and say 'Honey I'm home,'

The foyer was beautiful, dark wooden floors reflected and bounced light from the large crystal vase filled with large autumnal blooms placed on a delicate round table with spindly legs.

Blake pulled himself away from his dark thoughts. Trinity was strong, she knew her own mind. She'd be fine here. He'd just keep an eye on her. Maybe a bodyguard. But for now, he'd wait and see.

"Meet you at the top," he said suddenly, taking the stairs two at a time to beat her. She reached the top first.

She laughed seeing his disgruntled look.

"One thing you need to learn about me Blake," she said wrapping her arms around his waist and looking up at him.

"What's that?"

"I'm very competitive, and I'm currently fighting the urge to slide down the bannister to see who will reach the bottom first!" she admitted with a glint of a child at Christmas.

"No sliding Trinity," he warned.

"Spoilsport,"

"I'm serious." He moved them to the bannister and looked over. "Look how high we are. If you fall you'll crack your head open and you already know I'm rubbish with housework."

"Blake you have such a way with words. Now show me your bedroom."

"Our bedroom," he corrected taking her hand and pulling her down a long corridor.

"How many people live here?"

"Just me,"

"Why do you need such a large house?"

"I was waiting for you."

She pulled him to a stop, and he looked behind him, seeing her standing with her mouth open.

"I think that was the most romantic thing you have ever said to me," she whispered on a tear.

He pulled her along, smiling. "As you said. I have a way with words."

***

The following morning they were having breakfast, Blake was buried deep in three lots of newspapers, and he was reading one on his tablet as well as listening to the East Asia news.

"What time will you be back?" Trinity asked, already seeing a long empty day ahead of her.

"Around five, six at the latest." He'd answered automatically, and Trinity found she didn't like it.

She was going to set some ground rules and they started right now.

"Blake?"

"Hmm?"

"Can you please look at me when we're having a conversation?" The paper snapped, but he put it down.

"Thank you," she moved her plate setting up eight places and sat beside him. "Who set the table and made breakfast?"

Blake breathed in deeply.

"I don't have time to introduce you to the staff right now, but when I get back, we'll do it properly okay?"

It wasn't okay, but she wasn't about to argue with him on their first day.

"Okay," she moved onto his lap and wrapped her arms around his neck. "Have a nice day and be sure to think of me."

His hands moved to her hips, and she allowed him to rotate her bottom against him, already feeling how strong and powerful his arousal was for her.

"If I think of you, that will happen, and I've got back to back meetings today." He warned, nibbling her ear lobe and breathing in her soft vanilla scent.

"So? Just remain seated and all will be fine." She kissed his nose and tapped his cheek before sliding back into her own chair.

"Easier said than done." He murmured, finishing his coffee. He was pulling on his suit jacket when he stopped and felt around his pockets. "Here, your name is on it."

Trinity looked to see what 'it' was. A credit card.

"Thank you, but I don't need it." She dismissed.

"Of course you need it." He said, remembering how hard she worked after she had already put in a full day with her own business.

"Why?" She asked.

"Why?"

"Don't you raise your voice at me, Blake. I have my own money."

"I'm glad that you do. But you're living in my world now and will be under a lot of scrutiny. You need to look your best at all times. There'll be a lot of pressure on you."

Trinity may have been sitting, but she pulled herself up to her full height. "As I said," she said tightly. "I have my own money."

"Fine," Blake answered. "Keep it in case of emergencies." The card skidded across the table and stopped beside the slate placemat. A slate mat on top of a soft cloth placemat, she thought distractingly. Two layers before you even got to the plate. It reminded her of the pretentiousness of another time in her life.

She refused to look at him and took a sip of her tea, but didn't like the taste and put the cup down. She'd need to buy her favourite teabags she said to herself, ignoring the shadow that was Blake in the periphery of her vision.

"Thank you," she finally said, just so he would stop hovering beside the table and leave.

"Walk me to the door?" He asked.

She looked at him then, sighed and holding the hand he held out to her, walked him to the front door, gave him the dutiful kiss and watched as he was driven—he hadn't driven himself—in a huge black monstrosity of a vehicle off to the towers of steel and glass and a building with his initials on top that lit up at night.

Day one, Trinity thought, closing the door and looking at the staircase and already she was bored.

Two hours later, after duly introducing herself and relieved Lenny had already explained her presence to the staff, she called a taxi and took herself off. She was not the kind of person who could stay home all day dutifully waiting for the husband to come home from work.

She had an enjoyable afternoon, wandering around the area, buying her tea and making small talk with an elderly couple while sitting outside a bistro, eating thick tomato soup with a hint of basil, and watching people walk by as they went about their business.

Her phone buzzed.

"Where are you?"

"Hi sweetheart," she answered instead.

"Hi," he replied three whole seconds later. "Where are you?"

"Sat at a table eating tomato soup at a quaint little bistro on Riverside Street. Why?"

"I was worried. I called the house, and Malcolm said you'd called a taxi and gone out."

"Yes,"

"Yes?"

Trinity could hear a creaking noise. "Where are you?"

"In my office where I said I was going to be!"

"Are you shouting at me Blake, for leaving the house?" she asked quietly. The entire conversation was embarrassing enough, she didn't want her fellow diners to hear any of it.

She heard him breathe heavily.

"No, I'm shouting at you because you could get lost."

"Why would I get lost?"

"You don't know the area?" he shouted, completely irritated that she wasn't where she was supposed to be. Had the game playing already begun? "Look," he tried again. "You could have said you were going out. I would have left a car for you."

"Okay, I'm sorry."

"I'm sorry too."

"See you when you get back?"

"I'll be home early."

"Okay," she pressed the phone closer to her ear, wishing she could feel him. "I miss you," she whispered.

"I miss you too. See you later babes."

She smiled at his endearment. "See you later."

***

They didn't talk about her little excursion when he got back. He looked at her from head to toe and back again, asked if she was okay and at her nod, picked her up and carried her to bed.

They didn't come down for an hour.

"I spoke to Lenny earlier," Trinity said. "Apparently we're having a party here on Saturday?"

"This Saturday?"

Trinity nodded. "Family and close friends she said."

"How many?" Blake asked.

"How much family do you have?"

"Trinity I'm Italian," he said without smiling. "Family to Lenny will extend to all the third cousins and their offspring. We're talking hundreds. It's going to be a bloody circus!"

"Impossible, we can't fit hundreds here."

Blake looked at her strangely then took her hand. "Come with me." He pulled her out of the dining room and past the staircase and walked on. "You went gallivanting across London, but you didn't even bother to explore your own home!"

"Why are you shouting at me?" She stopped and asked.

"Because you should take more interest in your home!"

Trinity folded her hands over her chest.

"I wanted to have my tour with you," she said in a small voice, hurt that he was shouting at her, again. She turned and walked away, scrubbing the tears from her eyes.

Day one and they were shouting. It didn't bode well with her she thought, as she hooked her hand on the smooth wooden newel to give herself an extra boost up the stairs.

"Where are you going?"

She heard Blake ask, following her up the stairs to their bedroom.

"I'm going to bed."

"It's barely eight o'clock."

She didn't answer, but walked to his en suite bathroom and locked the door. Once inside she let the tears fall. Day one and she was crying.

She turned on the shower to drown out the sobs that escaped and sat on the edge of the bath.

"Trinity?"

She heard Blake through the door.

"Are you okay?" he asked.

"I'm fine," she dredged up some enthusiasm she didn't feel, injecting it into her voice. "Just having a shower."

A moment later a door she hadn't noticed because of the towel rail on it opened at the far side of the room, and Blake stood on the threshold. There was no denying her tears, but she did use a towel to wipe them away.

He came in and knelt beside her taking the towel from her and patting away her tears. His gentleness made more flow, and she sniffed.

"What's the matter?" he asked gently, his blue eyes darkening. "Why are you crying?"

She sniffed, "I'm being stupid,"

"You can be as stupid as you want as long as you're stupid with me. What's the matter?"

"I know you have to go back to work," she hiccuped, "but I wanted this first day to be with you. I wanted to explore the house with you."

Blake put the towel down and picked her up.

"Tomorrow I'm all yours," he told her gently. "Tonight I'm all yours," he kissed her temple. "Can I show you the rest of the house now?"

"Okay,"

The house was huge with one entire floor devoted to entertaining and another for fitness if the gym and pool were anything to go by. The whole house was spread over four floors.

"I see why we can have the party here," she said almost an hour later when they were back in the bedroom. She yawned. "Early night?" she invited.

"I've got one phone call to make," he reached into the bedside cabinet and pulled out a large tablet looking thing. "Here," he handed it to her. "This controls everything in this room."

"It says TV here, where's the telly?" she asked, seeing beautifully decorated walls, a painting and an impressive wall hanging.

"Press it and see," he grinned.

She did, and the wall opposite the bed slid open revealing a huge screen. "Oh, wow," she said with excitement. "I've gone to heaven." She knelt on the bed.

"The pool and sauna didn't impress, but the TV does?"

"I've got a brilliant pool and sauna at my local Leisure Centre," she said tongue in cheek and smiled at his affronted look. "Kidding! Come here and show me how to work this thing then you can go." She dismissed, flapping her hands at him.

He sat beside her and showed her how to work the device before giving her a kiss and going off to make his phone call.

CHAPTER SEVENTEEN

The following morning Trinity was waiting dutifully for the delivery Blake told her to expect and watched with excitement when a fancy car pulled up.

She watched from the front door as a uniformed man got out, nodded a greeting to her and opened the back door, only to pull out one cat carrier after another.

Trinity recognised the loud meowing of Mercy and pounced on her cat as she poked her fingers through the wire.

"Oh, baby. Have you missed mummy?" Trinity asked then turned to Soldier to ask him the same thing. He was sleeping and barely opened his eyes.

"Ma'am, shall I take the other one inside?"

"Yes please," Trinity answered. "What's your name?"

"Davis Ma'am,"

"Where did you pick the cats up from?"

"Mr De Laurentis requested my assistance late last night Ma'am, and I picked them up."

"Oh thank you very much," Trinity closed the door behind him. "You must be tired. Would you like a cup of coffee before you go?" she asked Davis and watched as a tide of red crept up his throat. "Don't worry I don't stand on ceremony," she advised graciously. "Relax, let's take the cats to the kitchen and get them settled."

***

Blake came home to find his driver Davis, his head of house Malcolm and the cleaning girl—Sheena or Sheila he thought her name might be—laughing and talking down in the kitchen.

He'd waited all morning for a thank you phone call from Trinity and when it didn't happen came home, thinking something had happened with the cats.

Yesterday he knew it would be easier for her to have her cats with her. Give her something to occupy her time with, so that she wouldn't be inclined to gallivant all over London. His phone call last night was to set everything in place. Getting Lenny to sort out Soldier and Mercy and wait for the driver to arrive. Blake did not come home expecting to see his staff hunkering down on the floor.

"Sir!" Malcolm said, being the first to notice him.

Everyone turned and melted away leaving Trinity and the cats. She came up from the floor, smiling and snaking her arms under his jacket and around his waist.

"Thank you for doing this," she reached up on tippy toes and kissed him.

"Why are you in here?" He asked instead.

She frowned, not liking his tone. He hadn't kissed her back she noticed, stepping back.

"Here?" She looked at him in confusion.

"In the kitchen," he seethed, "frolicking with the staff!"

Trinity stepped back and looked at him as though he'd gone off his rocker. She asked him.

Blake pulled himself up and adjusted the knot of his tie.

"I am not off my rocker! I want to know why you, the lady of the house, is sitting on the floor with my male staff!"

"Go to hell," Trinity answered in complete shock at his attitude.

"I came rushing over here, thinking something had happened only to—"

"Yes, find the lady of the house frolicking with the staff, oops male staff," she scoffed. "Yes, I know."

"Well?" He seethed.

"Well nothing. Get over yourself Blake," she turned her back and walked off to pick up both Soldier and Mercy, and she walked past him and into the sunroom just off the main dining room.

With Malcolm's help, they had chosen this room as the first to settle the cats in.

Trinity had used tissues to rub each cats cheeks and then rubbed the tissue against the furniture. It helped spread their pheromones and made it easier for them to settle. There wasn't any need to use butter on their paws. That was unless you like to mop, she'd told Malcolm and Sheena when they'd made the suggestion.

Mercy wasn't being very nice to Soldier though, but Soldier was taking it all in his stride. The poor cat couldn't be bothered with her attitude and meowed once, and she'd been somewhat subdued since.

"Please stop following me around Blake?" she instructed, putting the cats down beside their food bowls. "You're giving off bad vibes, and I'm trying to settle these guys."

She heard him leave and the door slam.

Day two she thought, she hadn't cried, but the tears were threatening.

She didn't understand what was going on with him. Why all the possessive jealousy? He couldn't be insecure about her feelings for him, could he? She thought, reflecting on their past few days together since the engagement. He'd become quiet and sullen the moment Lenny started planning their engagement party. Was that it?

Giving the cats a stroke each she went off in search of him. Only a quick perusal of their bedroom and a peek into his home office came up empty. She eventually sought out Malcolm and was upset to hear that he'd gone back to the office.

She rang him, but he didn't pick up, so she had a shower, changed into a woolly dress the colour of burnt orange with a scooped neckline. Added gold loops in her ears and arranged her plaits into a bun high on her head. Subtle gold eye-shadow, an extra coat of mascara and an orange blush that looked overly bright in the palette, but did, in fact, complement her complexion to perfection.

He'd never seen her dressed like this and that gave her pause. He'd only ever seen her running her café. He didn't know this side of her. He didn't know Trinity Melissa Johnstone Peters.

He had hidden who he really was, so did Lenny. She hadn't, but there were things he needed to know.

On an ominous sigh, she asked Malcolm to take her to his

office.

Trinity had always been proactive. If he thought their engagement was a mistake, then now was the time to end it. If he wanted out, then he wanted out, but she was not going to stick around wondering what she was doing wrong.

Announcing herself to the woman sat behind a low desk on the top floor, the crisp blonde raised an eyebrow and said only people who had an appointment could see him. The fact Trinity had reached so far in the building was testament to her confidence and stride. She'd looked neither left or right as she'd called the lift.

Trinity, in no mood for the big chill, swept past her and through a set of double glass doors only to pause mid step, unsure, seeing two other doors leading off it.

***

With barely a pause, Trinity chose the door to the left, knocked and went straight inside.

"Can I help you?" a man said, strolling towards her.

He was massive, all shoulders and bulk, handsome in a rough side-ally kind of way with grey, almost white hair. He looked too young to have a whole head of grey hair though. He suit was navy and his shirt sky blue and open at his thick throat. Blake wore his suits better, she thought.

"I'm sorry, I must have got the wrong office."

"Whoa whoa," he rushed towards her, his long legs eating up the space before she'd even finished her sentence. "A pretty little thing like you could never get the wrong office."

Trinity all but cringed at his slimy words. It wasn't very often that she didn't like a person on sight, she didn't like this man.

"Excuse me, I'm looking for Blake?"

"And why would you be doing that when you found me first?" he asked, trapping her between the door and his body, one arm above her head.

"Because I'm his fiancée," she glowered up at him pushing at his heavy bulk so she could breathe. His breath reeked of alcohol.

"And I would like to have lunch with him." Her hair fell around her shoulders when she shoved at him enough to duck under his arm.

"His fiancée?" he boomed in disbelief, before laughing to himself. He moved away and walked to a large walnut drinks cabinet to pour himself an amber coloured drink from a crystal decanter, tipping the glass to his lips and throwing the drink to the back of his throat, barely grimacing before slamming the glass down. "Oh I very much doubt you'll be getting married sweetheart," he went on. "Like me, Blake doesn't believe in marriage. He's as scared of the holy matrimony shit as I am."

"That's not true," she gasped, strangely needing to hear what he had to say.

"I'm his best friend. If he really wanted to get married, I'd be the first to know. You're not his usual type. Where the hell did he find you anyway?" he asked, strolling towards her with his hands in his pockets. "Scotland?"

"I live in the Midlands."

He smirked, the amusement apparent on his face as he tracked his grey eyes up and down her figure, staring at her breasts before tracking to her hips. He turned abruptly and poured himself another drink. He knocked it back just as quickly as the first.

"Poor Blake," he scathed. "He's been through all the women down here," he grinned at her knowing his words had struck a mark when he saw the flash of hurt. "Now he has to go out of town to play," he smirked. "When he goes back up there I might just tag along. We like to share." The implication was crystal clear as he looked at her knowingly. "Marry you?" he laughed, combing her body with a scathing gaze. "I doubt it." He pursed his lips.

Trinity had heard enough and fumbled, blinded by tears, with the door, slamming it behind her and leaning on it with relief.

"Trinity?"

Trinity started and scrubbed at her tears to see Blake standing with a group of men watching her. He strode towards her, took her arm and pulled her into what must be his office.

"What were you doing in Maxims office?" He asked as soon as the door closed behind them and he swung her around to face him.

She looked sensational, he noted, her dress clung where it should and flared where it should. Her perfect legs were on display and she was taller. About four inches taller by the looks of those sexy black patent heels with gold platforms and heels. He'd never seen her dressed like this before. Why was she dressed like this?

No, lovely to see you, what are you doing here or even why are you crying? Trinity thought in despair. No, Blake went straight to accusing her of doing something underhanded with this 'Maxim' person.

The door burst open behind him.

"Excuse me Mr De Laurentis," his secretary apologised, looking all flustered. "But she walked right past me and was in Maxims office, but then..."

"The future Mrs De Laurentis can sweep past any time Abigail," Blake said through clenched teeth.

"Oh, I'm sorry Sir!" She looked over at Trinity who was standing with her arms wrapped around herself with tear tracks and smudged mascara. "Erm congratulations Sir."

Blake made a shooing motion with his hand and the door closed softly behind her.

"That was rude," Trinity pointed out.

"What are you doing here?" Blake asked again as though they hadn't been interrupted.

"I thought his office was yours,"

"Why are you here?"

She walked to one of the two chairs in front of his large glass desk and sat down. "Can I have a glass of water please?" she asked, just realising how shaken she really was.

She looked around, seeing glass, vertical blinds pulled halfway down, cutting the harsh afternoon rays into manageable slices. Large leafy plants stood in corners and chrome. Lots of chrome.

"Are you feeling all right? Shall I get a doctor?" he asked handing her a heavy glass filled with ice cubes and water.

"I'm fine," she took a sip. "It's nothing." She concluded, giving him a weak smile.

Trinity watched as Blake went around the desk and sprawled in his leather chair, levelling her with his narrow blue gaze filled with suspicion. She waited.

"The last time I saw you," he began, steepling his fingers and rocking back and forth in his chair. "You were on the floor with the cats." He said eventually.

He made it sound like she was rolling around naked having an orgy, she noted.

Maxim was a horrible man, but this was so much worse. The only thing missing from this interrogation was a naked light bulb swinging from the ceiling.

Trinity took a deep, shaky breath, "I'm sorry I shouldn't have come." She made to go.

"Sit down,"

"No, I'd better—"

"Sit down!"

Trinity sat. Why was he so angry? She asked him.

"Because I see my woman coming out of another man's office and you ask me why I'm angry?" Blake replied tightly.

"I don't understand Blake."

"What are you doing here?" He asked instead, picking up a silver pen to tap on his desk.

"You left home in a sulk, and I thought we could go to lunch,"

"I did not leave in a sulk," he snapped, his eyes smouldering as he tried to rein in his temper.

"Why are you being so hateful right now?"

"Because my fiancée just came out of Maxim's office when I was in a meeting downstairs. How long have you been here?"

Trinity couldn't believe what he was implying.

"So you think I got all dolled up to come down here and have sex with any other man who was available because you weren't around? Is that what you're saying?"

The pen tapping stopped, and he got up to walk to his drinks cabinet instead. The cabinet was exactly the same as the one in the other office, she noticed.

Blake poured himself a glass of water as he tried to calm himself down. He was being unreasonable, he knew that. But seeing her here, where she wasn't supposed to be, looking sexy as hell when he had left her at home in dusty jeans and a t-shirt covered in cat hair! His imagination had taken over at a sprint.

"I'd better go," Trinity said into the silence, blinking rapidly as she fumbled around for her handbag. A fat teardrop dripped onto the leather, and she wiped her eyes before standing to face him.

"Let's go for some lunch," he invited, turning to her with a small, encouraging smile on his gorgeous face.

"No," she shook her head and pushed her braids over her shoulders. "I've kind of lost my appetite."

He was watching her carefully, she noted, one hand in his trouser pocket and his black suit jacket pushed back. At any other time, she would have got her phone out to take a photo. He was picture perfect.

This wasn't going to work. She knew that now. Day two and her heart had broken.

He walked over to her and cupped her face. She was so beautiful, but tears were about to overflow, and her bottom lip was trembling, he smoothed his thumbs over it and watched with regret when tears trickled down her face. He pulled her handbag off her shoulder and put it on his desk.

Gently taking her hand, Blake led her to another door, opening it to reveal a smaller room with a kitchenette, a sofa-bed and a bathroom.

He sat with her on the sofa.

"I'm sorry I exploded like that." He apologised.

She nodded and wiped at her tears. Day two and she did end up crying. It wasn't even lunchtime yet.

"I was already in a foul mood and then to see you coming from Maxims office, set me off."

"Who is Maxim anyway?"

"One of the directors and one of my best friends."

"He doesn't know you're engaged?"

"He's been in Russia for the past two months. I haven't got around to inviting him to our engagement party yet."

Was there even going to be a party on Saturday? Trinity thought.

She tried to smile.

"Have the babies settled?"

Babies! Trinity looked at him sharply. This was what was so confusing. He went from accusing her of having an affair to talking about their cats in the same breath! No wonder she was becoming an emotional mess.

"The cats are fine. Mercy keeps sending Soldier sultry looks, and he keeps ignoring her."

She took a deep breath and pulled her hands out from under his.

"What happened Blake?" she asked, feeling worn out as though she'd gone through every emotion known to man in twenty seconds.

She heard him sigh and watched when he stood up to look out of the window.

"If you don't talk to me I'm leaving."

He swung back, his blue eyes spitting fire. "One little fight and you're ready to run up north!"

She stood up and faced him.

"I meant your home Blake," she clarified quietly.

"Trinity I—"

"I don't know what's going on with you," she said. "But you have your own stuff to figure out." She took a deep breath. "Lend me your phone," she ordered, and when he gave it to her opened an App then typed something. "This is where I'll be staying—"

"Trinity no—"

She held up her hand. "I think we need a little space. I need a little space." She handed his phone back to him.

Blake looked at the address, recognising that the postcode was even more upscale than his.

"Who lives here?"

"I used to live there. It's my father's place," she explained. "It's empty most of the year."

"You know London?"

"Of course I know London. I'll take the cats with me."

"Trinity please, we can talk now."

She smiled through her tears but reached up and kissed him. She loved him, but she would not live like this. It ended now.

"Come around tonight. I'll make Spaghetti," she promised.

Dejected and knowing he had screwed up, royally, Blake shoved his hands into his pockets and walked her through to his office.

"I don't want to cause anything between you and your friend," she said, "but being drunk before lunchtime is never a good thing Blake." She advised, picking up her bag from the chair.

Then she was gone.

CHAPTER EIGHTEEN

Malcolm dropped her and the cats off.

Mercy was already familiar with the place and sauntered off to the kitchen. Soldier, the poor boy, looked as though he was at his wit's end. Three moves in one day.

Trinity hugged him close as she made herself comfortable at home. This house was very much dressed to impress. Platinum, gold and silver albums lined two walls, pictures of the 'The Never Blues' with famous people lined all the other walls in the massive hall. A living scrapbook.

Her dad was founding member of one of the biggest UK groups in the seventies and eighties. They'd ruled the disco charts across Europe and North America.

She smiled at a photo of her dad wearing electric blue disco pants and white platforms, a sequinned shirt open to his waist, showing off a huge gold medallion.

She loved her dad, but she hardly saw him these days. He preferred the steady sunny climate of California nowadays and toured within America. He said he spent less time in hotels this way.

Trinity had spent most of her years being tutored on the road with him and the band. She was never allowed a pet, no that's not true, she'd had a pet goldfish once.

"Come on Soldier," she said to the cat. "A shower. Then I'll go to the shopping district and pick up some stuff for dinner," she told him as she put him on her bed. "I'm not going to cry, but your daddy is being a jealous arse right now," she told him, scratching his chest. "But I'm not going to cry." She said again wiping away her tears as she undressed.

Later on in the afternoon, she walked home contemplating the office space she had seen and already pictured it as a cat café.

The people around here would love the quirkiness of it. She would get the cats from a rescue centre much like the one in Nottingham, and the cats would be adopted into homes of luxury. She liked the idea of it, could even picture it, but she would have to get a loan. Or she could just ask her dad for the money.

He would give it to her too. She'd been spoiled growing up, and it wasn't until meeting her half-sister Terry that she realised just how privileged she was.

From that moment she had paid her own way. Her mother may not have raised her, but her values had been chiselled into her by the time she was in her teens and ready for uni. Trinity paid her own way and wasn't afraid of hard work.

***

Much later the doorbell rang, and she smoothed her clingy white dress. It was a statement dress, sexy, completely backless and she'd worn it on purpose.

If she was off balance, Blake was going to be panting at her heels and be just as off balance she promised. Her gold strappy heels gave her some much-needed height as she walked along the dark marble tiles.

She opened the door, and there he was, wearing a tux and a sexy smile. He took her breath away.

"Oh my," she said, pulling the door wider to let him in. He'd driven himself, she noticed, seeing the sporty red car parked outside. "Hello,"

As the door closed, he swooped down and kissed her, pulling her close as he tasted her and filled his hands with her bottom, bringing her flush against him.

"Hello," he finally answered, releasing her with reluctance and looking around the black and gold hallway. "This is some place."

She laughed. "Completely over the top and ostentatious," she said with amusement, used to this reaction from those outside of the music industry.

"Who is your father again?"

"I'll show you."

Hand in hand she showed him the photographs.

"So you're like pop princess royalty?"

She laughed, leading him into the smaller of the three dining rooms. "Oh please. I was just the daughter to a superstar."

"You didn't like the spotlight," he deduced.

"I didn't like the spotlight." Trinity confirmed, "and when I was old enough to say no I was not going to pose in another photograph, and no I was not going to go on the road again, and no I do not like the new girlfriend, I was sent to my mother."

"How was that?"

"The very best thing to ever happen to me." Trinity moved a ceramic bowl of bolognese from the warming drawer to the table.

"Come on let's eat."

They ate and talked and it was like it used to be. The cats were at their feet. Soldier at his and Mercy by hers. Domesticated bliss.

"You're wearing a tux," she acknowledged remembering the last time he'd worn a tux, it hadn't been for her.

Trinity kicked off her shoes and curled up in the sofa after dinner. She'd moved them to her favourite living room. It was more like a snug, with a live fire and bookcases on all walls.

He shrugged, looking slightly embarrassed. "For you. Are you impressed?"

She laughed remembering why she had put on her sexiest dress, she'd wanted to make him pant.

After a moments silence, Trinity cleared her throat, knowing whatever was said next could end their relationship.

"I love you Blake, but I am not going to marry you if you don't tell me what's going on."

Blake nodded, looked at Soldier at his feet, reached out to scratch him behind the ears before taking a deep breath and looking at her.

Blake told her about Zoya, Maxim's wife from Russia. How beautiful and innocent she was. Maxim had adored her, gave her the world. He told her how she'd got caught up in the

wrong crowd and then the drugs. He told her about the time
he'd come home to find her naked in his bed. She'd been going
in a downward spiral, and Maxim wasn't listening to anything
anyone was telling him.

Blake had to watch as she almost destroyed his friend with her
behaviour, whoring herself out for drugs. Coming on to him all
the time and him having to rescue her more than once when
Maxim was overseas.

In the end, she'd died of an overdose after checking herself out
of rehab anyway.

"What else aren't you telling me?" Trinity asked. It was sad, but
she wasn't Blake's wife, his reaction was too extreme but what
if? Trinity gasped looking at him sharply. "You were in love with
her?" she whispered.

Blake looked at her and nodded.

"Did Maxim know?"

"I'm sure he guessed. We'd always liked the same things since
we met in boarding school."

"So it was just as hard on you?" Trinity scooted over to his seat
and hugged him. "I'm sorry."

He held her close and shifted on his seat so that she was lying
on his chest.

"Will you come back home?" He asked hopefully, sliding her
hair over her shoulder.

She reached up and kissed him on his smooth jaw before
answering. "I think it best if I stay here."

He kissed her temple. She needed space.

"I spoke to Maxim," he told her quietly. "You were right he was
drunk. He told me he frightened you and that he's sorry."

"Not good enough," Trinity said. "But it'll do for now. He's your
friend, but he has a problem."

"He does," Blake agreed. "Why isn't there a TV in here?" It was
a perfectly cosy room for lying around, cuddling as they were
doing now and watching TV.

Trinity giggled. "The only TV in the house is in my bedroom.
My dad said they distracted him from his creativity so banned

them from the house entirely."

They fell asleep on the sofa and of course when one, maybe it was Trinity, maybe it was Blake, whoever it was, placed the first kiss, Blake turned her so that she was beneath him.

He bathed her face lightly with his kisses, sweeping his fingers along her smooth skin, treating her like the precious person she was.

He was gentle when he pulled her dress over her head, then was fast and uncoordinated, his clothes flying in the air like confetti as he tried to undress without losing contact with her lips. He was gentle, when, with both hands, slid them up her ribcage to cup her breasts bathing first one and then the other in kisses as his tongue danced around her dark almost straining nipples.

Her back lifted off the sofa as she offered herself to him, smoothing her hands over his shoulders and down his arms, feeling the taut muscle as he levered himself above her, careful not to crush her with his strength.

Trinity whimpered when he moved down her naked body, sucking the shallow indent of her belly button before grasping her legs and placing them over his shoulders.

"Blake," she breathed, as her subtle body froze in anticipation of the pleasure he was about to unleash.

He stopped and looked at her, the pupils in his eyes were large pools of erotic bliss, and he was covered in a light sheen of sweat.

"Sarrio," he whispered, kissing the inside of her thighs. First on and then the other. "Call me Sarrio,"

She smiled and tried it in her mind first.

"What will happen when I do?" She challenged.

"I'll make you do this," and he watched as her body bowed taught as he pushed a finger inside her, hooking it around knowing exactly where to find her bundle of nerve endings.

"And this," he added another finger and pushed it in and out of her.

"Blake," she whispered, overcome with sensation. "Sarrio," she urged.

Blake replaced his fingers with his tongue and sucked away all her pleasure, only to lick and graze her with his tongue until she fell apart. Calling his name. His Italian name.

When she came a second time, he quickly put on a condom and finally entered her, pausing as he looked into her eyes. She was so tight, so beautiful and so snug the pleasure was almost too much, and he closed his eyes, letting go and just felt her. Felt all of her.

Trinity screamed more than once as Blake forged his way back into her heart. There was no denying their attraction, there was no denying they were made for loving each other.

She was his, and he was hers. Simple.

***

"Okay?" Blake asked much later. They were still on the sofa wrapped around each other with his head resting on the soft plumpness of one breast. His fingers stroked over her other nipple as though strumming a guitar to a love song.

"Hmmm,"

"Shall we cancel the party on Saturday?" he asked nervously, aware they hadn't talked about the wedding. She was still wearing his ring though.

"Do you want to?"

"I want whatever you want."

"No, you don't."

He shifted to look at her with eyes that were troubled. "Why do you say that?"

"Because I don't care about any of the wedding stuff. I just want to marry you."

His heart sang at her last words but then paused at her first words. "You don't want the big wedding, puffy dress and tiara?"

"You know how I feel about tiaras," she reminded him, remembering the day she'd chosen her ring. She looked at her hand now. "I like simple, uncomplicated things. If I could get away with you, me, a witness or two on a beach somewhere, I'd be happy."

"Why didn't you say?"

"Lenny was getting all excited, and you were getting quieter and quieter, and I thought you were maybe regretting making the proposal." She admitted, biting her lip as she looked at him.

"Never!" he shifted again, smoothing a finger along her bottom lip until she released it. "I thought you wanted the big wedding."

"Nope,"

He moved back into position against her chest.

"We have to do better Trinity," he warned. "I have a dominant personality and so do you. We talk, okay? No matter what, we talk."

"Okay,"

She closed her eyes already heavy with sleep.

"Trinity?" Blake said a few minutes later.

"Hmm?"

"Your heart beats the same time as mine." He said in awe.

She smiled and stroked his hair.

"Told you."

***

They were married two weeks later on the beautiful Caribbean island of Tobago. The wedding party consisted of her parents, his grandparents, her sister and Lenny and it was the most perfectly magical day.

They island-hopped for their honeymoon, with Blake promising they would go to Jamaica and visit properly another time.

CHAPTER NINETEEN

Trinity moved into Blake's house when they got back, but they drove up to Nottingham most weekends until they figured out what to do with her place.

Trinity didn't want to sell The Cat Café, and although Lenny enjoyed looking after it, it took up too much of her time, and it really wasn't fair, leaving someone else to look after her business. Blake had suggested hiring a manager, but she had yet to warm to the idea. So at the moment, they were travelling back and forth at the weekend.

The answer came with Annalise, Blake's step-grandmother. She and grandpop were going to buy the building, and as the council had agreed to regenerate the whole area, they were going to invest in two other buildings as well, knowing the council had plans to make Hockley into a Creative Quarter and market it as such.

Annalise planned to convert the second floor into a gallery and the third into artist studios. She also had possible plans for the other buildings, a recording studio as well as a small theatre. Annalise was definitely an advocate for the Arts, Trinity now knew, and they'd laughed when she told them how she had seen them peering through the windows all those months ago.

Trinity wasn't pregnant and found herself wishing she had been, but then again she and Blake were getting to know each other, sometimes at loggerheads when she said she was thinking about opening another cat café in London, the first in the city and him thinking it was too much responsibility.

She knew he still had visions of her slaving away from midday to midnight and beyond, being completely unavailable to him. But now she knew how to operate. Lenny's new system of moving the cat drop off and adoption days had freed up some time. Plus, she said, and what was her most persuasive argument, there were just too many homeless cats in London for them not to help.

***

Life was good. Trinity smiled as she sang along as her playlist shuffled to another one of her upbeat African Caribbean mixes that were going mainstream in the charts. She liked the new fusions.

Respecting Soldiers age, only Mercy travelled back and forth with them, and she was currently sleeping in a carrier held steady by a seatbelt.

Trinity settled in to enjoy the drive in her brand new white Range Rover Blake had bought her for Christmas.

The M1 was nice and quiet, with it going up to eight in the evening.

Travis was looking after the café until she got there as Lenny had plans for the weekend and Blake was driving up later tonight as he had an evening meeting. She missed him, she mused, as they normally enjoyed the drive up together.

Trinity was so happy. Married life certainly agreed with her as with every breath she took, she loved her husband even more. They were a perfect match. Absolutely perfect.

Trinity, knowing she wasn't able to park outside the café, parked illegally on the corner where she quickly slung her handbag over her shoulder, picked up the carrier and walked to the café.

Travis had obviously been looking out for her as he met her at the door.

"Hey Trin, good drive up?"

"Trinity," she answered, "and yes, it was a breeze,"

Travis looked over her shoulder at her new car.

"Imagine," he started, taking one of the carriers from her and following her into the shop. "If I hadn't made Blake come into the café that night, you wouldn't be looking as though the cat just got the cream!" he grinned.

She laughed, glad that Blake and Travis got on so well. Travis was a close friend of them all now and very much looking forward to the expansion.

"How's it been here?" she asked, looking around, strange to see a whole set of cats that she didn't know, except Miss Quaint that is and she recognised Gizmo sleeping on a tree limb.

"Guess what?" Travis went to the counter and held open the adoption book. "Look?" he pointed to an entry.

"Gizmo's getting adopted?" Trinity read. "By who?"

"Mr & Mrs Horncastle. They've moved house and can get a pet," he explained. "They want Gizmo with them."

"Aww, that's fantastic." She exclaimed, happy that Gizmo was going to be re-homed and with the elderly couple she knew so well.

She'd thought about asking Blake if he could come and live with them, but she knew Blake had visions of cats taking over his house, and she didn't want to push it, well not just yet anyway she thought, smiling secretly to herself.

"Let me take Mercy upstairs and then I'll relieve you." She said, picking up Mercy's carrier again and going to the door to her old flat.

The light on the stairwell flickered once, twice for longer this time and with an accompanied buzzing sound that hadn't been there before. Trinity thought to buy a new bulb. It would be the fourth or fifth bulb in as many months she remembered, unlocking the door.

The flat looked exactly how she and Blake had left it last. Another home away from home only they never slept here, going back to his flat instead.

Annalise wasn't sure what she was going to do with the flat yet but had suggested she maybe might let her granddaughter, who was at Nottingham uni, have it as she would be leaving the Halls next year. Everything depended on the sale though, and who knew how long that was going to take?

Trinity washed her face, fed Mercy and then went back downstairs where she had a pleasant conversation with Travis over a cup of tea.

She told him her tentative plans about the building she was eyeing. He was full of encouragement and enthusiasm, and he told her about this hot nurse he liked and wanted to ask out.

"Make sure she likes cats," Trinity suggested and they laughed.

***

As Travis had to pass Blake's building, she asked him to park her car for her over there as parking a top of the range vehicle in the middle of the city centre on a Friday night was asking for trouble. She might wake up to a smashed windscreen and wing mirrors hanging off.

After the last customer had left she locked up and got to know the new cats.

They were a happy bunch, twenty-five in all and she played and stroked and said goodnight to each and every one of them before climbing the stairs to get her purse. She was going to nip across and say hello to the girls in the taxi office, knowing she wouldn't have time to say hello tomorrow and then get herself a tray of cheesy chips from Mo.

She was still smiling from her conversation with Mo when she got back and rang Blake, but it went straight to voicemail, so she left a message telling him that she was sleeping at her old place tonight and he was to ring her when he got here.

***

Blake checked the time and closed his laptop. He'd get to Nottingham by nine, ten at the latest he thought as he got up to go, shrugging into his jacket, and loosening his tie.

His door opened and Maxim walked in.

"Hey!" Maxim roared, swaying on his feet. "My best friend in the whole world is here!"

"Maxim are you drunk?" Blake asked as his friend closed the door with exaggerated softness, only for it slam anyway.

Blake noticed his bloodshot eyes and high ruddy complexion.

"No, of course not," he answered taking exaggerated steps forward.

"I think you are. Want a coffee before I go?"

Maxim made a face and went to his drinks cabinet instead, but Blake beat him to it.

"I think you've had enough mate," he warned taking the decanter of whisky from him and leading him to the chair instead.

"Where is that beauty you married?" Maxim looked around the room putting his hand over his brow as though looking out at sea. "She's so hot," he whistled or at least tried to. "I want to try her," he smacked his lips, "you know have a little taste."

"Careful my friend," Blake warned.

"She has a tight little—"

Blake grabbed Maxims shirt-front and gritted his teeth. "That is my wife you're about to insult," he warned. "Watch it."

Maxim laughed and peered at Blake.

"That time in my office," Maxim made a rude gesture and Blake hit him.

"Hey, what the hell was that!" Maxim held his jaw, stumbled to his feet and took a swing at Blake. "She came on to me, and you hit me. Your best friend."

Blake took an easy step backwards, and Maxim swung into thin air and lost his balance. He caught himself on Blake's desk, and the laptop slid to the floor.

Maxim looked at it and made to pick it up, but Blake beat him to it. Grumbling all the while, saying Blake always had to win, Blake always got the pretty girls, Blake's new little wife would make the perfect mistress.

"Stop Maxim. Or I won't be accountable for what I do next." Blake growled.

Maxim swayed and placed his hand on Blake's shoulder looking at him dead in the eye.

"You love her?" Maxim asked.

"I love her."

"I loved her too, Blake," He said in a small voice. The words spilling out over and over and running together like two rivers colliding.

Somehow Blake knew they were no longer talking about Trinity.

"She was the sweetest thing I'd ever seen." Maxim fell into the chair and held his head. "She was sat outside on her grandmother's doorstep wearing the ugliest jumper, but her smile." Maxim smiled as the tears started to fall and he remembered. "Her smile lit me up inside." He gulped and stared unseeingly at the London skyline, remembering that day in Russia.

"I know it did Maxim," Blake soothed putting his arm around his friend as he began to cry. He could feel his phone vibrating in his pocket but knew he couldn't answer it. Not now.

"I loved her with all my heart," Maxim cried. "What happened?"

Blake rocked his friend back and forth knowing it had taken him two years to let out his grief, two years to finally let go. He couldn't leave him like this. Trinity would expect him to see to his friend.

***

It was almost three in the morning by the time he pulled into his parking space. Trinity's vehicle was in the adjacent spot, and he smiled getting into the lift and quickening his steps as he walked down the corridor to their flat.

It was dark inside and strangely quiet. He poured himself a glass of water and then turned on a lamp, aware that something was wrong with the skyline. It was orange and thick with dark fog. Only there hadn't been any fog when he was driving in Blake thought, as he walked to the windows.

Something wasn't right. Fog didn't tunnel up to the skyline like it was doing, nor move in bulging swirls like that. It was smoke, and it was coming from the direction of May Hill Lane. Trinity!

Dropping the glass of water, he raced into the bedroom. Knowing before he actually got there that it would be empty.

"Trinity!" He yelled as panic took hold.

The flat was empty.

***

It would normally take ten minutes to walk, Blake ran it in two.

Trinity's building was on fire. Several fire trucks squeezed along the top of the lane battling with the flames that had already engulfed most of the buildings nearest to the tram lines.

Crowds of people gathered to watch in morbid curiosity. Their phones recording the goings on as flames finished off the empty warehouse behind the café and jumped over to lick and tease at the buildings on either side of it.

Blake shoved his way through, completely oblivious to who and what was around him. All he could see was the café and black smoke billowing from the floors above it.

"Oi!" someone grabbed his arm. "You can't go any further mate,"

Blake swung round to see a police officer.

"My wife," he said, his eyes wild with fear. "My wife is in that building."

"Come on!" The officer held on to Blake's arm as they ran down to the front of the café. "Let us through!"

They reached a line of firefighters who were looking dejectedly up at the building. A heavyset man in a white shirt was calling out instructions through his radio and swearing about the lack of water.

"This man says his wife is in the building." The officer told him.

The fireman swung around to them and swore. "Where?" The man asked harshly, he'd been told no one was in the building except for a bunch of cats, and he'd already made sure the cats could escape through a broken window.

"The café with the cats. There's a flat to the side." Blake pointed, and as the firemen turned to see, he took off and was already running for the door, but they caught him by the shoulders and dragged him back.

He tried to fight them off and almost made it to the door again just as someone's fist slammed into the side of his face.

"Sorry mate," one of the men told him. "It's not safe. We'll get her out."

Blake was dragged back and held by two men, but his eyes

remained glued to the door.

"Tell us where she is?"

"The side entrance, up some steps, the door is on the left. It's the only door. Our bedroom is to the back. Please hurry." He pleaded. He pulled out his phone and rang her.

"What's her name?"

"Trinity. She's all that I have. Please save her," Blake cried just as there was an explosion and the whole street shook.

***

Trinity woke in a panic.

Mercy was stamping on her head and flexing her claws.

"Why are you doing that?" she scolded the cat while fighting through the fog of sleep. Her eyes were stinging, and there was a smell of burning. Trinity closed then opened her eyes again thinking she may be having a dream, but no, there was definitely smoke in the flat.

Looking around she could see globs of blue and red lights shine onto the walls from outside, and Trinity ran to the window.

It was a bizarre scene. Fire trucks and police cars and crowds of people clogged the top of the street, and another group of firefighters were below her window.

"Oh God." She said in her panic trying to think what to do, all the while trying to remember the emergency training she'd once had as a Girl Guide.

She ran to her front door and felt it carefully. The door handle was hot, and the paint on the wood was bubbling in places. "Oh God," she said again and ran to the window. It was a sash window that opened inwards. It had been installed way before Health and Safety and any other safety remit and was covered by a hardened sheet of plastic that had been nailed in years ago. It was just last summer she'd tried to open it but to no avail. She couldn't get out.

She saw a commotion below and screamed when she saw a man in uniform hit Blake, dragging him away. "Blake!" She yelled knocking frantically on the window.

It was surreal and everything seemed to be in slow motion. Trinity could see cats everywhere and people running around trying to capture them.

"Blake," she said again as he looked up and their eyes met.

***

Instinct took over. She needed to get out. Thick black smoke was seeping under the door and coming through the vents. The air was getting too thick to breathe, she knew she only had a few minutes, or she'd suffocate to death.

Running to the bathroom, she grabbed a towel to wet it only nothing came out of the taps. She couldn't even stem the smoke coming in from under the door! No water.

In desperation, Trinity picked up a saucepan and threw it at the windowpane, but it bounced against the plastic. She needed to get the heavy perspex off first.

She ran to the kitchen, grabbed an eating knife and used it to wedge between the plastic and the frame. The frame was rotten and crumbled easily under the abuse. She was getting weaker she realised, so fell to her knees, breathed in and out, twice, held her breath, stood up and using her fingers dragged the perspex off. She then picked up the saucepan again and turning her face away, slammed it against the glass. Clean air gushed into the room, and she breathed it in with relief.

Her hands were stinging, and there was blood everywhere, but she didn't care.

"Trinity!"

She could hear Blake, and she searched the crowd for him, seeing him waving frantically.

There was another explosion, closer this time and it knocked her off her feet. She fell, hitting her head and for a split second gave in to the blinding panic and closed her eyes.

She couldn't do it. She was too tired. The window was too far away. She sank further, feeling the heat beneath her. It was so warm and comforting. The crackling she could hear reminded her of the bacon she'd cooked for Blake one morning, but she'd burnt it to a crisp, and he'd taken over, not doing much better. Trinity smiled at the memory.

"Trinity!"

Blake? Her eyes snapped open. He was calling her.

"Trinity get up!" She could hear him yell. "Let me go!"

"Meow,"

Everything was happening at once, and Trinity could just about make out Mercy. The cat was clinging to her bare legs.

"Trinity!"

Trinity dragged herself up and pressed her fingers to the back of her head. She peered at the blood on her hands and then looked over at the door, seeing the strip of bright orange glow under the door. The fire was here.

Picking up Mercy and tucking her under her arm she stumbled on her knees, keeping herself as low to the ground as possible as she picked her way to the window. She knelt on broken glass but kept going, brushing a path for them as she crawled to the window.

"Trinity!"

She could hear his panic. Blake, she had to get to him.

She made it to the window just as the door made a weird groaning noise.

"Trinity!"

She edged up and pulled herself up.

"Blake?"

"I'm here," he yelled. "Jump!"

Trinity pulled the curtain and used it to protect her legs from the shards of glass sticking out of the wooden frame and levered herself up. Mercy dug her claws into Trinity's side as she clung on.

"Hurry up!" Blake shouted. "Jump!"

Everyone was watching and just as she was about to jump, the door splintered, Mercy jumped out of her arms and flames licked their way inside.

Trinity screamed falling back inside.

"No!" Blake yelled, beside himself with fear.

***

She looked back for the cat. But couldn't see for the smoke. Flames danced into the room, frolicking with the sofa and licking at the walls. The heat was unbelievable.

She scrambled to the window, hauling herself up. She could feel the heat on the back of her legs.

"Trinity?" Blake shouted above the roar of the flames eating away at the building.

She looked at Blake.

"Jump!" he ordered. "Do it now!" he said sternly.

Trinity couldn't do it. It was too high, she thought in a panic looking down and seeing some sort of silver blanket thing with a square bullseye in the centre below her window, the edges held by men in black uniforms and yellow hard hats.

She couldn't do it.

Blake saw it happen. Saw the light going out in her eyes.

"Trinity! No." He yelled in desperation, viciously pulling away from the arms that were holding him back. "Look at me!" he commanded. "look at me," he shouted to her. "We have the same beat. Our hearts have the same beat," he thumped his fist over his heart. "Jump and do it now!"

Closing her eyes, Trinity jumped.

***

There was a scattering of applause as she was caught by the firemen below.

Blake stumbled towards her and held on to her for dear life. Kissing her face, her hands, everywhere he could touch. He couldn't believe he had almost lost her as he cried and she cried.

It was only the intervention of two paramedics that made Blake finally let her go, although he still held her hand as they walked her to a nearby ambulance.

They turned to see the entire building in flames. All floors, the fire already licking away at the roof.

"Look!" Someone in the crowd shouted. "There's a white cat!"

Blake and Trinity turned to see Mercy on the second floor. Somehow she had crawled through the bathroom window and was now perched precariously on the narrow ledge.

"It's Mercy," Trinity whispered flapping her hands at the paramedic and trying to remove the oxygen mask.

"You have to stay here Miss," one of them told her.

"Blake?"

She didn't need to say anything more.

The fireman tried to hold him back again, but a glare from Blake and they let him a little closer.

"Come on Mercy, come on kitty." Blake coaxed, but the cat clung to the little strip of wood, meowing loudly.

"You need to step back," he was told. "The window is going to blow out."

They could see the flames behind Mercy.

Blake moved closer to the building. The heat licked at the hairs on his arms and scorched his skin, but he only stopped inching forward when he was right beneath Mercy.

"Jump," he told the cat. "I've got a treat," he coaxed, shuffling his pocket like he used to when she was in training all those months ago. She'd only jumped on him once before.

Mercy looked at him, her blue eyes trained on him with trust. She blinked slowly at him and he imitated her blink.

"I've got you Mercy," he whispered, spreading his arms as the cat jumped.

CHAPTER TWENTY

"Ready?" Blake asked, walking into their bedroom and looking over at his wife who was dressed in a soft pink dress.

"You stay right there," she warned, knowing how turned on he got seeing her in his favourite colour.

"We have twenty minutes," he suggested, wriggling his eyebrows lasciviously.

"Behave," she teased. "Okay one kiss, but that's it," she relented lifting her head up for his kiss.

"Since becoming pregnant you've become an absolute shrew," he said with all seriousness, moving his hand over her tiny bump as he sucked at her bottom lip.

"And you've become as lovely and as irresistible as ever," she pulled him down for a lingering kiss, before turning back to the mirror to redo her lipstick.

"It's showtime Trinity." He said looking at the time on his phone before dropping to his knees and sliding her shoes on for her. Even though she was now able to use her hands, he had gotten into the habit of putting on her shoes and hadn't been in any great hurry to stop. He pulled her to her feet. "Ready?"

It was her turn to wriggle her eyebrows. "Like never before De Laurentis."

***

Together they walked to the front of their building and opened the doors with a flourish.

The Kitty Parlour was now open for business and London was ready for it.

Streams of people came in drinking glasses of champagne or orange juice or a mixture of both as they sat around talking and relaxing in the up-scale atmosphere surrounded by cats.

The Parlour was almost three times the size of what the café was and was divided into three separate sections. Only the veterinary clinic was closed off to the public at the moment.

Trinity had had the place professionally decorated in purples and golds, in rich, kitty enticing fabrics. It was one giant scratching post, Blake had joked. The Parlour was luxurious enough to match the posh postcode.

"Trinity!"

Trinity turned at her name.

"Travis," she hugged her friend. "Glad you could make it." She smiled at him.

"As if I would miss this," he turned to a pretty dark-haired girl beside him. "This is Sarah," he introduced. "The nurse." He tagged on after Trinity hugged her.

They chatted for a while, and as she was about to excuse herself, Travis told her that Sarah wasn't allergic to cats, or dogs for that matter and Trinity laughed.

"Well this is beautiful," Lenny said coming up beside her and Trinity put her arms around her shoulders.

"Isn't it just."

"I'm so proud of you. Of you both." Lenny said with a tear in her eye, and she flicked it away. "You've come so far. Done so much." She took Trinity's hands turning them over. "They've healed really well." She pointed out knowing Trinity had had second-degree burns on the palms of her hands from the fire and several deep lacerations from the glass.

Trinity looked at them also, remembering the heavy bandages on her hands and knees and her four-day hospitalisation for smoke inhalation. If it wasn't for Mercy, she might not be here today.

She turned just as Blake came up behind her.

"How do you always do that?" he asked wrapping his arms around her thickening waist and pulling her against him.

"My heart skips a beat when you're near," she said with a smile, and he looked down at her frowning.

"Seriously?"

"You'll see,"

179

He looked at his aunt who had a dreamy look on her face. "What?" He asked, his frown still in place.

"Who'd have thought my stuffy nephew could be so in love," Lenny questioned the small group.

"Stuffy?" Blake growled but ruined the effect by kissing his aunt on the cheek.

"Trinity came along with her cats and look what happened." Leonora looked around. "We're developing an entire postcode in Nottingham for their Creative Quarter, still bought that burnt building and we have started the Cat Café franchise." She listed. "And best of all we have a great great grandchild on the way and —"

"Children," Blake interrupted with a smug expression.

"What?" Lenny gasped grasping Trinity's hand. "Oh, my goodness children?"

"Children," Blake confirmed cupping his large hands over Trinity's small bump.

After another round of congratulations, the parlour emptied, and only their closest friends and relatives remained.

"How's Mercy doing?" Travis asked sitting on a plush velvet sofa coaxing a cat to jump on him.

Trinity smiled, it had been touch and go with Mercy for a few days, but Stevie and the whole nation had been praying for her.

Her jump into Blake's arms had been recorded on someone's phone, and it went viral. It had been featured on the news in several countries, and Blake said the banks stock had skyrocketed. He was called the Banking Hero, and there were pictures of him online covered in black soot holding Mercy close to his heart.

"She has a slight limp on her hind leg, but she's working it into a sexy sway," Trinity answered and they all laughed. "Her paws have healed nicely, and her fur has grown back, so she's doing well. Of course, she rarely has anything to do with me. She's Blake's little darling." She said smiling at her husband.

Trinity and Blake later learned that the fire had been all over Social Media. Mo and Lorraine and all the taxi drivers had been on hand rounding up the cats, and the taxi drivers had locked them in their cars to keep them safe during all the chaos. They'd only lost one cat that night, but she, Miss Quaint had turned up the next day on the other street.

Even Steph, the young lady Trinity had counselled all those months ago in the taxi office had helped. She'd been on a night out with her new boyfriend when she'd heard what had happened.

She'd since adopted Miss Quaint too.

It was tremendous and heart-warming, the love and respect his wife got and Blake watched as she approached him where he was sitting with his grandpop, Annalise and Lenny. Trinity's eyes were shining bright with love and promise, and then he felt it and put his hand to his chest.

His heart had just skipped a beat.

THE END

LOVE TO BELONG

Chapter One

She was beginning to dislike it, but plunged ahead.

"Okay guys, I'm super excited. I'm at St. Pancras train station and finally on my way to Paris. Got my portable chargers, my favourite bag with all the pockets. Remember, it's about convenience when you're travelling," she advised, with a swiftness she was famed for. "And look at this beauty," Chilli aimed her camera to showcase the furry pink, totally impractical suitcase at her feet. "How cute." Angling the camera back to her face, she fluttered her freshly in-filled eyelash extensions and giggled. "See you on the other side."

With a sigh of relief, Chilli swivelled the camera screen into its housing, signed off and carefully placed the expensive camera into her bag, before grabbing the outrageous suitcase, entering the train, and making herself comfortable in First Class.

Ten minutes later, she was joined by her friends and fellow influencers, Candace Mason, and Vinny Sang.

They'd been friends via cyberspace for years, but had only met physically two years ago at a media conference in Berlin.

Fortunately, although beauty vloggers, Candace took the healthier, hemp, aloe vera, au natural approach, and Vinny's content was wild and theatrical.

"So, what's the deal?" Vinny asked, re-arranging his bucket hat on his head. His clothes were loud and vibrant, his hair shaved on one side from the left temple, right around the back of his head to the opposite ear and he sported a chin-length fringe tipped in platinum blonde. Last week it had been deep purple.

"We have the fashion shows and the after-party at the hotel." Candace explained, checking her emails.

They talked about fashion, influencers, designers, who they wanted to interview and definitely what they'd hoped to be gifted.

For the three of them, content creation was big business. They each had followers in the millions. Two years in a row, Chilli was voted Social Influencer of the Year.

Yep, life was good, and she revelled in it.

"Love the hair, Chilli Pepper," Vinny teased, using his nickname for her and reaching across the table to tug the strands sweeping over her shoulders.

Chilli leaned back out of his reach and shook her head. "You know the rules, Vinny," she scolded seriously. "Don't touch the lace front." She wagged her finger at him in warning. She was wearing a prototype for a collection they had approached her to endorse from an American wig manufacturer. It was a shoulder-length brown bob with a deep parting on the left. Apparently, if she sprayed a little water on it, the bone straight strands would turn into a tousled wavy beach babe look. She was going to try that later when she changed for the party, although she had a long wavy lace front wig as backup in case it didn't work.

Chilli had been creating content for years and covered everything from fashion trends and makeup to talking about her daily life and pop culture.

She collaborated with large, well-known brands. Wearing their clothes and using the products that had been sent to her. And also shopping in their brick-and-mortar shops. Almost everything Chilli did was documented via video, and she shared her views publicly and was paid handsomely for it.

Anything Chilli endorsed, sold out and her last makeup tutorial had received over three million views in a few days. She was liked and in high demand.

She was aware she couldn't rely on content creation as a stable income. The money was good but influencing fickle. Trends came and went. Popularity could disappear like a puff of smoke. It was becoming saturated, and Chilli was missing the enthusiasm she had had when she had started out. With the help of her staff, she was looking at other ways to monetise her brand.

Born in England, Chilli, whose real name was Chillitara Laurent, was bi-lingual and as comfortable in France, where her beloved grandmother lived, as she was in Britain and frequently travelled between the two countries.

"How's life with the boyfriend going?" Candace asked, interrupting the pleasant thoughts of her grandmother, whom Chilli intended to visit before she left France in a few days.

Chilli sighed, thinking of Paul. He'd lasted all of three weeks and was only a boyfriend on paper. She couldn't get past his large sweaty hands, much less have him kiss her. Besides, it soon became apparent he'd wanted to use her for her contacts for his T-shirt business.

"It's not," Chilli answered without remorse, barely concealing a shudder.

Vinny laughed. "You go through men like I go through–"

"Men," Chilli finished for him with a teasing wink.

"Oh, *touché*," he waved his hand about.

"Who knows, maybe we'll both find somebody rich to snog at the after-party tonight," Vinny declared.

Chilli laughed. "That's right, we're only snogging rich men from now on," she proclaimed.

They high-fived each other as they laughed. None of them had much luck with relationships. Candace flittered from man to man. Vinny was continuously looking for a lover who could support his extravagant lifestyle and Chilli wasn't looking to be in a relationship at all, but played along, contributing to their outlandish list of what Mr. Rich Man should be like.

***

Arno Tournier cringed and swiped his finger across the surface of his tablet a little too aggressively. The passengers in front of him laughed and talked loudly about their love lives. Generation Z, he thought, knowing he'd just about escaped that label being thirty-four himself.

Arno couldn't concentrate on the blog he was reading and with a huff, put his tablet down and glared at them. The Generation Zs were gossiping with no consideration for the other passengers.

He was tired. He'd been in England for a nine o'clock appointment, and because of the lateness of one of his suppliers, the meeting hadn't started until after eleven, ruining his entire day.

Arno slumped in his seat to rest his head against the headrest and closed his eyes. He wanted to return to the vineyard. He was a vigneron at heart, but with his grandfather's steady decline in health, there was no one else to manage what he liked to call the sterile side of things.

Arno hated it. Hated life in Paris and couldn't wait to head home. But his beloved grapes had to wait because of a conference in the morning.

A loud burst of laughter captured his attention, and there was nothing for him to do but look and listen to the conversation going on not three feet from him. Unfortunately, he'd forgotten his headphones so couldn't tune the world, *them*, out.

The girl directly opposite was beautiful in a lanky blonde sharpness kind of way. She was probably a model or something, seeing the long willowness of her arms. Her shoulders protruded rather sharply from the cut-outs of her black top, and her breasts were small. She did nothing for him. Paris was full of women who looked like her.

He shifted his gaze to the girl sitting beside her. She was smaller, wearing a hot pink felt hat placed at a jaunty angle on her head. Her features were soft, and her face was round. A dimple played by the side of her mouth. Her complexion was dark gold, and the hair poking out from under the hat was slightly darker. She was wearing a long-sleeved black, V-necked,

T-shirt thing, and the hands that she waved expressively about were tipped in hot pink too.

He mentally rolled his eyes. High maintenance was stamped all over her. And as for the vicious way she dismissed her boyfriend, Arno knew the poor bastard had had a lucky escape.

He closed his eyes and didn't open them again until jolted by someone landing on his lap.

"I'm so sorry," Chilli apologised in a rush, trying to get up. But between the table at her back and the hard-muscular chest at her front, not to mention the arms now holding her, she couldn't move. "I tripped on something." She explained, trying to wriggle free.

Arno looked at her. Up close, her skin was flawless, her eyes the darkest brown he had ever seen. They could even be black. Her eyelashes were very long and thick and her lips full and tempting. He had to force the inappropriate urge to lean forward and run his tongue along her succulent bottom lip from his thoughts.

"I'm sure that you did," Arno drawled, gritting his teeth when his body reacted to the soft cushion of her bottom. She was well within her rights to slap his face and call him a pervert, knowing she couldn't help but feel the hard ridge of his lengthening arousal beneath her. He'd gone too long without a woman and couldn't remember the last time he'd enjoyed the smoothness of a woman's thighs locked around his waist.

Chilli gasped at his harsh tone and heaved herself up. Or she tried to. She'd noticed him earlier as she'd waited for her friends. He was hard to miss with his deep olive skin tone, and dark wavy hair she'd had the mad compulsion to touch and remembered curling her fingers into a fist to control the tingling.

From a distance, she hadn't been able to make out his eye colour, although they hadn't looked run-of-the-mill brown. Now, with only inches between them, Chilli was fascinated to see they were deep forest green. Funny how the colour reminded her of the dream she'd had this morning.

It was weird, and she knew there was some psychobabble

explanation about it, but she dreamt in one colour. She thought it was some kind of premonition or something, so whatever colour it was, she'd always wear it close to her skin that day. The dark green of his eyes matched the colour of her satin bra and panty set perfectly.

His shirt was unremarkable, plain crispy white. She glanced down to see what colour his trousers were. Please don't be black, she prayed silently to herself and looked down to stare at the patch of cloth between her legs. His trousers were dark. Black, or maybe navy, she mused curiously, but with a stripe running through it and she peered to discover what colour the line actually was.

"Do you mind?" Arno barked. The girl was practically looking at his crotch. Did she have no shame?

"What?" Chilli looked at him wide-eyed.

Arno all but growled. "Get up!"

"Oh, I'm sorry," Chilli declared, with an embarrassing gasp, "you see I have this thing about colours," she explained quickly. "I wanted to see what colour your trousers were, if they were like your eyes or boring like the rest of the suits on the train." She tipped her head towards the businessmen in the carriage, clear by their white shirts, generic ties, and black trousers.

Chilli, feeling the heat still scorching her cheeks and thankful her skin was dark enough to disguise her embarrassment, wriggled about, trying to lever herself up without touching his chest or wrapping her arms around his neck.

"I'm really sorry," she repeated with difficulty. It was as though he'd sucked in all the air surrounding them and her heart was struggling to beat. He continued to stare into her eyes as though she were a crazy person, before dropping his gaze to track all over her body. "Can you at least help?" she ordered eventually. Everywhere his eyes touched sent tiny flames of awareness through her. If she could, she would fold her arms over her breasts to cover her peeking nipples.

Chilli wasn't fat, but half-African genes ruled over her figure. She had curves. Curves that when growing up had been embarrassing, especially beside her petite French grandmother. Now she embraced them, but unfortunately, they were still the first thing men noticed.

Arno opened his legs, and she slid between them. He didn't dare look at her, having already lost the battle with his body and just wanted to move her on as quickly as possible to save them both further embarrassment. He'd seen the heat in her eyes, the brazen sexual awareness as her nostrils flared. Her scent had changed, reminding him of the shift in the air when a summer storm was coming. He was close enough to see a flush of red gently touch her cheeks to sweep down her neck. He wanted to map the enticing colour with the tip of his tongue, knowing she was as aware of him as he was of her. The ever so slight rocking of her hips told him so. But this was neither the time nor the place. He did not pick up loud young women on trains.

Turning to his left, Arno twisted away, placed one hand on the back of the seat, the other on the table, and hauled himself up.

Chilli quickly scrambled out and stood to face him.

"Thank you, and again, I'm really sorry," she said, hoping she didn't sound as breathless as she felt. She didn't know what this was, but wow.

"Think nothing of it, *Mademoiselle*," his tone was formal, icy, and unpleasant.

Chilli gasped and stepped back in indignation. He made it sound as though she had intentionally fallen on him, and she wouldn't be surprised if he checked his pockets for his wallet. Forget the wow, she thought, pursing her lips. She wanted to smack that arrogant sneer off his face, and she wasn't a violent person.

Instead, Chilli tipped her chin up and spoke to him as he towered over her. He was tall, with broad shoulders she didn't want to think about. He could be an athlete, she guessed, trying not to notice the distracting broadness of his chest. "I really did trip," she defended tightly.

They both looked down, staring at the pale blue carpet with

a narrow red line running through it. There was nothing to trip on.

"Run along," Arno said, sitting down to pick up his tablet in a blatant display of dismissal.

With a chilling look, completely wasted as it landed on the top of his head, Chilli straightened her spine and went to the bathroom.

On her return, instead of sitting in her old spot, she sat beside Vinny. Her back to the rude Frenchman.

CHAPTER TWO

It was almost one in the morning.

After a late meal in the hotel restaurant, Arno made himself comfortable in the foyer. It was a beautiful space, decked out in creams, golds with deep red trimmings, that reminded him of the full-bodied Cabernet he produced.

His mouth twisted, and he shook his head at himself. He was such a wine freak and was precisely what one past lover had called him.

Five, no, six generations of prized winemakers coursed through his veins.

One past relative had planted vegetables with the vines and they had lost much of the vineyard to disease, and it had taken another generation to recover.

A sexy server walked over to him in a tight black skirt and white shirt that strained across her breasts. She flirted outrageously with him, and the thought of asking for her number almost tumbled from his lips. Paris was perfect for a one-night-stand.

Once he went home, it was long days in the vineyards and even longer nights in the office, doing the sterile admin things that bored the life out of him.

His last girlfriend had left him months ago or was it a year now? He mused, trying to recall what she looked like. He clenched his fists. The server, although pretty, wasn't doing anything for him. He'd gone about his business with the girl on the train skirting the periphery of his mind all day, distracting him. The subtle scent of her perfume had clung to him. He'd felt the whisper of her breath across his skin when he should have been listening to one of his distributors. And he definitely remembered how her luscious bottom had felt pressing against him. Added together, and the memory of her had kept him in a state of semi-arousal all day. He wanted her. He should have got *her* number.

Arno declined the server's invitation with a polite smile and ordered a glass of red wine. Hell, if he was in Paris when he wanted to be home, he may as well check out the competition, he thought, relaxing into the plush armchair.

The server walked away with a swing to her hips, and a look over her shoulder to let him know her offer was still open.

Arno pulled out his phone and checked his messages instead. There were plenty of emails, and he steeled himself, hating all the paperwork, and thought about hiring a firm to manage it all. Although felt like he was betraying his ancestors.

Tournier Wines was one hundred percent family-owned. He and his grandad were the only ones left. Past generations had killed off his workforce by not reproducing enough, Arno mocked, saluting them with his glass.

The elevator doors opened with a soft ping, but it was the raucous laughter skittering across the polished porcelain tiles that made him look up with annoyance, and his breath caught. It was the girl from this morning with her loud friends. Did they never shut up? He thought with irritation, watching them and then *her* as she tipped her head back in laughter.

Her dress was sexy as hell, electric blue and soft looking. It looked complicated to put on. Much less take off. Rope-like things crisscrossed her otherwise bare stomach, connecting the top half of the dress to the skirt.

The rest of her body was covered from the hip down. Tight sleeves bellowed at her wrists, covering her fingers. It was dramatic and seductive, and he found himself wanting to lick those patches of skin on display at her waist.

Her hair was longer than this morning, and he frowned, knowing he'd thought it to be shoulder length on the train. Maybe it wasn't her. Perhaps it was someone who looked like her? he thought, watching her closely. But no, her laugh was the same, her lips ripe and as kissable as he remembered, and, oh yeah, her bottom was definitely the same, peachy and pert, he noticed with a smirk appreciating her curves as she turned to link her arms with her friends when they made their way to the bar to his right.

He had been tired, but Arno suddenly felt excited, like when his grapes were ready to harvest.

The server brought his glass on a dainty brass tray, hovered for a moment, then, realising he really wasn't interested, walked off without a wiggle to her bottom. Women. Arno laughed to himself, how fickle is thee, he misquoted.

With the glass held loosely in his hands, he looked at the colour, swirled it around, sniffed and then tasted, letting the wine slide along his tongue and fill his mouth. The flavour was good. His was better. Without thinking, he walked towards the bar with his glass, his tiredness gone.

***

Chilli saw him enter the dimness of the room and her heart skidded to a halt.

She was still on a high because style icon Annika had said her name in greeting and that high now shot to mega heights.

After pausing in the doorway, the man from the train sauntered over to one of the semi-circular seats and sat down, sliding to the centre. He was directly opposite to where Chilli was standing at the bar with her friends. She moved, turning her back to the room, knowing she could watch him openly via his reflection in the mirror behind the glass case.

The soft lighting from the five-fingered brass chandeliers scattered here and there lent a romantic feeling to the intimate room. It was a new modern hotel, yet the bar had a quaint 30s feel about it. A white piano with an enormous vase of red roses on top dominated an elevated stage, but Chilli didn't see any of that. She was locked on him.

He was beautiful. Definitely French by the aristocratic angles of his cheekbones and jawline. His hair, brushed back from his face, was thick and glossy, but it could do with shaping, she noted.

Funny how this morning she took him to be a boring businessman, probably an accountant. Watching him now, his long fingers slowly smoothed up and then down the stem of his wine glass, she would say he was an artist or something else, passionately creative.

He could do with a makeover, though. His clothes were as boring now in dark trousers and a plain shirt as they were this morning. Yet there was an exciting restlessness about him. Chilli could feel it. The sleeves of his shirt were rolled up in defiance of rigid formality. He didn't want to be here.

Their eyes connected via the mirror and Chilli could not look away. Neither acknowledged the other, and Chilli was grateful when the shots arrived, and she had an excuse to escape his intense gaze to pick up her glass.

Only she couldn't help herself and watched him surreptitiously under her lashes, very much aware of him staring when she clinked her glass with her friends, toasting the success of the day. She spilt some and licked it from her fingers.

Almost defiantly, Chilli did another shot, even though her first drink still scorched a trail of fire down her throat. She raised her chin, noticing a single dark eyebrow lift ever so slightly as he watched on.

Chilli loved Vinny and Candace, but after twelve hours of togetherness, they were rattling her nerves. Thankfully, they were returning to England in the morning. However, she was staying on.

Tomorrow she was going to an all-day AXP Centennial Conference, a foreign exchange programme she had taken part in a few years ago. She was a guest speaker. Afterwards, she was going to spend time with her grandmother.

"Okay," Chilli suddenly turned to Vinny and Candace, "I'm going to do a quick update, and then I'll be back," she promised, digging into her designer bag shaped like a gold cherry tomato and pulling out her beloved camera.

Chilli was looking for a quiet corner to film when he spied him. Boosted by the alcohol, she straightened her spine and walked over.

She really needed to call him something else 'the man from the train' made him sound like a serial killer, she acknowledged, giggling to herself before stopping in front of his table.

"Bonjour," she greeted in French, "remember me?" she finished in English.

Chilli hovered by the table and licked her suddenly parched bottom lip. Now that his dark green gaze was trained on her, she'd lost her nerve. The tiny amount of alcohol she had consumed had rapidly evaporated under his sizzling stare. He was intense, his regard giving nothing away, although the fingers skimming his wine glass had stopped.

"I remember you," Arno replied.

Chilli scooted in beside him. "Can I borrow your table for a moment?" she asked.

He canted his head to one side, then looked around the room before pinning her with his gaze, his forehead pleating into a puzzled frown.

"What for?"

Chilli beamed. "I'll show you," she invited. Opening her handbag, she carefully pulled out her beloved camera she called Frankie.

Knowing exactly how her camera worked, she adjusted the settings to facilitate the dim lighting in the room. She fluffed her hair and angled the camera just where she liked it–slightly above her–before turning somewhat. Then, clearing her throat, she smiled into the lens.

"Hi guys," Chilli said, then talked excitedly about her evening and everything that had happened throughout her day.

Arno listened as she talked into her camera. She was talking about herself and reeling off names and details of her meal as though she were writing a diary.

She talked and talked and said something about rating her

foundation ten out of ten.

Then repeated everything in French.

Arno found her speech fascinating as he listened keenly and deduced she didn't live in France. Her pronunciation, though perfect, was accent-less.

"And finally," Chilli turned towards the man from the train, "I'm going to find out his name," she angled her camera at him for a split second, "And then ask him to buy me a drink." She winked. "When in France...?" Chilli left the rest unsaid.

"Thanks," she said, placing her camera carefully on the table.

"What was that?" Arno asked.

"I'm a content creator," she explained, but at his baffled look went on. "Vlogger."

"Blogger?" he'd heard of the stuff people wrote on the internet were called blogs and read many articles on the winemaking industry, but he didn't delve much further than that.

"No," Chilli explained. "Vlogger. I don't write about things so much anymore. I film myself talking instead. It's more exciting."

"Isn't that, how you say?" he cocked one silky brow at her. "Pretentious oui?"

"What's pretentious about giving people an honest diary of my life?"

"The fact you are giving people a diary of your life?" he shot back.

He didn't quite sneer, but it was there, hovering in the corner of his well-shaped mouth. Chilli really hoped he would not disappoint her and be an arse, she thought. Good looking, but still an arse.

"Everyone loves my content," she defended, losing the excitement of the day to his moody disapproval. "I have my own YouTube channel." She announced, tipping up her chin.

His dark eyebrows dipped, and he reached over to pick up his glass. He swallowed down his wine disrespectfully–wine was supposed to be honoured across the palate–before turning to look at her.

"Is that what you will do?" he inquired. "Put it on YouTube for people to watch?"

"Yes."

"With me on it?"

Oops. Chilli should have seen where this conversation was leading.

"Not necessarily," she hedged. But by the tilt of a single eyebrow, knew he knew she was lying.

Time to go. He was an arse, she thought, fighting her disappointment and scooting across the seat, but he grabbed her camera and put it on the other side of him, out of her reach.

"Hey!" Chilli gasped in horror, nobody touched Frankie, "give that back!"

"As I see it," Arno charged, fighting to keep from smiling. "You took my image without my consent. I own that image." He declared. "I now own your camera."

"I'll erase it."

"You will."

"Give it back. I will do it right now."

"What is your name?"

"Chillitara Laurent."

"You are French?"

"West African father. French mother. Live in England." She revealed automatically, as she mentally calculated how fast she could dash across the table and get her camera back. It was worth over two thousand pounds.

"You speak French?" He asked, stating the obvious.

She looked at him then, hearing the curiosity in his deep voice. This morning she hadn't noticed the gravelly sound of his speech, being distracted as she was by his moss-coloured eyes, but now she did. She liked it. "Why?"

"Curious."

"What's your name?" she thought to ask.

"Arno Tournier."

"Nice to meet you, Arno," Chilli repeated his name in her head. It suited him. Masculine and sure. "Can I have my camera back now, please?"

"No," he shook his head slowly and tipped his mouth down before saying, "I will erase it myself."

Chilli gasped in horror. "Are you crazy!" She sputtered, thinking of all the videos she had made today. She would make a fortune when they were uploaded. Not to mention all the new followers. Followers meant revenue. "You know nothing about Frankie."

He looked at her in confusion, his wide forehead pleating into a tight frown. "Frankie? Who is this, Frankie?"

"My camera," Chilli could feel the sting of tears behind her eyes. Frankie meant everything to her. Her grandmother had bought it for her twenty-first birthday.

Arno leaned forward. She was closer than she had been a moment ago, her arm brushing his as she sneakily inched nearer to launch for her camera. Arno hadn't had this much fun in years. He moved the camera further away, out of her reach, even if she did lunge for it.

"How old are you?" Arno asked.

Chilli pursed her lips and rolled her eyes. "Old enough to tell you I'm not interested," she answered harshly, her tears forgotten as she planned how to retrieve her camera.

Arno laughed; he couldn't help himself. She didn't seem to have any of that British stiff upper lip thing they were famous for, and had more of the French passion he appreciated.

Winemaking in South Africa and Ethiopia aside, he knew little else about Africa. However, he was looking forward to exploring that side of her culture, preferably tonight.

"Then why are you breathing so," his eyes dipped to her chest, "erratically?" Arno usually wasn't like this; he never teased or showed his interest in a woman so blatantly. He didn't need to. But she was an exception. She wanted him. Had wanted him from the moment she had landed on his lap this morning.

"Because I'm upset!" Chilli shouted with annoyance, wanting to thump him or the table. The table won.

Arno laughed at her outburst. She was so fiery. Was she like this in bed? "It is only a camera."

"But it's mine, and I want it back," she charged. "Right now!"

Without thought, Chilli lunged across him and touched her camera, but instead of capturing it, she ended up pushing it beyond her reach, and she was lying across his lap in an even more intimate position than this morning.

"Tut-tut Mam'selle," Arno quickly rearranged her on his lap, sitting her up and placing one of his arms on the table at her back. He placed his other arm below her breasts to grasp the edge of the table, ultimately caging her in when he leant forward. Anyone looking from afar would think they were taking advantage of the shadows and kissing. "Now look what you have done," Arno accused softly.

"Let me go," Chilli breathed. Erratic didn't explain what she was feeling. His masculine scent bathed her all over, vanilla, spicy bergamot and the subtle smell that was all him. She remembered it from this morning. His thighs were rock solid beneath her bottom, and his warm breath fanned her ear. She was one massive pulse of awareness for him. She had never been so turned on.

"Why?" he whispered, close to her ear.

If Chilli were to move her head just a bit, those lovely lips of his would caress her ear when he spoke. She so wanted to turn her head.

"Because you're a stranger," she answered softly, feeling his finger insinuate itself between the soft latticework of her velvet dress, to find her skin and make small circles on her side. She stopped breathing.

"We met this morning." He shifted and spanned both hands around her waist.

"What are you doing?" Chilli whispered. This was improper on so many levels. But she couldn't move. Her usual confidence had dissolved with the alcohol, she reasoned, because if she'd had her wits about her, she would have slapped his handsome face already. Why did he inspire such violent thoughts? She went from wanting to run her fingertips under his shirt to wanting to throttle him!

"Rearranging you," Arno lifted her slightly and, with one hand going to the small of her back, brought her forward. Liking that she didn't resist.

"We are French," he declared, with great importance, "we greet each other properly, oui?"

Before she could answer, he kissed one side of her cheek, and then the other.

His lips were warm and soft against her skin. She didn't know when it happened, but her hands were on his broad shoulders as their movements synchronised and they flowed together like water running over pebbles in a brook.

"Hello Chillitara Laurent," he whispered, ever so close to her lips. Like this morning, he knew she could feel his arousal, and like this morning, he felt the subtle rocking of her hips.

"Bonjour Monsieur,"

"How old are you?"

"How old do you want me to be?"

Arno smirked, his eyes smouldering as they trailed over her delectable curves. He flexed his hands, wanting to stroke the inner softness of her sex until she bathed his fingers.

"Twenty-six." He answered honestly.

"Lucky for you." Her smile was small but confident when she walked her fingers from his shoulders, up to his neck, to spear her fingertips into the long hair at his nape. She leaned in close to whisper. "I'm twenty-six," she paused, allowing the tip of her tongue to skim the sensitive spot below his ear. "And a half."

They looked into each other's eyes. A secret moment shared.

"Will you come to my room?" Arno asked, his lips almost, but not quite, touching hers.

Chilli's body ignited all over.

She knew what he was asking. What he wanted. She wanted it too, she convinced herself.

Dark green, she remembered. This morning she'd woken to the harmonious glow of her dream on her mind. She'd felt excited. Safe.

She licked her lips and watched as his eyes dipped to track the movement. There was a heavy pulsing of promise beneath her bottom. He wanted her, was blatantly reacting to her, and didn't mind her knowing it.

The stars aligned.

She squeezed his shoulders as though needing to hold on as her next words sent her into an emotional free fall.

"Yes."

DISTRACTING ACE

CHAPTER ONE

'Kill me now!' Nina pressed her head against the cool glass of the windowpane and watched, with what should have been scenic excitement, as the panoramic skyline of New York City whizzed by to her right.

The Statue of Liberty was just a thin, blurry, one-inch line in the distance.

A few hours, and what should have been the best solution for getting to New York from Baltimore, had turned out to be the journey from hell.

If hell could be described as sitting in an ancient model American car with loads of metal at the front and back, no air conditioning, the windows unable to go down and cracked leather seats that scratched the back of your legs-then this was it.

If hell was occupied by fraternal twins Shereece and Nicola sitting up front, continuously bitching because they had to have dinner with their Grandmother, then Nina was definitely in hell. Add her once favourite Gwen Stefani song Hollaback Girl being on loop for the last hour, and she was ready to open the door and fling herself into the flames.

Nina shared the back seat with the twins' friend Devonia; an elfin like Chinese girl who could be the 'poster child' for travel sickness! Devonia was doped up and sleeping with her head thrown back against the head-rest; her long hair in braids and bunched up at her neck, acting like a satin pillow as she slept. Devonia had tagged along at the last minute and, because of her, they'd had to pull over countless times while she brought up her stomach lining. The car still reeked of vomit. Yes, her trip to hell had begun at six o'clock this morning. She would have been better off taking the bus, Nina thought once again but had craved another All-American experience, a road trip, in a Cadillac no less, before she left for Europe in a few days.

"Nina?"

Nina tried not to grimace as Shereece turned in her seat to address her.

"We're just going to pull into a convenience store, or gas station, to get some flowers for the old lady, drop them off, then New York is ours!" She ended on a flourish, raising her hand to her sister Nicola, who had taken her hand off the steering wheel to slap Shereece's palm in a hi-five.

Nina made a tooting horn gesture and stretched her lips into what she hoped was a smile.

Her phone vibrated in her hand and a genuine smile lit her face as she rapidly began texting her best friend, Andy. Her flight had arrived, and she was currently taking a taxi to their hotel.

Nina couldn't wait to see her; it had been three months. They'd never before gone more than a month without seeing each other. Now her time as an overseas student at the University of Maryland was over; she had two nights and three days in the city with her best friend to look forward to, then back home to England. Nina couldn't wait. She liked America, had enjoyed her stay on campus, but nothing beat the nightlife of Essex. Both she and Andy were born and raised Essex girls, and proud of it.

Screams, and a screeching of tires, jolted Nina out of her daydreams and she watched in horror as the heavy car fishtailed, in what seemed like slow motion, stopping a hairsbreadth away from a silver SUV with darkly tinted windows that had been about to park in the same spot.

They were too close to the other car for Nina to open her door so, taking off her seatbelt, she scrambled across Devonia, who was looking around in a daze, and rushed around to the front of the sky-blue vehicle.

Shereece was already in the face of a tall, athletic-looking guy. If the scene weren't so tense, Nina would have taken a moment to appreciate the man's thick shoulders, displayed in a black 'muscle shirt' and his long muscular legs in khaki shorts, but Nicola was now out of the car, and the three of them were screaming at each other. The twins were like yapping, blonde, cheer-leading Chihuahuas; the man like a fierce German Shepherd.

"This is disabled parking!" The man blazed down at the girls for the tenth time, stabbing a finger in the air.

Nina looked around, spying the blue disabled parking sign you couldn't miss, as there was one smack bang in front of each parking bay.

"Oh yeah," Nicola stood up on tiptoe getting in his face. "You don't look like a cripple to me!"

Alarmed, Nina watched as the man practically turned purple, and she quickly squeezed between them all, pushing Nicola out of the way.

"Stop it!" She yelled above the din of accusations, placing her back to his chest and shooting daggers at the girls before turning to look up at the man. "I'm really sorry," she soothed, taking a chance and touching his forearm.

He looked down at her, his sharp frown not detracting from his handsome face. God, he is a looker, she thought, taking in his dark blond hair, straight eyebrows and blue eyes. She wanted to starfish her fingers and trail them over his chest. "I'm sorry," she apologised again. "Nicola, move the car," Nina ordered over her shoulder.

"Not before we get those flowers," Shereece huffed adamantly, before flouncing away, Nicola close behind as they went into the shop without a care or thought of apology.

"Friends of yours?" The man drawled, capturing her hand and turning slightly, so they both could follow the drama of the twins as they squabbled over the dismal selection of bouquets.

"Certainly not," Nina clarified, stepping away. "Look, I'm ever so sorry. If the car weren't so big, I'd move it myself." She stated.

He was looking down at her with a sparkle of interest, his mouth tipping up at one side as he stepped into her personal space. She thought she heard him mumble something about being surrounded by fucking Brits, but she couldn't be sure.

Nina stepped back; she was tired, hungry, and had reached her wit's end. Cute guy or not, she wanted to get to the hotel, right now.

"Where are you from?" He asked, tipping his head to the side.

Shit, she really wasn't in the mood for this conversation and smiled briefly, before spying Devonia who, now that it was safe, had gotten out of the car.

"England," she said rapidly, in a tone that didn't invite further conversation as she edged towards the car. "I should say they," she nodded towards the sisters in the shop. "Don't normally act like that, but I'd be lying."

He grinned at her, then looked at his own vehicle as though remembering something.

"Don't worry about it." He walked to his SUV, got into the drivers' seat and, as the engine had still been running, swiftly reversed and manoeuvred the vehicle into the next bay, then with another smile sent her way and a tip of the head, made his way into the shop.

With her mind made up, Nina turned to Devonia who was leaning against the bumper, looking pale.

"I'm going now."

"Now?" Devonia turned to her.

Nina opened the door on her side of the car and checked the pockets to make sure she hadn't left anything behind in the door and seat pockets before pulling out her bag. She didn't want to have any reason to seek the twins out ever again in this lifetime or the next.

Opening the boot, or trunk as she was told to call it, she heaved out her rucksack, placed it on the ground and slammed the door shut before glancing down at her clothes. She'd dressed for comfort this morning, grey leggings and trainers, but her white crop top wasn't really appropriate for public transport so, rummaging in her rucksack, pulled out her favourite T-shirt with the university logo on the front, and without thought, quickly stripped off her top and pulled on the T-shirt over her bra.

She thought she felt eyes on her, but Devonia was dramatically panting into a paper bag and Cuteness, as she now called him, was chatting and laughing with the twins. Men, Nina thought, shaking her head, were so bloody predictable.

"You're going?" Devonia asked, between huffs.

"There's a subway station over there," Nina pointed, she'd spotted it earlier. "I'm sure I can find my way into the city from here."

"Maybe I should come with..." Devonia started.

Nina knew it wasn't for her benefit. Devonia was a follower, she never made a decision that was her own, how she managed in this world Nina didn't know, but what she did know, with absolute certainty, was that this escape she was making by herself.

"Nah, I'll be fine," Nina deliberately misinterpreted her meaning and hoisted her rucksack onto her back before giving Devonia a quick hug. "Tell them thank you for the lift, but I'll make my way from here." She instructed, hoping to make her escape before the girls came out of the store. She turned away after watching Devonia go into the shop.

"Oh, thank God." She breathed in relief as she checked her phone. Andy had arrived at the hotel and was ordering a bottle of champagne for them. Nina grinned.

"You forgot your bag," someone said behind her, as she was about to set off and cross the street.

Startled, Nina span around, looking for the person behind the deep voice.

"On the bonnet."

Nina turned to see the top half of a man's face looking at her. Everything below his lips was hidden behind the tinted window. She hadn't even realised there was someone else in the SUV. She couldn't see much of him as a navy baseball cap, as they said in America, was pulled down low on his face, shadowing his eyes. The hair peeking out at his neck was dark, and a single thick curl played in his ear. He was very masculine; all hard angles and she could see the start of a neatly trimmed shadow of hair framing his face. A tiny gold earring caught the sun, winking at her.

He must have seen her get dressed, she thought. Creepy.

"Pardon?"

"On the bonnet," he nodded towards her car. "Your bag."

Knowing he was watching, Nina moved to pick up her bag, bounced her knees to reposition the heavy rucksack, before placing her other heavy bag on her shoulder. "Thanks," she turned to him and watched as he dipped his head in acknowledgement.

For some reason reluctant to move, she stepped close enough to see that his hair was chocolate brown and his facial hair a mixture of colours. Mario's Let Me Love You was playing softly from his car.

"Erm, do you know how long it will take to get over there?" She pointed to the famous skyline.

She thought he wasn't going to answer and turned to go when he said. "On the train? About an hour or so."

He was British, West London if she wasn't mistaken, but as she hated when this kind of thing was pointed out to her, decided not to mention it.

"Thank you."

His head dipped in acknowledgement again before adding, with a smirk. "It was a good thing you changed."

Nina gasped, he had seen her and was letting her know that he had. Oh my, his smile changed his face, Nina thought, feeling a warm blush creep up her neck and she crossed her arms over her breasts as her body reacted to him. She took another tentative step closer.

"Erm, I'm sorry about the parking thing—" she began, but he turned to the front, giving her a quick view of his profile before the window slid up and Nina only saw her reflection looking back at her.

His rudeness took her breath away and with lips puckered with annoyance, turned and walked to the subway.

On the other side of the street, she turned and, because she knew he was watching, waved before descending the subway steps.

CHAPTER TWO

"Oh my God, it's so good to see you!" Nina exclaimed once again to Andy, who was laying on the opposite table as they both had a massage.

Andy hadn't been joking about the champagne or the 'Before You Head Out' package she had treated them both to. They'd been waxed, plucked, rubbed and polished to within an inch of their lives, and they still had something called the 'Rain Forest' shower experience to have, then nails, hair and make-up.

"I know," Andy exclaimed with a grin. "I don't know why your parents thought it would be a good idea for you to go to America."

"We'd been going out too much,"

"I told you that weekend in Marbella was a bad idea," Andy stated.

Nina laughed, remembering the infamous weekend when they'd taken off to the Spanish coastal city at the last minute, with two other friends, and spent three nights partying hard. Hard. So hard, she didn't remember one night at all.

"You wouldn't have met Gareth if we hadn't gone though, would you?" Nina reflected.

Andy sighed with a stupid grin on her face. "I think I'm in love."

"I know," Nina answered. Andy fell in love quickly and often.

"Who'd have thought it."

"I knew you'd think that too."

"You aren't offering much to this conversation, are you?"

Nina giggled, "I only met him that one time after Marbella and that was just before I came here, so I never got the chance to vet him, but he seems okay."

Andy turned onto her back and waved the masseuse away.

"Thank you, but that's it," she dismissed with a smile, sitting up. "He's a bit clingy." She revealed.

"Clingy, how?" Nina asked, following suit and wrapping the huge, white, hotel towel around her lightly oiled body, as she helped herself to another glass of champagne and handed one to Andy too.

Andy shrugged, but Nina knew her friend too well and asked again.

"He thinks you're a bad influence," Andy admitted ruefully, with a twinkle in her eyes. "And that you'll introduce me to a gorgeous American footballer type with massive shoulders this week."

"Is that on your wish list Andrea Duke?" Nina asked, with her hands on her hips. "How could he think I'm a bad influence?"

"I told him it's the other way around, but he remembers that night in Marbella when you danced on the bar and dragged me up there with you."

That was the night Andy had met him.

"Didn't you tell him it was your idea?"

"Sort of." Andy evaded.

Nina laughed, not the least bit perturbed by her friend's evasiveness. Nina did get blamed for all of their escapades, mainly because she was the one to follow through on Andy's dares, with Andy herself somehow never getting caught. It was the blue innocence of her eyes, added to her dark straight hair, pale skin and sunny disposition–you couldn't fault her friend for anything, and Nina wouldn't have had it any other way. Andy was the little sister she never had. Although technically speaking Andy was older by twelve days.

"It's a good job I love you." Nina hugged her tight as they moved into the living area of the suite and flopped onto the huge suede sofa that faced the flat-screen TV. The whole suite was white, with brown and gold soft furnishings throughout—all very five star.

Nina's parents had treated them to two nights in the hotel, flying Andy over to be with her, before Nina returned to

England.

"I know." Andy tucked her legs under herself, picked up her phone and started playing Snakes.

"Can I ask you something?" She asked, after a moment, putting her phone into the pocket of her complementary white hotel robe.

"Since when have you ever had to ask permission?" Nina went on but sat up straight when she noticed how serious Andy had become. "What is it?" She asked, her forehead creasing in concern.

"Is everything okay with your mum and dad?"

"Yes, why?"

Andy bit the inside of her cheek; she'd been deliberating whether to ask or not. Ever since Nina had been in America, her parents had been acting strange.

"There's a rumour going around that your parents have filed for bankruptcy."

Nina laughed. "That's ridiculous,"

"I'm serious, Nina. Your dad has put the house you have in Cornwall on the market."

Nina frowned. She'd been speaking to her parents every Sunday, like always, and they hadn't even hinted that they had money worries. How could they have money worries anyway? She thought. They'd opened a new Caribbean restaurant just last year, bringing their outlets to twenty-four around the country.

"We hardly go to that house anyway, so maybe he's just getting rid of it." She reasoned.

"Your mother loves that house. Why would he sell it?

"I don't know, do I?!" She replied sharply, then reached for Andy's hand. "I'm sorry, I didn't mean to shout."

"It's okay. Maybe it's nothing. Forget I even mentioned it." Andy grabbed the complimentary basket off the glass coffee table and placed it between them. "What do you want?" She asked, rummaging through the indulgent calorific goodies.

"No more snacks!" Nina shouted, slapping her friend's wrist playfully. "What are we having for dinner?" Nina asked, feeling a little light-headed. The champagne had landed on top of the chocolate bar she'd bought in the subway station that morning; she needed proper sustenance.

Andy was the organiser; she always had been, and Nina referred to her when it came to organising her life. It had always been like that. They worked so well on every level, and they both knew they couldn't cope without the other.

"We're eating dinner in the hotel," Andy paused dramatically. "And then we're going to that Irish pub I told you about."

"Irish? You don't want to go to a sports bar? Check out the jocks?"

"Yes, Irish. Do they even call men jocks anymore? It sounds so ancient,"

Nina shrugged. This was how they were, conversations all over the place.

"I don't know. It's a great word."

Andy rolled her eyes. "I take it you're still into this whole linguistic thing?"

"It is what I've been studying all these months, you forget?"

"Nah, but that gap year to travel around the world kind of made me forget." Andy went on as she picked up a brownie from the complimentary gift basket, unwrapping the delicate tissue paper it came in and took a bite. "Mm." She rolled her eyes to the back of her head and sighed. "Lush."

"As if you weren't there with me," Nina went on. "Remember the time you started chatting up that cute customs officer in Indonesia? We ended up having a full-body drug search!"

"How was I supposed to know that's what drug mules did? He was so cute! Dimples and everything!"

"and—"

There was a knock at the door.

"Saved by the knock," Andy chimed, going to the door. "Time for that Rain Forest thing."

***

While waiting for dessert, and Andy, who had gone to the loo, Nina took a moment to remember her earlier conversation with her dad. She'd rung him as she was getting ready for dinner.

He'd been happy to hear from her; listing everything that had happened that day with meticulous detail, as he always did. When she'd asked him about the sale of their holiday home, he said yes, they'd decided to get rid of it as they were buying a newly built six-bedroomed, four-bath roomed, detached up the road. He said it made better economic sense and that their coffers were still overflowing.

He always used the term coffers instead of money, and she'd laughed, reassured that all was well. She'd reminded him of their flight times and rang off with a chorus of I love you's down the phone.

Andy came back to the table just as their dessert arrived, 'spotted dick' for Nina and 'key lime pie' for Andy. As soon as she sat down, Andy began talking about Gareth again.

"What do you mean he's hiring a personal trainer?" Nina said, interrupting Andy's animated flow of words.

"Yeah, he says he loves my body, but wants me to get fit."

Alarmed, Nina put down her spoon and focused on her friend. "What do you mean he wants you fit?"

"Yeah, that's what he said." Andy shrugged her shoulders and looked down at her pie. "Maybe I shouldn't eat this, huh?"

"Back up missus," Nina said. "You don't think something is wrong when a man tells you he wants you fit?'"

"It's not like he called me fat, Nina," Andy answered, pushing her plate away, leaving three-quarters of her pie. "Not everyone can be five seven and a size eight." She defended cattily.

Nina frowned over at her friend. Something was going on, and it all pointed to Gareth.

"I'm sorry." Nina soothed, pushing her plate away. She was not going to fight with her best friend over a man, especially tonight. Their time in New York was about the two of them. When they got back to England, it was back to their busy lives,

Andy working for her parents' party planning business and Nina, hopefully preparing for the next chapter of her life.

"I'm sorry too." Andy apologised, her phone buzzed, and she picked up the pink metallic Motorola and flicked it open. "It's Gareth," she said unnecessarily.

Nina watched as Andy bit the inside of her cheek, something she always did when she was anxious. When she glanced at her, she snapped her phone shut and, with what Nina knew was forced brightness, asked.

"How was it anyway? Did you meet anyone? Have rampant sex with an American jock?" Andy made bunny quotations over the word 'jock'.

"It wasn't how I thought it would be," Nina admitted, ready to change the subject.

"No sex?"

Nina shook her head.

"Feeling up of your perky bits?"

Nina chuckled. "Nope."

"Oh dear, three months without getting any?"

"It was okay, really. Everyone was nice—"

"The word nice is insignificant. It doesn't have much of a meaning you told me so yourself. You said nice was up there with—"

"Moist, yes I know," Nina rolled her eyes at her friend. "I just wasn't attracted to anyone, plus—"

"What?"

"There's a different kind of atmosphere here," she looked around the room, seeing all the affluent people of different nationalities and leaned in close. "I felt my blackness."

Andy, who had also leaned in close, reached for her friend's hand.

She had been Nina's friend since forever, well from the age of seven. Nina had been one of three black kids in the entire school. It got better when they went to boarding school in France, but not by much. She'd had to wipe her friend's tears when she had been referred to because of her skin colour by stupid, insensitive white people. But things were so much better in Europe nowadays, especially in England.

"I'm sorry," Andy squeezed her hand.

"It's okay," Nina shrugged, moving back into her chair and sipping her wine. "I buckled down," she took a deep breath. "And applied." She revealed softly.

Andy gasped, knowing instantly what she was referring to. "Oh, my God! You did?!"

Nina grinned and nodded, catching her friend's excitement. Andy was the first person she'd told.

"I'm so flipping proud of you. Oxford; I can see you now," Andy picked up her napkin and dabbed at the corners of her eyes.

"Are you crying?" Nina asked, spying the tears.

"No, it's an eyelash," Andy sniffed. "When will you know?"

"I'm expecting an email any day now."

"Oh my God," Andy said again. "We need to celebrate." She signalled the waiter.

"How about we head out?" Nina suggested. Although the hotel was beautiful, it was too exclusive. She was ready to let her 'Essex' out.

"To the pub it is!" Andy grabbed her hand and pulled her from the table, took a few steps then looked at what they were both wearing. "But we have to change. Essex has come to New York!" She laughed, knowing exactly what she was going to dress them in and rushed them over to the elevators.

CHAPTER THREE

"This place is amazing," Nina said again, slamming down another shot glass. She'd lost count of how many she'd had, maybe five or maybe seven. But she knew she hadn't yet reached her limit. The fiasco in Marbella was her measuring stick from now on. There was no way she would ever drink to the point of passing out ever again. Get to the buzz, drink water, maintain the buzz. That was her new motto. She should get a T-shirt printed, she thought.

"Glad you like it!" Andy shouted over the music.

They were in Heathers, an Irish pub in Manhattan. Andy had been here once before and knew the atmosphere was just what they needed to celebrate Nina applying to Oxford University. Oxford! It was huge! What an achievement.

Nina had always been super-intelligent, forever on the 'Talented and Gifted' programmes throughout school and was one of those irritating people who never really applied herself, but always managed to pass exams with flying colours. While Andy's parents had to employ every tutor for every subject, to ensure she got a passing grade. Nina going to Oxford to study linguistics was massive. She was so happy for her.

"You know what this place reminds me of?" Andy said.

"No, what?"

"That bar in Coyote Ugly," she explained, looking around, spying a bunch of bras hanging from the ceiling, alongside glittery, home-made four-leaf clovers. "You know the one with the girls dancing on the bar, pouring drinks and singing—" she flapped her hands with excitement as they both burst into song. "Can't Fight the Moonlight!"

***

Ace watched from the far corner, he'd seen them when they'd walked in, and he'd been unable to pull his gaze away from her ever since.

She was as beautiful as he remembered her to be. He'd felt a pull then when she'd apologised for her friend's rudeness that morning, and he felt an even bigger pull now; dressed as she was in a deep red pair of shorts that cupped her ass and showed off her toned legs, and a black, sparkly vest type thing that clung to her breasts; no man could resist that package! She was fucking supreme, he thought.

Her skin was brown; a perfect deep, sun-kissed brown that looked both smooth and healthy. He'd been admiring her body while she talked to his cousin that morning. A year ago, he would have been out of the car like a shot, and she would have been under him right now, those long legs of hers wrapped around his hips as he fucked her. Last year, that was.

Ace snarled, raised his beer bottle to his mouth and watched as she bumped hips with her friend, threw back her head to laugh—showing him the long kissable column of her throat—touched her glass to her friends and drained the glass before slamming it on the bar in triumph.

The group of men milling around them cheered, egging them on. One guy even put his hand on her ass, and Ace felt possessive anger stake him. He was relieved when she removed the dick's hand and wagged her finger in the guys' face. Good, Ace thought, pulling on his beer as he continued to torture himself by cataloguing everything she did.

What the hell was he doing here anyway? He looked around; it was his fucking pity party to help him make up his mind. Time was running out. His cousins had dragged him out because, as they put it, he was wallowing in self-pity and needed to get his dick out. Their words. How the hell could he be any fun when he was like this? He slapped his thigh. Didn't they know what he was going through? And if he wanted to—Jesus fucking Christ! He interrupted his gloomy thoughts; someone had turned up the music, and the girls had climbed onto the bar to dance.

***

Nina graciously took the hand that was offering to help her off the bar. She and Andy had danced, taken some shots and danced some more. Knowing her limit was near and the height of the bar making her dizzy, she climbed down. It was time to pull back and have a glass of water, she thought.

"Thank you," she told the guy, only looking at him when he didn't let go of her hand. "Hey, it's you!" She grinned up at him.

"Yeah, it's me."

"Cuteness."

He raised his eyebrows and smiled. "If you say so. You took off before I could get your number," he said in her ear, wrapping an arm around her waist, but looking over his shoulder as he pulled her flush against him.

"You're so full of it," she told him playfully, pulling out of his embrace. "You already have the twins' phone numbers, why do you want mine?"

"Ah," he touched his heart dramatically. "You broke my heart today and didn't give me a chance to get to know you." He wiggled his eyebrows, feigning innocence. "Can I get yours?"

She shook her head.

"Who's your friend?" Andy said, sliding awkwardly off the bar to stand beside them.

"I met him earlier," Nina explained. "When we almost crashed into his car."

"You didn't tell me about any crash," Andy gasped. "What happened?"

Nina watched as Cuteness slung his arm over Andy's shoulders, leaning heavily into her, to tell her about their earlier mishap.

Nina took that moment to go and freshen up in the bathroom.

After using the facilities, she patted her face with a tissue and looked at herself. She looked good. She wasn't vain or anything like that, but she knew she was pretty and had a fabulous body. Gymnastics and ballet all her life made for a toned body. She could drop into the splits with a gust of wind if she wanted to.

The hair and make-up team had done an excellent job on her. Her make-up wasn't as obvious as she liked to wear it in England, but it was nice; her eyes smoked up and lined with black liquid liner, layers of mascara and fake lashes. Her hair had been washed, and her extensions replaced. She looked good.

Turning on the tap, she ran water over her wrists for a moment and thought about the other blonde guy in the SUV today. Cuteness–she really needed to ask him his real name–was here, maybe his friend was too. Hmm, perhaps she would get a chance to tell him off for his rudeness.

Turning off the taps, she dried her hands, and with renewed determination walked out. She was on a mission. Nina didn't like bad manners.

Andy was by herself when she came out. "Where is he?"

"Who?"

"Cute-the guy, I left you with?"

"He was too busy talking to my girls," Andy looked down at her boobs.

"Since when has that been a problem?"

"I didn't like him okay," she replied sharply. "Want a shot?"

Nina frowned at her friend; something was off. "Did he make a pass or something?"

"It was the 'or something'."

Nina could see the tears threatening in Andy's eyes and pulled her friend close. Andy was a big girl. In England, a shapely size eighteen and all lush curves. In body-conscious America, she would have to shop at a specialist shop for clothes.

"Do you want to go?" Nina asked with concern, forgetting her mission.

"No, he's an arse." Andy wiped her eyes and grinned. "Let's dance!"

They danced with each other, they danced in groups, and they danced with different men. They only stopped dancing when the music changed to slow songs and, sitting at the bar and fielding offers of drinks and more dancing, Nina looked around.

That's when she saw him.

***

Ace watched her all night; his jaw was aching from all the clenching he'd been doing, and he'd wanted to smash his cousin's face in when he'd gone over and talked to her when he'd specifically told him not to.

Now, his brother and cousins had gone on to another bar, reluctantly leaving Ace behind when he told them he 'didn't need a fucking babysitter'.

All night he'd remembered the man he used to be. He held the record for getting laid the fastest out of all his cousins, he reflected without humour, remembering the night he'd talked up a woman and was deep inside her up against a wall, in eighteen minutes flat. His cousins had timed him, he remembered. Now he was sitting here, limp as a squid, stalking a woman who didn't know he was here.

Ace didn't even know why he was torturing himself like this. It wasn't as though he was going to walk over and talk to her or take her to bed. He rubbed his leg as he continued to watch her dance. God, she had moves, he appreciated. He decided he'd get pissed, then go home.

She turned suddenly and looked straight at him.

Shit! Don't do it, don't do it. Don't. Fucking. Do it, Ace thought in a panic. She did it anyway. She walked over to him and he, dumb shit that he was, had nowhere to go.

She sat down without asking if the seat was taken, even though the table was full of empty beer bottles and shot glasses that he couldn't have drunk by himself.

God, she was beautiful. She needed to leave. Fucking Christ, he was all over the place and needed to get a grip, he thought, trying to calm his heart rate down.

"Help yourself to a seat," he drawled, in what he hoped was a casual sounding voice. She tied him in knots, and she hadn't even said a word yet.

"I was hoping you'd learned some manners between this morning and now," she answered, leaning back in the chair and drinking him in. He was wearing a darkly coloured shirt, open at the neck. His shoulders were broad, and his shirt sleeves rolled up, showing his hard forearms. When had forearms ever been sexy? She thought, fighting the urge to touch him.

"And why would you think that?" Ace weaved his fingers together and placed them at the back of his head in studied casualness.

She crossed her arms over her chest, dragging her eyes off the column of his throat and shrugged. "Oh, I don't know, slamming the door in someone's face is the epitome of rudeness maybe?" She challenged.

He frowned and leaned forward, placing his right forearm on the table, pushing the bottles forward. "We must have been at two different places, lady," he drawled coldly. "Because I didn't slam no doors."

Nina tipped her head to the side, not only listening to what he was saying but also how he was saying it. He was British, but he'd lived in America a long time. His words and sentence structure were Americanised, she noted curiously.

"Winding up a car window is akin to slamming doors!" She retorted. This was a weird conversation. "Aren't you going to offer to buy me a drink?" She asked playfully, edging for normality.

If she had reacted to him by seeing just half of his face this morning, seeing him full-on like this, without the baseball cap, was making her all hot and light-headed. She clenched her legs together.

He was beautiful, the low lighting cast shadows over his face, but what she could see she liked. The angle of his chin, his lips, oh my, they weren't smiling at her, but there was some sort of teasing movement going on, as though he was holding it in. His eyebrows were thick, with a small landing strip leftover from an injury scarring the right brow. His nose was long and his hair thick and shiny. He must have had it tied back in his baseball cap, she thought, as it was now touching his broad shoulders in dark waves.

"You've had enough to drink." He answered.

She gasped, jolted out of her appreciation of him. "You've been watching me?"

"No."

"Yes, you have," she teased, placing her elbows on the table and cupping her cheeks. She'd been feeling eyes, other than those close by, on her all night. Now she knew why.

"It was hard not to,"

He made it sound as though she'd been eating fire and prancing around naked.

"Do you want to dance?" She suggested, hearing Mario's Let Me Love You for the second time that day.

"No."

"Shame. What's your name?" She'd never had to work so hard to get a man's attention in her life, but she couldn't, wouldn't, leave it alone. Mario playing was a sign.

"Ace."

She laughed and rolled her eyes. "And I'm the Queen of Hearts."

He frowned at her. "Seriously, my name is Ace."

"Nina," she held out her hand and waited. Just when she thought he was going to leave her hanging, he moved forward and grasped her hand. That's when she realised why he didn't want to dance and why he hadn't got out of the car that morning.

He was in a wheelchair.

CHAPTER FOUR

He had to give it to her she didn't flinch or falter as his large hand engulfed hers.

"Nina Mae," she repeated, with a smile.

"And I'm Ace."

"Nice to meet you properly, Ace. No last name?"

"What would be the point?"

Nina shrugged, he was still being stubborn, if the short sentences and hard glare were, anything to go by.

"Well," she looked around as though seeing the place for the first time. "We've got two," she listed. "Probably one and a half nights to get better acquainted before I go home."

"Home, being?"

She noticed how he'd avoided her reference to getting better acquainted. But she'd leave that for now. "Oh, come on. I know you're a Brit and I know you know I am."

He smiled. A proper smile that went to his eyes. Nina wished she knew what colour they were.

"Now that was a helluva sentence, wasn't it?" She mused.

"It was." His lips twitched, trying to keep up. She was so full of sunshine and bubbling vitality. He really shouldn't encourage her. "What gave me away?" He asked reluctantly, needing to satisfy his curiosity.

"This morning, you said the magic word."

He frowned and Nina could see he was turning over their brief conversation in his head.

"You got me. What did I say?"

"Bonnet."

The rich sound of deep laughter filled the air, transforming his face. Nina wasn't surprised by how much she liked the sound of his voice or how young and approachable his features had become.

"Guilty." He put his hands up, admitting defeat, and relaxed into his chair. He could be her friend, for a night, he decided charitably. He wasn't a complete ass-hole.

"Well?" Nina prompted, with a slight nod.

"My family moved to the States when I was thirteen."

"From London? Chelsea perhaps?"

His eyebrows snapped down into a tight frown. "How did you know?" He demanded.

"I like languages; accents, the whole British English, American English, to-mar-toe to-may-toe thing." She explained, lapsing into her fascination with words and languages.

To give him his due, he did listen and accepted his bottled water with barely a glance at the waitress.

"So, all your family are here, in America?" She asked a bit later.

"Yeah, you've met my cousin Kyle—"

"Kyle?" Nina frowned, "Oh, you mean Cuteness!"

Ace didn't like that. "If you mean the guy you were feeling up this morning, then yes, Kyle." He gritted, as he remembered.

"I was not feeling him up!"

"It looked like it from where I was sitting."

They stared at each other, Ace realising, in dismay, that he had inadvertently said way too much.

Nina took a swig of the water he'd ordered for her and carefully put the bottle down as she tried to keep from smiling. The music had changed in tempo, and some Latin beat was playing, but it faded into the background as she observed him.

"The only person I want to touch now is you." She revealed, with honest softness, her dark eyes reflecting her vulnerability.

They looked at each other and Nina held her breath, waiting for his response.

Just as he opened his mouth, about to say something, Andy came up to the table.

"Hiya," she greeted them with a bounce.

"Hey Andy," Nina would have done anything to know what

Ace had been about to say. "Pull up a chair." Nina invited, watching her friend sit down before making the introductions.

"I'm ready to head off."

"So early?" Nina said.

"It's after one, and I want to email Gareth before I go to bed. I just don't understand why we can't get internet service in our suite for crap's sake!" Andy lamented.

Nina stood up to leave, unable to hide her dismay.

"You can stay," Andy said, catching the look and touching Nina's arm to stop her from moving. "And I'll take a taxi."

Nina looked at Ace, who was listening to the exchange but giving nothing away. Nina didn't want the night to end.

"Okay, but we'll walk you out," she looked at Ace and, with a cheeky wink, added. "Although hot wheels here will wheel out beside us." She walked off, not daring to see how he'd reacted to her little joke.

Outside, Andy hugged her close. "You sure you're okay? I can stay a little longer if you like. It's just that Gareth wants me—"

"No, go ahead." Nina interrupted. "Text me when you get there."

"And you be sure to text me if you leave here to go anyplace else," Andy ordered right back, sending Nina a knowing look and nodding towards Ace.

They grinned, hugged and kissed each other's cheeks.

"I will," Nina confirmed, and she watched as Andy stepped out into the road and raised her arm to signal a yellow cab like a native. She waved as her friend disappeared.

Nina held the door open for Ace as they went back inside and to his table. Someone had cleared it while they'd been gone. It smelled of pine disinfectant.

They sat down and looked at each other. Nina didn't know him well enough to know what he was thinking; yet, she added to her thoughts.

"So, do you come here often?" Nina teased, to fill the silence. She needed to lighten the mood after the bombshell she'd dropped earlier, but at least he was still here which was encouraging, she thought, dashing away her anxiety.

"You and your friend are close?" He asked, ignoring her question.

"Oh yeah, we're sisters."

"Sisters?"

"Not blood related," she explained. "We've known each other since primary school."

"Tell me about your life Nina Mae." Ace invited.

"I'm a golden child. Very much a daddy's girl and a mummy's darling." She began conversationally, not the least bit embarrassed by her admission. "Spoilt. An only child of only children. There's just my mum and my dad and little ole me, but I'm not a brat." She told him. "I'm an Essex girl. Do you know what that is?"

"No,"

She smiled at him. "You'll have to visit me in England to find out." She went on. "Are you going to dance with me?"

He scowled. "No."

"Why not?" She pressed.

He crossed his arms over his chest and frowned at her again, Nina realised it was his way of telling her to shut the hell up.

"Let's play a game," she said instead, determined to get her way. "If I win, we dance and if you win you get to ask whatever you want."

Ace pulled in a deep breath and let it out in a noisy whoosh. Why was he still here, he thought, but already knowing the answer. She wanted him, had made it damn obvious with all the nervous chatter and hair flicking. She was desperate enough to keep him guessing, and he was curious enough, egotistical enough, to want to know how this would play out. "What's the game?"

"Things that go together," she explained. "But as pairs."

"Pairs?"

"Yeah. For example, I have to say something that is always referred to in a pair, like Kings and Queens and bricks and mortar, things like that."

Ace shook his head; he'd never come across anyone so complex and playful in his life. But he was game. The pub was emptying, and if he lost, it would be no hardship to wheel around by the table pretending to dance. Jesus Christ, this is what his life had become, playing fucking party games to get his ego stroked.

"You start," he ordered. "Wait," he held up his hand. "How many pairs to win?"

"How about until one of us stops?"

"Cool."

"Left and right. Your turn.

This was going to be so easy, he thought. "Brush and comb."

They played for almost fifteen minutes; Ace was getting into it but knew he was going to lose. She was just too good and too fast. He eventually faltered, and she clapped her hands, declaring herself the winner, of course. His lips twitched into a smile.

"Come on." She stood quickly, eagerly heading over to the dance floor, but turned back when she saw that he hadn't moved.

"Not out there," he said. "Here."

"Okay." Nina agreed, grabbing the back of his chair because it didn't have any handles and, without asking, positioned him so that his back was to the bar and he was facing the wall, where a large mural depicting fields of heather gave the impression, they were in County Tipperary. It was a beautiful focal point.

His wheelchair wasn't bulky at all and was easy to manoeuvre. She'd never seen one like this before, it was compact, with large thin wheels. Then again, had she ever really looked at a wheelchair? Or the person in it? She shook away her dismal thoughts and rolled her shoulders as she stood in front of him, her legs shoulder-width apart as she waited for him to look into her eyes.

She would have preferred softer music but didn't want to chance breaking the mood by asking for a request from the DJ, 50 Cents' Candy Shop would have to do.

She picked up the beat and moved around him, undulating

slowly as she danced for him, stretching and moving her body to the music. Strippers and pole dancers had nothing on her, she thought confidently, as she lifted her leg to her head, holding the pose as his eyes fed on her legs and her privates, hidden away by her velvet shorts. With another twirl, she placed her leg on his right shoulder before leaning closer, hooking it around his neck. She watched him swallow, before rereleasing him and twirling away, smoothing the backs of her hands down the sides of her body as she danced for him.

Ace was transfixed and as hard as he'd ever been in his life. Some part of him computed the fact that his pipes worked. She danced so close, barely touching him, but he could feel her heat and smell her arousal. He wanted to reach out and smooth his hands up and down her legs. He wanted to lean forward and bury his face in her thighs. She was a tease, and she knew exactly what she was doing to him—the little minx.

"Do you like it?" She asked in his ear, touching her tongue to his lobe with the earring.

He didn't reply. He was too busy enjoying his first full-blown hard-on in months. He wanted to grab her hips and press her down onto it in case it went soft, never to come back.

"Closer," he growled, when she turned her back, pushing her ass nearer, her legs on either side of his. Her dexterity was amazing; she was folding herself around him, without needing to hold on to anything for balance.

Nina looked over her shoulder at him, then turned to face him again. She angled closer and picked up his hands to place them on her hips. Finally, he was touching her. She flicked her hair to one side and ran her tongue up his neck. The saltiness of his skin was a massive turn on.

He turned his head slightly, and their lips met. Their first kiss wasn't tentative or delicate. They didn't ponder their newness. No, with another deep growl Ace grabbed the back of her neck with one hand and her waist with the other and took control.

Nina had been kissed before. Many times. She enjoyed kissing, but this? This was like something she had never felt before. She felt as though she was now his, as though they were now a couple. His lips were familiar and comfortable, as though they'd already shared a lifetime of stories and intimacies.

She knew she wanted to keep on kissing him. Never mind that they had just met, that was irrelevant, her parents had met and married within two months of meeting each other. Nina knew Ace was already a part of her; she felt it.

Wanting to be even closer to him, she bravely sat on his lap and looped her arms around his thick neck, matching his aggression. His erection seared her bottom, and she rocked into it.

Someone dropped a load of glasses or bottles because the loud crash was enough to jolt them both and Nina shot off his knee in surprise. The room fell silent, and the music stopped.

"Sorry!" Someone called out and after a few seconds, the music resumed. We belong together by Mariah Carey.

Ace and Nina looked at each other and Nina, not knowing why grinned down at him and waited.

It took ten long seconds to come, but he eventually smiled, and she flung herself onto his knees again, wrapped her arms around his neck and buried her face in the curve of his neck, squeezing him tight, but his entire body went stiff, and she heard his breath catch.

"Oh my God, did I hurt you?" She asked, leaning back. His mouth was tight, and even in the dim light, she could see that his skin had paled. Alarmed, Nina scrambled off him.

"Oh my God," she said again, watching him rub his right thigh and close his eyes. "I hurt you. What should I do?" She asked, worrying her bottom lip in distress.

"It's okay, just give me a minute," he breathed. The pain up his right leg, hip and lower back sliced through him in waves. How could he forget his injuries like that? Fuck!

"I'll call an ambulance,"

"No!" He grabbed her wrist as she made to leave. "It'll pass. It's going already," he lied. "Just give me a minute."

Stricken by guilt, Nina pulled out a chair and sat beside him.

She had no idea why he was in a wheelchair. Hadn't wanted to seem too forward and insensitive by asking. She'd just assumed he didn't have any feelings from the waist down because his legs were held in place by two wide Velcro straps over his jeans.

"I'm sorry," she said, reaching for the hand closest to her that was in a tight fist on his leg. She rubbed her thumb over the white knuckles trying to give him what little comfort she could. "I'm really sorry," she repeated, in a small shaky voice.

Ace opened his eyes to see tears pooling in hers.

"Come here, baby," he ordered softly, as he laced his fingers through hers, pulling her closer so that he could open her hand and kiss her palm. "There's nothing to be sorry about okay?" He captured her chin, forcing her to look at him, and he gave her a reassuring smile. "Want to get some air?" He asked.

She nodded.

"Where are you staying?" He asked, to distract her. Seeing her in tears brought out a tenderness he didn't know he had. Nina named the hotel. "It's just a few blocks from here. Come on." He held out his hand and smiled when she took it.

***

"You called me hot wheels." He said when they'd walked a few feet in silence. New York was never quiet, no matter what time it was and even now, the roads were busy with theatregoers, mixing with people going to and from nightclubs and whatever other social events people went to. They were all vying for the attention of the stream of yellow cabs that snaked up and down the street as though it were midday.

Nina giggled. "So I did,"

"Yet you called me rude."

"It's my term of endearment for you."

"So we have terms of endearments now?" He asked with a smirk.

"Of course. You've seen me naked."

"You weren't naked."

"But very close."

"Hmm," he moved off again, remembering the acres of brown skin on display before she'd pulled her T-shirt on this morning.

They moved on in silence.

They'd only just met, but Ace knew she had something on her mind as she was unusually quiet, and her stride had lost its bounce. She hadn't been this quiet since they met.

He wheeled a little faster then stopped in front of her, blocking her path. "What is it?"

She shrugged and tried to step around him. He blocked her again.

This wasn't good, he thought, realising how much she had come to mean to him in just a few hours. He wanted to hear her non-stop chatter. She made him forget the decisions he had to make.

"Peanut butter and jelly."

"What?" She glanced at him confusion evident in her gaze.

"Moon and stars."

Nina grinned at him and put her hand on his shoulder as they walked. "Nuts and bolts."

"Bows and Arrows."

"Cops and robbers."

"Good one," he praised chuckling. "Ben and Jerry's."

"I won that round I think," Ace said, after a little pause.

Her tinkle of laughter lightened his heart. "I'll tell you what I want later," he said, winking at her as he zigzagged his chair playfully on the sidewalk.

Later, she thought. They had a later. She smiled as she rushed to catch up with him with a renewed spring in her step.

CONVINCING KYLE

Chapter One

The waiting room was packed with three very distinct families. The blondes; the Asians and then his family, the Italian Americans with the odd Brit within their midst.

Kyle Mannino looked around, bored out of his mind. Why couldn't the birth of a baby be scheduled between nine and five, or something equally decent?

When he'd received the phone call from his cousin and best friend, Ace, that Sabrina was in labour, Kyle had just uncovered the lace offerings of a pair of real double D's. If it weren't for the persistent ringing of his phone at ten o'clock at night, he would have missed the whole baby landing event.

But why was it taking so long? Kyle watched through the doorway as Ace walked Sabrina up and down the corridor. Sabrina was leaning heavily on him, she looked tired, but had a determined glint in her eyes and Ace had his arm around her shoulders, taking all of her weight.

Although Sabrina had dilated enough at one point, the baby had decided to stop just before the pushing stage Kyle had been told. 'Stubborn little fucker', he thought, plastering a smile on his face and offering a thumbs up when he caught Ace's eye. Ace frowned darkly at him over Sabrina's head, and Kyle laughed to himself. Ace knew him like no other.

Kyle felt his phone vibrate in the pocket of his jeans, and he dug it out. His date had sent him a picture of her cleavage with a wiggly trail of whipped cream over them, and he chuckled. He would recognise these anywhere, but what was her name again? Tiffany? Or was it Stephanie? Anyway, something 'iny'; she wasn't a conversationalist, but what she could do with her thighs was like shit.

"You get that smirk off your face right now, Kyle Mannino,

before I take that phone off you!"

Kyle turned to look down at his Aunt Greta, who was sat beside him and giving him an irritated look. He quickly stuffed his phone into his pocket.

Aunt Greta was Ace's mother, and his mother's baby sister; yet Aunt Greta was the matriarch of the family. A round, diminutive, four-foot eleven tornado, with long dark hair with a wide white streak at the front. She wore lots of costume jewellery and ruled the family, as her plastic earrings bounced with enthusiasm. When Aunt Greta spoke, they listened. The thing is, they just didn't want to disappoint her anyway.

Kyle leaned over and kissed his aunt. "Sorry, Auntie. It was an important email." He lied smoothly, but with the lift of one tattooed eyebrow, he knew she had seen the image, and she was letting him know that she had.

A tall, thin man came rushing into the room with a wide smile and announced to the family of blondes that the baby had arrived. It was a boy and, to a chorus of claps and congratulations, added that mother and baby were fine.

The blondes rushed out into the corridor, and for a moment, it was quiet again. Kyle resisted the urge to look at his phone, feeling the trio of vibrations in his pocket and looked at the clock on the wall instead. He'd scarcely been there an hour. Damn.

"Do you need me to get you anything, Auntie?" Kyle asked. He needed to get out of here. The room was boring and uninspiring. Pea-green walls with framed, printed posters of differently coloured calla lilies in groups of four. A grey rug partially covered the pale, laminated floor with a wooden table, piled with battered, out of date, magazines and Breast is Best leaflets.

"Water please, Kyle." Aunt Greta replied, and he moved to the water fountain, poured her and himself a cup of water and went to sit beside her again.

It took another hour before there was any news, but it wasn't their news. The Indian family did a round of back-slapping with the arrival of a baby boy. Apparently, the newcomer had a lot of hair, looked like his father and weighed a whopping ten pound eleven ounces.

Kyle grimaced. He hoped the baby Sabrina was carrying weighed nothing like that, as Sabrina was petite. He looked out into the corridor but didn't see his cousin or his new wife.

Kyle smiled, he loved Sabrina and always ribbed Ace, because he had met her first. Ace had smacked him in the head and told him the only reason Kyle had met her first was because he'd been in a wheelchair at the time.

Kyle sobered at that memory. It had been a bad time for the family. Ace had almost died. A stuntman; he'd fallen from a building and broken eighty per cent of the bones in his body. They didn't think he would ever walk again.

Ace was supposed to do his surgery but was dithering about the risk. It was now or never, and he was leaning more towards the never, much to the despair of the family.

He and Ace had met Sabrina; she had been God sent. Kyle only went to church for weddings and christenings. They had yet to have a funeral in the family, thank God. But that year, that week, Kyle had chatted to God constantly and found himself in church. Get Ace through this, he'd asked. Get Ace walking, and he'd never ask him for anything else ever again.

In forty-eight hours, Sabrina had met and got Ace to the hospital, giving him hope and something to work for; her love. Kyle would always love Sabrina for that. Hence, he was sitting here on a chair made for someone with a metal backside, but he would sit here for her and Ace and their baby. The baby really needed to hurry up.

"How much longer do you think?" Kyle asked his auntie.

"Will you stop asking Mom that!" Kelly said, from across the room.

He grinned over at his cousin, Ace's baby sister. "I'm sure that little tyke you pushed out didn't take this long," he said.

Kelly rolled her eyes at him and huffed in annoyance. "That's because you came at the end. I'd been in labour for eighteen hours."

"No, shit."

"Kyle, watch your mouth, please."

"Yes, Auntie." He reached over and kissed an apology on her cheek. Aunt Greta always smelled of gardenias. She was like a breath of fresh air wherever she went. A tornado of fresh air, he amended, kissing her again at her snort.

He'd been doing that his whole life, apologising to Aunt Greta. His own parents rarely disciplined him growing up, and it was left to his aunt to keep him in line. It didn't always work, and he was once sent over to England, to boarding school for a term, to cool off. But otherwise, Aunt Greta and her English husband Uncle Charles were the disciplinarians, and he loved them for it.

A pretty girl from the Indian family came into the room and looked around. He'd noticed her before, and he'd noticed her checking him out. If her grandfather, father, brother and uncles weren't around, he'd probably be walking her to her car and getting her number, but the people around her were better than any chastity belt. He knew that first hand and steeled himself against the memory.

"Lost something, sweetheart?" Kyle asked as she moved to a pile of magazines on the table between his chair and the empty one on his left.

"Just my new magazine," she glanced at him from under her eyelashes, "But it doesn't matter, she smiled. "I can always get another one."

"You can." Kyle waited. He knew what was coming next. It had been coming from the moment he'd turned fourteen. Women loved his dark blond hair and blue eyes and, apparently, he was charismatic, but had a devilish attitude, their words, he was just him. But the women flocked around him; always had. It was just too easy, sometimes.

She picked up a magazine, which Kyle was sure had been stuffed in her handbag a moment ago and stepped closer, bending at the waist and giving him a glimpse of her cleavage. Not quite double D's, but nice enough. Was it written on his forehead that he was a breast man?

"You might like the article on page fifty-six," she whispered breathlessly, placing the magazine beside him. With another smile and a wink from her dark eyes, she looked over her shoulder and was gone.

Kelly burst out laughing. "Really?" she scoffed. "She really just hit on you, when her sister has just pushed out an elephant?"

Kyle smiled and spread his arms. "What can I say?"

"Not a whole lot." Kelly went on with a shudder. "I just don't get it." She shook her head and rolled her eyes.

"It's the Latin in him, Kelly." Kelly's sister Charlene said.

"No, it's that bad boy image he goes around with. Ace, Kyle and Matthew treat..."

"Excuse me, I left boyhood years ago and why are you even discussing me like I'm not even here?" Kyle interjected darkly, glaring at his cousins across the room.

"You're a great topic of conversation little cousin," Charlene replied, pursing her lips in that no-nonsense way of hers.

Kyle grimaced, knowing what was coming next; he managed to count to one before her list started.

"You don't work," she began, "globe-trot around the world at a whim, and now that you don't have Ace to keep you company, you've gotten worse. When are you..."

"Enough," Greta interjected quickly, used to the pace at which this topic could disintegrate into a shouting match. Her children and nephew would revert to teenagers if she let them carry on.

Kyle smirked over at his cousins, then looked at the magazine in his hand. It was a woman's magazine called Miss Asia USA. If all the subheadings were anything to go by, the women who read this would discover where their G-spot was, eat chocolate and still lose weight and knit a sweater in five days. Kyle shook his head and leafed through it casually as baby Ace– as they'd taken to calling the baby–was not about to make an appearance any time soon, he thought.

Kyle turned to the page as instructed, took out his phone and took a picture of the girl's name and number written in what looked like liquid eye-liner across the page. Her name was Harpreet.

"For goodness sake."

He heard one of his cousins say across the room, but he ignored them, settled into the chair and, turning to the first page, began to read.

The magazine was quite good. The few articles were well written and informative. Kyle was in the middle society pages now, glancing at all the beautiful women, some in traditional saris, others' inexpensive designer wear. Then he settled in to read the film and book reviews. He was reading the review of a Bollywood film when turning the page, his breath hitched.

He didn't breathe, as he looked closer, stood up, and moved directly under the bright tubes of fluorescent light. It was her, Camille. The caption under the photo said her name was Camikara.

"Well?"

Kyle looked up, thinking his auntie was talking to him, but Ace was standing in the doorway, looking tired and dishevelled, but with the widest grin on his face.

"It's a girl."

***

Kyle dropped off his aunt and cousins and drove through the not so quiet streets of Manhattan. Now that Ace had bought an apartment in the exclusive Four Thirty-Two Park Avenue building, Kyle stayed at his old apartment whenever he was in New York.

He parked and rushed inside. The magazine was burning a hole in his back pocket, and Kyle only stopped to pour himself a whiskey and grab his tablet before sitting on the couch.

He did a Google search on the film, an Indian adaptation of Wuthering Heights, called The Mumbai Plains. It had gained five stars. Camikara, Camille, was playing the lead and was apparently Oscar Nominee amazing.

Kyle went to images, and there she was. It was her, the dark skin, even darker hair and startling grey eyes and the dimple in her chin. There was no mistaking her. She was still incredibly beautiful, if not more so.

She was in town. A premier of the movie was showing not far from where the apartment was. Kyle looked at the time; it would still be going on.

Now that the wait was over and the baby had finally arrived safely; a sweet six pound eight ounces, Kyle was free. He was going to the première. He wanted, no needed, to see Camille. It had been nine years.

All the pomp had died down when he got there half an hour later, but hundreds of people were still waiting around, and the air was filled with a spicy, succulent fragrance, that made him remember the flower stands in Jaipur market.

As Kyle waited for the film to end, he got talking to a 'paparazzi' reporter from England. His name was Kev Taylor and didn't look what Kyle thought a sleazy pap would look like. Kev wore a dark suit, white shirt, red bow-tie and a flat tweed cap, turned slightly backwards. A dangly earring in his right ear and a full beard completed the look. He was character personified.

Kyle had lived in England for three months and hated everything about it. He was a New Yorker born and bred, upstate, but still New York. The boarding school had been in Derbyshire; surrounded by mile upon mile of fucking green fields of various shades, but still green. He hated green.

There was nothing for a boy like him to do. That was until he'd discovered the sister school, St Ann of Hope for Girls, just a tiny green field away.

Every night, in the last of his three-month term, he took a bunch of guys and would sneak out to meet up with some girls. Kyle smiled at the memory. Boarding school girls were just as hot and kinky as the porno videos made out. The things they all did. Fucking A!

Then he'd met Camille. She'd been out riding a massive chestnut coloured horse; a special privilege, one of the other girls had said scornfully.

Camille had sat, with her back straight, looking down her elegant nose at them all. Kyle had actually hidden his cigarette behind his back, hoping she hadn't seen it. She had, and the look of distaste on her face made him feel all sorts of embarrassment.

With a flick of her riding crop, directed at them, she'd trotted off.

He didn't see her again until the official school fête when the two schools met in the middle field to play traditional games like apple bobbing, conkers and rounders.

Camille had been sat on a bale of hay, looking bored out of her mind. She'd been wearing tan-coloured pants, a light blue shirt, tucked into the waistband, a brown jacket and brogues. Brogues in a field; Kyle smiled at the memory, her hair had been in a long thick braid over one shoulder.

He'd bought her some pink cotton candy, and went to talk to her. She'd ignored him at first, but he'd continued to talk and talk, exaggerating his accent until she'd laughed. She'd looked at him then, and accepted the cotton candy that seemed to have lost some of its fluffiness. They'd argued over the proper name for it; cotton candy versus candy floss. He'd let her win.

They'd been inseparable after that; meeting in the village for ice-cream. He'd gone to a 'revision group' he knew she'd be in and fell in love for the first time in his life. Two fucking weeks before he was to leave England!

"They'll be coming out in a minute, mate." Kev Taylor said, lifting his camera and jolting Kyle out of his memories. The pap scrambled about in his hunt for a better view of the double doors. "Get ready."

Kyle tipped his head at him, then said. "Nice to meet you and thanks for the info." That pap knew more details about Camille than the Google search he'd done earlier.

She was Bollywood Royalty; super-rich, and it was rumoured she was retiring. This was to be her last film, hence all the interest. But there was also the rumour that she was going to play a role as a smouldering sex siren in a Hollywood film that would be frowned upon in conservative India.

There was movement from inside the building and straightening up behind the gold velvet rope that matched the gold carpet; Kyle watched as the enormous 1920's style glass doors opened. The long, tubular brass handles reflected and threw candle-light into the crowd from the millions of fake tea lights on the ground. Beautiful people–that matched the pages of the magazine he'd been reading earlier–came pouring out.

Kyle was pushed out of the way, and his feet trampled on, by a group of teenage girls who had somehow managed to stand in front of him, their phones at the ready. Just then, their screams got louder, and they started jumping up and down excitedly, shouting the name Camikara and declaring their love for Parmer Christopher Abdul.

Camille came out on the arm of a tall, handsome, dark-haired Asian man. They looked like a couple, laughing and leaning into one another. Kyle felt a fire ignite in his lower belly as he watched.

Camille wasn't in traditional Indian dress, but she was in a shiny white gown, elaborately embroidered with dark gold threading, sequins and stones, from the hem to the knee. The skirt was full, hanging from her shapely hips, and fell to the ground. When she walked one long slender leg played hide and seek within the folds. She was wearing sky-high heels, with barely-there gold straps.

There was a gold stone in her belly button, and her stomach was bare, right up to the low cut, white bodice type thing, with tiny sleeves, on her shoulders. He didn't know what to call it, as it had a bit more fabric than a bra, but not much more. He just knew it displayed a whole lot of skin, and the guy beside her was busy looking at her boobs. Kyle wanted to punch him in the face.

They ambled down the steps to shouts and flashing lights, all smiles, stopping now and then to take pictures with fans or sign autographs. It took them fifteen minutes to walk twelve steps. Kyle knew because he'd been counting. This was fucking ridiculous.

Then she was there, taking pictures with the group of girls in front of him. Her beautiful long hair, still as long as he remembered, was parted in the centre, reaching the curve of her bottom and covered by some sort of glittering gold headdress of small pearls and gold gemstones. A thick, gold chain sat along her parting to cascade in an array of intricate chains to lie on top of her hair. A large tear-drop shaped gemstone lay perfectly in the centre of her forehead.

Nothing she wore could detract from her natural beauty.

"Camille," Kyle said clearly, over the din of gushing. She heard him.

Kyle watched as she looked through the crowd, still smiling, still taking pictures, but looking for him. He knew she was. She would never forget his voice, and he would never forget hers. She'd whispered to him and screamed at him. She'd cried to him and said goodbye to him. He would never forget her voice.

She saw him then. Her body froze for the millisecond she looked into his eyes. Recognising him, and just like that, turned her back to be swept away by a tide of people wearing black, with orange lanyards swinging around their necks, to a waiting limousine.

Kyle didn't move. She'd blanked him?! She'd fucking blanked him! After everything, they had shared?! He watched as the gold limo pulled into the street and he stood still as the crowd dispersed and he lost sight of the car.

Only then did Kyle turn to walk back to the apartment; he felt hurt beyond belief.

***

"Are you ready?" Camille turned to her co-star, Parmer, and placed her hand into the crook of his elbow.

"Ready." He replied.

With a nod to her publicist, the doors opened, and they were hit by a blaze of flashing lights and screams.

The film had been a success, and with the number of people

still waiting two hours later, just to see them, Camille knew this was going to be another box office hit. Twelve in a row for her.

They took their time, signing autographs, taking selfies with fans. Parmer was dragged off to one side by his publicist, and she was pulled to do on the spot interviews for celebrity TV shows as Parmer wasn't too bright.

Camille didn't mind it. Being a film star had saved her, and she showed her appreciation and paid her dues by slowly making her way down the line, chatting and smiling until her cheeks hurt, to her loyal American fans who had come out to support her.

Another interview then pictures by camera phones; Parmer joined her as she felt his arm go around her back. Their names had been linked in the press recently, and she knew it was his office that had done the linking. He was a good actor, looking to up his career via her. She was used to it from her single male co-stars. It came with being one of few unmarried Bollywood actresses. If she looked at a man too hard, for too long; she was linked.

She posed for some pictures, even took the phone off one hysterical teenager and turned around for a close-up of them both. She was smiling and telling the teenager not to cry when she heard his voice.

"Camille."

No one called her Camille any more. She'd intentionally lost that, and all the memories attached to it, the moment her feet had landed in France at the age of seventeen, all battered and bruised with a heartbroken into a thousand pieces.

She searched through the crowds, careful not to look too long at any one person. There were too many cameras, from every angle. She may be a megastar in Bollywood, but her stardom had followed her across the continents. The paparazzi was out in full force.

She saw him then, standing behind a group of screaming teenagers. She met his dark gaze, saw his lovely mouth slide into a smile and knew he was about to say something to her.

Quickly, she turned her back and allowed herself to be pulled towards the waiting limousine. Parmer got in beside her, laughing and winding down the window for one more chance to have his picture taken.

Digging into her bag, Camille pulled out her personal phone and spoke in soft French once it was answered.

***

The constant banging on the door woke him. Kyle had taken a shower, knocked back three, or was it four whiskies, before heading off to bed to torture himself; reliving the feeling of her walking away. How could she do that?

He shoved the single blanket aside and stomped out of the bedroom.

"What the fuck man?" Kyle wrenched open the door, not even thinking about his safety. No one should be able to get up here; they had security. It was a rich person's building. Ace was paying a fortune for shit like this not to happen, he thought belatedly.

Two burly men, dressed in black, stood on his threshold.

"Kyle Mannino?" One of them asked.

Kyle was about to deny it but was not a wimp. He could take these guys on, he wanted too. He folded his arms high on his chest and widened his stance.

"Who wants to know?"

The two men moved to the side.

"Camille?" Kyle whispered.

"Hi, Kyle. Can I come in?" Camille asked, but already she had slid past him into the apartment.

The men, her bodyguards, went straight to the large windows and pulled the sheer curtains shut with loud swishes, before walking to stand on either side of the front door.

Camille turned to him then and pulled off her baseball hat.

"Hi," she said again.

Chapter Two

They stood staring at each other. Or rather he stood staring at her as she looked around the apartment. He didn't see what she was seeing but remembered he'd left his shoes in the middle of the living room. The whiskey glasses were still on the glass side table, the sofa cushions askew where'd he'd taken his nap that afternoon, and he was sure he hadn't hung his sports jacket in the closet when he'd gotten home from the hospital earlier.

"Still untidy, I see," Camille said to him, with a soft smile.

"Yeah go figure." Kyle tried to stuff his hands in the front pockets of his jeans, but only then realising he was wearing a pair of black cotton boxer briefs. Briefs, she was now looking at, and Kyle felt himself react to her look. "Excuse me," he stated, folding his hands to his front. "I'll go put some clothes on."

Kyle closed the bedroom door with a silent click and leaned heavily against the cool wood. Camille was here; in his apartment. The last time he had seen her this close he'd had blood pouring out of his nose, one eye had been slammed shut, and he'd just swallowed a piece of his incisor. She'd been screaming for them to leave him alone, with tears streaming down her face.

Kyle shook his head at the painful memory. Camille was here and, with a deep breath, he rubbed his chest as he calmed his heart rate, before pulling on a pair of blue jeans and a black T-shirt and then going into the en-suite to splash cold water on his face and brush his teeth.

Rotating, then shaking his broad shoulders, Kyle opened the bedroom door. She was standing exactly where he had left her; dead centre of the room. Her two bodyguards were gone, he noticed, glancing over at the front door.

"I sent them out," she said, seeing his questioning look.

Kyle walked up to her and stopped in front of her. She was wearing white, non-branded sneakers and white tracksuit bottoms that rested low on her hips and were held in place by a rope-like tie, a plain white shirt and a black hoodie. Her hair was parted in the centre, and two long, fat, plaits fell down the side of her body. She looked like Rapunzel or Pocahontas, he mused, tipping his head to one side to sweep his gaze down her slender body and back up again.

"Do I get a hug or something?" Camille asked, holding her arms out to him, but her small smile seemed nervous and unsure.

Kyle didn't know what he was feeling. He'd never felt like this. Camille, his dream, his fantasy, the one person he'd ever shared a part of himself with was here. Seeing her was like seeing his truth and his deepest secret staring right back at him, only with grey eyes. He wasn't sure if he wanted to face their truth just yet.

She took the moment from him, stepping into his space and wrapping her arms around his waist. Kyle pulled her closer, and they hugged.

She was average height, with a petite frame. He was a giant, six-four and muscular, but somehow she fit him. Her dips and curves had always slotted perfectly into his. He felt her body shake as she buried her face into his chest, and he pulled back, cupping her face to tilt it up to his. Her lovely eyes were awash with tears that now ran into her hairline. Kyle thumbed the rivulets away.

"Don't cry Cami, please." He choked, as he felt his own throat constrict as he kissed her temple and pulled her into his embrace again.

They held each other a moment longer and then, by mutual deep breaths, pulled apart.

"Sorry Kyle," Camille apologised, stepping away to sit on the soft grey suede sofa and picking up a square, charcoal coloured cushion to hug. "I don't know what came over me."

"Don't Camille," he said simply, his shoulders curling in defeat, knowing they needed to share the tears. "Would you like a drink or something?"

"Water please."

"Got it." Kyle went for a bottle of still water from the kitchen and brought one back for himself too.

"How did you find me?" He asked, settling into the sofa

beside her.

"I had Jai follow you from the première."

"What was that shit, Cam?" Kyle blazed, remembering the humiliation of just standing there when she'd turned her back on him. "Blanking me like that?"

"Please don't be angry," she turned fully to him, one knee on the sofa, she put the cushion aside. "If I'd reacted to knowing you, you'd be on the front pages of all the celebrity blogs and papers and someone–probably Kev Taylor, as you were standing right beside him–would be digging into your background trying to link us by now," she rushed, reaching to touch his thigh in apology. "I was protecting you."

"Yeah well," he chugged down some water. "I didn't like it."

Camille watched him drink. Tipping his head far back, the column of his throat thick and strong and slightly shadowed with dark blond hair. He'd become a handsome man.

"Are you really going to sulk about me protecting you like that?" She asked with a raised brow.

Ah yes, Kyle thought, trying not to smile; his Camille was back. She told it like it was.

"After nine years I wanted my moment," he clarified, slicing her a look. "Then."

She laughed at him, remembering how emotional he could get and moved to stand in front of him again with her arms open wide.

He laughed, stood up, pulled her into his arms and twirled her around and around as he kissed her neck before settling her gently onto the sofa again.

They grinned stupidly at each other.

"Hello Kyle," she said again, as she reached for his hand.

"Hi Camille," he laced their fingers together. "Where have you been? How have you been?"

In a calm voice, Camille told him how she'd finished her schooling in France and then went on to university in Germany. She was discovered by a modelling scout while out shopping one day, the rest, she said, was history.

Kyle looked at her. He hadn't seen her in years, but he knew her. Her words lacked emotion. She was telling him the abbreviated version, he knew. But he wouldn't push, not just yet.

"What about you?" she asked.

"I fly."

"I remember your father owned planes?"

Kyle laughed, thinking of the tiny airstrip his parents owned. "Small planes," he clarified. "I pilot all sizes."

"Doing what?" she leaned forward. "Going where?"

He shrugged. That was it, he didn't do much. He'd been a commercial pilot for a while, but that got boring. Then he flew tourists around the Caribbean Islands until he was bored of that as one island of blue seas and white sands blended into another island of blue seas and white sands. Now he simply took a map out, closed his eyes and wherever his finger landed, he flew to, explored for a bit until the boredom set in and he'd get his map out again.

"Nothing much," he shrugged again. "How long are you in the States for?"

"What day is it?" she asked instead, releasing their hands to smother a yawn behind her hand.

"Tuesday."

"Until tonight." She revealed.

"Then where are you going?"

"England for a few weeks and then who knows." She picked up the cushion again, hugged it close and rested her chin on it.

"Can you put that off?" he asked, feeling a sense of urgency. He'd just found her. Granted, he'd never looked for her but now that she was here, sat on his sofa, in his space, he wanted her close to him. It was an odd, profoundly unsettling feeling. "Stay with me for a while?" he urged. "We have a lot to talk about, catch up on."

"I can't, Kyle."

"Please," That word felt foreign on his tongue, but he would beg, and he held her hand again.

She lifted their hands and nudged his knuckles with her

cheek. "I'd forgotten just how convincing you can be," she laughed. "You should be a solicitor."

Kyle smirked over at her and tugged their hands so that she fell across the empty space between them, he caught her and sat her on his knee.

He was comfortable doing this. It was as though they'd never been apart all these years. The two weeks they'd had brought them right back to this moment. Forget all that had happened; all the time that had elapsed, what he'd been doing, what she had been doing. This moment was what mattered.

"You were always pretty Camille, but now?" Kyle said with quiet reverence, smoothing his knuckles down her cheek and watching for her irises to expand in her unusual eyes. They didn't. "Beautiful." He whispered.

Unless you asked, you wouldn't know what her heritage was. Her great grandfather was Ugandan and her great grandmother Asian Indian. They had married against the wishes of both families and travelled from Uganda when the awful dictator Idi Amin wanted all Asian people expelled from his country in the 1970s. Camille had dark skin, bone-straight black hair, high cheekbones and clear grey eyes. She was unusually beautiful.

"Thank you."

"I guess you hear that all the time now, huh?" He said, noticing her automatic reaction with a frown. Once upon a time, she would have dipped her head in embarrassment and told him to stop looking at her. It had been so cute. "Adoring fans, paparazzi wanting your photograph?" He was annoyed as hell and didn't know why.

"I'm not just a pretty face, Kyle." She answered sharply, moving off him, but with his large hands on her narrow hips, he held her down.

"Hey!" He pulled her back, scooted her around until she straddled his thighs and was facing him. There was nowhere for her to hide. "It was a genuine compliment. I knew you when you were a skinny teenager, with no boobs and a scattering of pimples on your forehead. You were cute then."

"Are you actually having a conversation about my lack of boobs?"

Kyle laughed at her look of outrage. He realised she must have been wrapped up in that pink celebrity bubble of hers for too long and laughed out loud, before going on to sweep his gaze down over her chest with deliberate slowness.

"Yeah. They've gotten bigger." He reached up and cupped her breasts, taking liberties that were only his to take.

Camille slapped at his hands. "What are you doing?!" she screeched.

"Playing with you." He chuckled, pushing her forward with his hands on her narrow back. "Do you still taste the same, Camille?"

"Maybe not." She answered, leaning backwards.

"I think maybe you do. Sweet." He said. "Your mouth was always so sweet. Your lips the sweetest I'd ever tasted."

"It was all the candy floss you used to buy me," she answered. "And did you actually just bring other women into our conversation?" She went on, giving him a fierce look.

He laughed, leaned forward and skimmed his lips quickly over hers, before settling her beside him again.

"I came straight here. Have you got anything to eat?" Camille asked a moment later.

"I doubt it," Kyle mentally ran through the cupboards. He always ate out. "We'll have to order in or go out."

"Order in, please. Pizza."

"You always were a bossy little thing, weren't you? What if I want Chinese or Italian?"

"You don't,"

"I might,"

"But I know you don't." She went on confidently, and he laughed.

Kyle stood, and she followed him into the kitchen and watched silently as he went to a large draw beside the fridge and rummaged through hundreds of take-out menus.

"Close your eyes," he ordered, fanning several menus out in

his hands. "Choose one."

Camille indulged him. It was nice to have some normality in her life. She chose a menu and opened her eyes at his throaty growl.

"I'll have bell peppers, pepperoni and extra cheese on mine." She ordered smugly, seeing the pizza menu.

"Please."

"Please." She repeated, not used to being taken to task. It had been a long time since anyone had ever questioned her manners. In fact, she didn't think anyone ever had.

She liked playing with Kyle. He was her friend. For years she was scared her darkest secrets would be plastered in the papers or found on the internet. He never told. He'd never said a word.

"I see you have not lost your princess tendencies," Kyle said.

"And disappoint you?" she laughed, coming back from her not so pleasant thoughts. "I think not."

"The world always did bow down to you."

"And so it should," Camille answered softly. "It owes me enough."

They looked at each other then, the horrid memory of that night intruding on their moment and he pulled her close and kissed her forehead tenderly, before letting her go to order the pizza.

When the large pizza came, they sat on the floor and talked. She ate more than he did and Kyle watched, amazed, as she drank half a bottle of coke as well. When he commented she burped indelicately and laughed, saying she was celebrating her new beginnings.

"I read this was going to be your last film." He said, a while later, as he wiped his mouth and threw the napkin onto the open cardboard lid of the pizza box.

She shrugged as she picked up her fifth slice and bit into it. "Where did you read that and how did you know I was in town anyway?"

Kyle told her about his night, the magazine, the girl with her phone number and the baby as he watched her pick off an oily pepperoni disc and pop it into her mouth.

"All you used to talk about was your cousin Ace," she said between chews.

Kyle's smile was wide. "Yeah, he's my boy."

"I wish I had someone close like that." She revealed honestly, as she chased a string of cheese with her tongue.

"What happened to that girl? What was her name? Red hair, pale long face, really skinny?" Kyle listed.

"Chloe?" she sighed. "When I made my first box office hit, she sold the story of my so-called 'Rich Girl Life' to the press."

"Shit."

"No matter." Camille took another bite from her slice, licked her lips, put it down then shrugged.

"That hurt?" He asked, not really expecting her to tell him the truth. But she did with her acute nod.

Kyle watched as her eyes turned dark, and she became lost in thought. It had hurt her. In school, she was called the snobby rich girl. Everyone at that boarding school was rich, but apparently, Camille was super rich and standoffish, but Kyle hadn't been fooled. There was a vulnerability in the slump of her shoulders when she thought no one was looking. He was always looking.

"I'd better go," she scrambled up and dusted off the backside of her sweats as though she'd been sitting in a pile of road dirt.

"Why?"

"Because it's getting light and I've had a long day."

"You're as pumped as I am right now Cam."

"No."

"Yes." He followed her backward steps. He was not letting her go. "You've been waiting for me to kiss you all night."

"No."

She almost walked into the wall that separated the kitchen from the rest of the apartment, and Kyle pulled her away.

"Yes," he repeated. Her coordination was always off. Her sense of direction was pitiful. She'd even gotten lost one night when he left her midfield to find her way back, and she'd rung him from her phone. She'd actually ended up in the field behind his lodgings, and he'd laughed so hard and even harder at her stiff shoulders and furious dark eyes.

"Look behind you." He ordered and watched as Camille looked over her shoulder, seeing his room, his bed and the sheets all messed up where he'd been tossing and turning.

"We can't, Kyle." She whispered, looking up at him with huge eyes.

"Why not?"

"Because we've just met."

"Are you involved with anyone? That guy I saw you with tonight with the toothy grin?"

She laughed. "No, he's my co-star Parmer; but he wants more. He's gay but hasn't realised his truth yet."

Kyle leaned his body into hers.

"What about you?" Camille asked. "Hot sexy man like you must have someone in the wings."

"Hot and sexy, huh?"

She punched his shoulder.

"Only casual. Nothing serious."

"Ever had a serious relationship?" Camille asked, waiting watchfully.

He'd once talked about taking her to America and marrying her. He told her they were going to have three kids, two girls and a boy. They were going to have a dog called Popsicle, and he was going to write poetry, paint and sculpt.

He sighed and looked into her eyes, watching for a flicker of emotion. "You were my serious relationship, Camille."

Roughly she pushed away from him, and he took a step back from the violence of it.

"Then what happened?" She asked bitterly, turning her back. She hadn't intended to bring it up, but she couldn't help it. "You took the money and ran." She gritted.

ABOUT THE AUTHOR

Caroline Bell Foster

When I described myself to my friends, I called myself an introvert, and they laughed so hard I should have really been offended.

As you can probably tell, I adore cats.

The Cat Café began as my NaNoWriMo (50K words in 30 days) project. I wrote it in 19 days.

I hadn't planned on publishing it, but then a real cat café called Kitty Café was opening in the exact location I'd set the book. I considered that to be a sign. I added more words to make the purrr'fect novel for cat lovers everywhere.

Almost all the cats featured in The Cat Café are known to me.

I consider myself to be very lucky, as although born in Britain; I spent my formative years mostly in Jamaica, with a long detour through Canada and Kenya.

I married my college sweetheart David, and we have two amazing kids. I've come full circle and live in Nottingham, just 12 miles from where I was born.

To keep up with me and my projects, I'm on most of the social media platforms, although active on some more than others.

www.carolinebellfoster.com

BOOKS BY THIS AUTHOR

More Books

Love To Belong - Coming Spring 2023

Country Boy – It was a young love, but tragedy struck before Kerry and Noah could explore their lives further. Now adults, could the politician and the country singer reconnect? Free via Newsletter sign-up

Convincing Kyle – (International Heroes Book 2)
First, love and family interference spelt disaster for Kyle and Camille. Years later, they tried again but even more, interference threatens their love.

Avoiding Matthew – (International Heroes Book 3)
Special Government Operatives Matthew and Lacy hooked up every chance they got. But wanting to make the world a better place, Lacy has to avoid Matthew at all costs. But it's so hard!

Distracting Ace – (International Heroes Book 1)
It took thirty-six hours for Ace to fall in love. But longer to find it again and keep it.

The Cat Café. London banker Blake enters the cat café by mistake. Not only is he shocked to see so many cats in one place, but to also fall in love with the mad cat lady Trinity Peters.

The Pussycat Trap - Who knew it only took the pitter-patter of tiny paws to melt the hearts of these powerful men?

Amazon bestselling Call Centre Series:

Call Me Lucky. Teddy could not believe the foul-mouthed girl he once knew had changed so little. He needed to show Felicity the world could be better and brighter with him.

Call Me Royal. Della now lived her life by one word, safe. Could long lost love Spencer remind her how it used to be?

Spicy Tropical Romances:

Saffron's Choice. Engaged to a man she hadn't seen in 5 years. Saffron gives in and falls in love with the man that had always been in front of her.

Caribbean Whispers. Could Merrissa escape her past and take a chance on Alex, or does her past continue to haunt her?

Ladies Jamaican. Three friends, three kinds of love. Could they make it?

www.ingramcontent.com/pod-product-compliance
Lightning Source LLC
Chambersburg PA
CBHW071136170626
46809CB00002B/644